Fromage à Trois

VICTORIA BROWNLEE

Fromage à Trois

AMBERJACK PUBLISHING

IDAHO | NEW YORK

AMBERJACK
PUBLISHING

Amberjack Publishing
1472 E. Iron Eagle Drive
Eagle, ID 83616
amberjackpublishing.com

Publisher's Cataloguing-in-Publication data available upon request

ISBN: 978-1-948705-13-4
E-ISBN: 978-1-948705-25-7

For Jamie and Clementine, my little Paris family

One

"What happens to the hole when the cheese is gone?"

—BERTOLT BRECHT

HOPPING ABOUT ON ONE FOOT, I spied a patch of unshaved hair on my ankle as I struggled to roll up my stocking. *Damn*, I thought, swinging my head to check the clock and see if there was time for an emergency shave. There wasn't. I pulled out a tiny red number I'd found in a sale bin the day before on my lunch break and stepped into it. Zipping up the slightly crinkled dress and standing tall, I checked the effect in the mirror and winked at my reflection. *Not bad, Ella.* It was a size smaller than I'd normally wear—pinching more than slightly around my already-ample bust—but it looked good, and I wanted to look good tonight. I was heading off on a potentially life-changing date.

I was hunting for my black heels on all fours under the bed when my phone started vibrating softly. I scrambled to get myself upright in the restrictive dress and started flinging clothes and books aside in search of it. It could be Paul calling to alter our plan.

"Hello," I said, picking up the phone, panting.

"Ella, darling. I wanted to see how you're feeling."

"Mum," I sighed. "It's only you. I'm fine. Just getting ready."

"Did you get any more hints this morning before he went to work?" Mum had been preempting this proposal since my first date with Paul. She always referred to him as a "good catch."

"Mum! Please stop. I have no idea if anything is going to happen." Even saying it out loud, I wasn't convinced. I had a sneaking suspicion tonight was going to be special.

"Just tell me exactly what he said when he asked you to dinner."

But Paul hadn't revealed anything. He'd casually told me that he'd booked a table at Francine, our favorite French bistro, and had asked me to meet him there. I assumed he wanted to keep some element of surprise.

"He *must* be planning something . . ." she said.

And then she began to rattle on about how Paul might sneak a ring into a glass of champagne, or perhaps nestle it into dessert. Listening to her made me visualize the possible proposal and butterflies began to flutter in my stomach. For the past eight years, it had felt like Paul and I had been working up to this moment. Of course, as the years rolled on, I'd had the standard midtwenties' doubts about how compatible we were—me, an indecisive drifter, and Paul, a realist on a fast track to becoming a hedge fund partner—but our lives had continued to become further entwined and now it felt like our future was all but set in stone. Then again, there'd been anticipated proposals before this that had never come to pass: weekends away, holidays overseas, sunsets on the beach; and every time I would find myself at the end of it, gazing down at my ringless finger. I figured there was no point getting overly excited that something would happen tonight and I'd been trying to stop my imagination from running away from me all day. I'd even hunted around the apartment for a jewellery box earlier that week while Paul spent another evening at the gym, but sadly found no trace.

"Mum, seriously, stop. I've got to go and finish getting ready. I'll give you a call if anything happens. Love you."

"Good luck, darling. Keep me updated."

It was a relief to get her off the phone. Her nerves had the tendency to rub off on me and I wanted to be composed at dinner, at least in appearance.

I went to the bathroom to apply another layer of deodorant and put on just enough makeup to enhance my dark-green eyes, while still looking like the type of girl that a guy would want to marry. After a few failed eyeliner attempts that resulted in more of a lady-of-the-night rather than potential-wife vibe, I nailed it and marveled at my work. I'd tied my hair up into a messy bun, which tamed some of the wild, dark curls. Demure but sexy, a desirable combo.

Climbing the stairs to the open-plan lounge and kitchen, I grabbed Paul's car keys and slid them into my clutch. I couldn't help stopping a minute and admiring his apartment—our apartment—and the glittering lights of the city that you could see through the floor-to-ceiling windows that lined the far wall. We'd moved in in January after nearly a year of searching for the perfect place, and it was finally starting to feel like a home. My mind went back to when we walked in at the sale inspection, nudging each other, both realizing without saying anything that it was perfect. While I had baulked at the price, Paul had reassured me it would be fine. After all, he was paying; he had money to burn after a recent promotion. He was, as he would say, "kicking goals" at work, and this apartment was his celebratory gift to himself, and to us. I could almost feel Paul behind me now, whispering into my ear, as he had done when we were placing our fictional furniture, that he was going to buy it for us.

The night we moved in, and before all of our stuff had arrived, Paul had set up a makeshift bed and we'd stayed up all night reminiscing about our first apartment—small, cramped, and run-down; a lifetime away from where we were now—and talking about how we were going to decorate this one. Thinking about how far we'd come had been exciting, and the new apartment felt like the opening paragraph of a new chapter for us. We were in a good place, and despite our drastically different career choices, I'd increasingly attached myself to him and this new life we'd chosen. While previously the idea of settling in one place with one person scared me—the prospect of being a wife or mother had made me feel physically sick—I gradually started to see the joy in having a beautiful home and reliable car, of having job security and an income. While sitting on that makeshift bed with him, I swear I even heard my uterus yelp.

After a few months in our new home together, I'd hinted at Paul that I was ready to commit. I hadn't been sure he'd registered this, but when a few weeks later he told me he'd started saving again, I quietly rejoiced. And since then, I'd been on edge thinking about when he might pop the question. My flighty solo days of backpacking around the world having adventures were becoming remnants of my past. They were happy memories, but now I was on a new path.

I checked the time on my phone and snapped out of my daydreaming.

Shit, shit, shit, I was going to be late.

I slammed the front door behind me and, hearing the lock click into place, walked excitedly down to the garage. It was raining outside—*a sign of good luck? Or was that reserved for wedding days?*—and I drove the few kilometers to Bistro Francine. I was so on edge that I had to take care to drive extra carefully.

A crash in Paul's car on the way to dinner would not set the right tone.

Paul was already sitting at our regular table, having squeezed his tall frame into the booth seat. Not that I minded taking the chair and facing away from the restaurant's action; I only wanted to look into Paul's eyes tonight. Everything else was simply ambiance, background noise for the big question. I leaned over, allowing him a nice view down my dress, and kissed his clean-shaven cheek before sitting down and shaking the drops of rain from my curls. I smiled. I was ready.

The waitress came over to our table and I hesitated before asking Paul if we should order a bottle of champagne. He shook his head and pointed at the vodka soda he'd ordered before I arrived. He seemed distracted.

But then, who isn't nervous when they're about to propose?

We scanned the menus in silence. I felt too jittery to start a conversation and Paul was concentrating intently on the specials, probably deciding which dishes wouldn't break his Paleo diet.

When he looked up, he smiled and asked me how my day had been, immediately breaking the tension. *Maybe I was overthinking things?* I tried to remain casual while I told him about how I'd had to spend the whole afternoon photocopying a book on Victorian-style gardening, and then caught myself. Ranting about my job was *not* sexy. I changed the subject and asked about his day, which had been equally frustrating. He'd been trying to close some big, secretive deal before the weekend and it'd fallen through at the last minute because the guy's wife had been in an accident.

"Oh my God, is she OK?" I asked.

"I don't know. I didn't think to ask. I really needed him to sign today. I can't believe my luck."

I nodded politely, deciding that Paul was probably a little off because he was worried about work. He wasn't usually so thoughtless.

Nothing a surprise engagement couldn't improve, I told myself. I wasn't going to let anything spoil my good spirits.

The night went swiftly and things began to warm up between us as we moved between courses. Paul even ordered a bottle of expensive Yarra Valley pinot noir for us to share. But despite the improvement in mood, I was still struggling to relax and ended up sipping my wine with greater gusto than I normally would. By the time we finished our main courses, I was tipsy, flinging my head back and laughing loudly in an effort to put Paul at ease and hurry him up a little. It was meant to be one of the happiest moments of our life and I didn't want him to be anxious about it.

I was jubilant on the outside. Inside, I was biding my time until dessert, hoping to find a glittering diamond crowning the top of our favorite apple tart.

Paul looked at me sideways as if he was about to say something important, but our server's untimely arrival at the table interrupted the moment. She asked if we'd like to share our usual *tarte tatin* or if we fancied something different for dessert. I looked hopefully over to Paul, waiting to see what he would order. Could it be an indicator of where he'd hidden the rock? I figured that must be why he'd gotten here early, to arrange it all with the chef. He smiled softly and paused, and after a few anxiety-inducing seconds, asked for a sixteen-year-old Lagavulin with one ice cube. I pouted, the waitress nodded at Paul's request and after emptying the remains of the bottle of wine into my glass, walked away.

Paul gazed at me across the table, saying my name quietly. I felt my heart start to beat uncomfortably in my too-tight dress that seemed to have shrunk during dinner.

This is it, I thought. Of course my Paul wouldn't go the cliché route of a hidden ring.

"We need to talk about something," he said.

Oh God, it's happening. Try to look calm.

"Yes," I whispered, eyeing his mouth impatiently, willing his next words to hurry. I watched him inhale deeply while looking out the window.

"Ella, I've decided I'm leaving . . ."

Chapter

2

I LEANED ACROSS THE TABLE, not sure I'd heard him correctly. My long necklace smashed into my water glass making a loud clang, which drew all eyes in our direction. I looked at him, wide-eyed and astonished.

What the fuck is going on? This wasn't the plan!

"Leaving?! Leaving me?"

"Leaving Melbourne," he said quietly. "And, well . . ."

"Leaving Melbourne? Where are you going?" I didn't want to hear the end of that sentence.

"To find myself . . ." he said, an air of calmness washing over his face as though he was now completely unburdened, having told me.

"Paul, what the hell are you talking about?"

"Ella, it's complicated. See, I earn all this money and I'm doing so well at work. I feel like I'm getting lost in my own success."

"But you love your job. You love being successful."

"But is that enough?" he asked. "I need to get away to find out how to take the next step. All the top partners are doing it. If I'm going to make it even bigger, Ella, I need to do it too. It's not enough to rise through the ranks at work anymore. I also need to challenge myself spiritually."

I sat poised, ready to laugh. He was about to tell me this was all a big joke. But his stony face hammered home quite the opposite. He was being serious. I tried to figure out what this decision meant for us as a couple. Paul had been known to get swept up in wellness trends and health fads, the latest of which were his CrossFit and Paleo obsessions, but generally these "hobbies" hadn't affected us. If anything, they just made Paul more attractive to me.

"So, where are you going?" Despite feeling apprehensive, I decided to try and be supportive.

"It's a three-week retreat on a secluded beach somewhere in Thailand. The organizers won't even give you the address before you arrive; they just pick you up at the airport and take you there. This particular retreat is really hard to get accepted into. You need at least two recommendations from former participants."

"So it's like a glorified rehab or something?"

"No, it's a meditation and wellness retreat. It's apparently very enlightening. I'll probably come back a different person," he said earnestly.

I tried not to roll my eyes. I couldn't imagine Paul—the man I'd known for close to a decade—changing who he was, or even wanting to change.

"OK . . ." I said slowly, buying myself some thinking time. "And when are you meant to leave?"

"My flight out is tonight so I'll leave directly after dinner. I've got a bag packed and I'm ready to go."

What? Why didn't he tell me about this earlier?

"And how did you find out about this retreat?" I asked, trying to remain calm despite the fact that my stomach was anxiously poised and ready to jump out of my mouth.

"Oh, it's a cool story, actually. You know my trainer at CrossFit? The one who's really into mindfulness? Well, she went away on a retreat last year and said it completely changed her life."

I couldn't believe what I was hearing.

"When I was telling her about my recent promotion," he continued, "and how I wasn't even excited about the huge pay rise I got offered, she recommended I go. She's really on my wavelength."

Really on my wavelength, I scoffed. *What fucking wavelength? And why the hell is he taking life advice from a meditating CrossFit girl?*

"Why now?" I asked instead. "Couldn't you have gone on this soul-searching 'journey' sooner?"

"I didn't feel like I had the support before," Paul said, a serious look on his face. "But now my boss has agreed to give me time off work, and Jessyka has been coaching me on how to tell people in a neutral environment and what to expect when I do . . ."

He paused and I furiously wondered how my boyfriend could be taking life advice from someone who spells her name with a 'y' and 'k'. When I first saw Jessyka's name come up on Paul's phone, I thought he must have entered it in wrong. But things were about to get worse. "She's also helped me figure out how to manage people who might not support my decision . . ." he said, trailing off.

"Like me?" I suggested.

"Ella, please. This isn't about you. It's just something I have to do for myself. It's a big life journey . . ."

I could feel my blood pumping more and more angrily in my chest. This retreat had all the hallmarks of a typical Paul stunt: him acting like he could fast-track his way to enlightenment in one easy three-week course. I reached out for his hand, mustering all my reserves of calmness and self-control.

"I'm just trying to understand, Paul." I cleared my throat, trying to squash my anger. "So this different person you're coming back as, does he envisage a future with me?"

"Ella! Don't be like that. I don't know what will happen when I get back. Everyone experiences these retreats differently. I can't predict how I'm going to feel. I also can't promise anything. It's probably best to wait and see what happens when I get back . . . Sound good?"

Now I was confused. Was Paul leaving me or not? Waiting around for his return certainly wasn't the proposal I'd been hoping for.

"And is that what you want?" I asked. "For me to wait for you? Are you able to at least commit to our relationship before you go?"

"What are relationships, anyway? What is commitment?" he asked, almost to himself. "I've been meditating a lot on this recently . . ."

I looked at him stunned, unsure whether to attempt a response.

"And what does it matter if and when we commit?" he continued. "We're here together now, having a lovely dinner before I go away. Isn't that enough?"

Why is he being so infuriatingly vague?

"And did you think to ask me about any of this?" I asked.

"Ella, you know *we* can't be happy if *I'm* not happy, right?" he said.

"Are you being serious, Paul?"

"One hundred percent serious, Ella. I wouldn't joke about something as important as this."

"But I've done everything for you. I settled in Melbourne and got a nine-to-five job. I stopped traveling. God, I even got a savings account. I thought that's what you wanted from me. Now you're leaving me for some kind of hippie cult."

"Don't call it that. And I never asked you to change who you were; quite the opposite. The Ella I met all those years ago, that girl in Paris, was the type of partner who would support me on this journey. The Ella I met back then was open to change. I don't really know who you are anymore. Perhaps we're just not on the same page. But don't worry. It's not you; it's me. I'm changing too."

I frantically tried to piece together what was going on. Any notion of me supporting Paul had swiftly disappeared and been replaced by rage. Questions spun through my head: Why did he bring me to our favorite restaurant to dump this news on me? Did he really believe I would just sit back and get on board with his plan? How could I have thought he was going to propose? Did I really waste the last eight years of my life with this fool? My God, was he sleeping with this meditating CrossFit girl?

"Are you sleeping with this meditating CrossFit girl?" I blurted out.

"Who? Jessyka? Don't go there, Ella. And even if there were someone else in my life right now, it wouldn't change anything. I always figured that we were just a bit of fun, nothing too serious. You feel the same about us too, right?"

The problem was that I *didn't* feel the same. After eight years together I was deeply committed, and up until dinner, I'd thought that Paul was too. I was sure that I'd wanted him to propose. God, I'd even started imagining the lavish wedding ceremony: my poufy white dress that would have to be tamed by my half-dozen bridesmaids, the epic flower arrangements that would visually represent our ever-blooming love. I'd even made a mood board. *Ella, you idiot!*

"Paul, we've built a life together. And I love that life. I thought we were moving towards the same goal." I was coming across more desperate than I wanted.

"What goal?"

"Getting married . . ." I started.

Paul looked stunned. "Married? We've never talked about getting married before. I didn't even know you believed in marriage."

"Where did you *think* this relationship was going?"

He was mute.

I didn't even bother bringing up the idea of us having children together. The life I'd been envisaging for us as a couple was quickly imploding.

"And what about our apartment?"

It was Paul's turn to lean towards me. His eyes narrowed as he said, "Ella, that's my apartment. I paid for it. It's my name on the mortgage."

I gasped. There was the financially-ruthless Paul I recognized. Granted, he had paid the deposit and was paying the majority of the monthly mortgage payments, but it was definitely *our* place; we'd chosen it together. I'd been there at every inspection and had supported him when he was making the offer. I'd even helped choose the furniture. It hadn't even crossed my mind that he might claim it as his territory. What the hell was happening?

He continued, avoiding my gaze. "Yes, you helped me find it

and I'm grateful for that. But if you can't support my chosen path in life, I don't know where that leaves us."

Paul pulled out his wallet—no ring box in sight—and motioned to the server to bring the bill.

"Ella, I need to get going or I'll miss my flight," he said. Our relationship clearly wasn't up for further discussion.

I looked at the man in front of me, and suddenly the future I'd spent the past few months dreaming about began to seem absurd. Nothing that Paul was saying made me feel like I could, or should, wait for him to get back. For the past eight years I'd compromised my own plans and goals to fit in with his life, and he'd just strung me along. The realization hit me hard. I felt like I might throw up.

Enough is enough, girl! Where's your pride?

"Paul, I think we should break up!" I half yelled, shocked as the words came tumbling out of my mouth.

"Seriously?" he asked. "You don't want to wait until I get back and see if I've changed or not?"

"I don't think I do," I said.

"Oh well. I guess some things just have a natural 'expiration date,'" he said, air-quoting the last two words with his fingers.

I grabbed my clutch and made to leave, feeling trapped at the table, at the restaurant, in my dress, but Paul put his hand on my arm, wanting me to sit for a minute longer. I searched his face for a sign of something, anything, that would bring us back together, still hoping that this was all a big joke and that maybe he'd propose after all, but his face remained somber. He sat there in his purple shirt with the hideous dollar-sign cufflinks that screamed finance-douche rather than meditation master. He was my Paul. But now he wasn't.

"What?" I snapped, still trying to hold in my emotions, desperate to get away from him so I could scream in rage, burst into tears, or perhaps try both simultaneously.

He patted my hand patronizingly and I brushed him off. "When do you think you'll move out?" he asked.

"I'll be gone by next weekend," I said dramatically.

"Ella, you don't need to rush. Take all the time you need. If you're still there when I get back, we can talk some more."

"I'll be gone by next weekend," I repeated. "Now are we done?"

Paul nodded, an infuriating air of zen descending over him.

"One last question, Paul," I said. "When you told me you were saving for something big, what the hell was it?"

"The retreat," he said, like it was the most obvious thing in the world. "I've booked the more expensive Chakra Cabin. It has its own outdoor shower and private plunge pool."

"Of course you did," I said. "How very mindful of you."

Standing up, I caught my stocking on the wicker of the chair, which set off a chain reaction and made me spin around too quickly and knock over what was left of my wine. The liquid ran about the table dramatically, and I envisaged it as the blood pouring from my heart into Paul's lap—how fitting that we'd ordered a bottle of red, I thought. He let out a manly squeal and started patting his trousers furiously with a napkin. I muffled a laugh, not surprised to see that his zen state could be so easily shaken.

Given that we were already making a scene, I decided to amp up the action some more and threw my remaining water in his face. "And that's for cheating on me!" And even though he hadn't—or perhaps he had—it felt good. Really good.

Turning on my heels, I left the restaurant with my head held high, holding in the torrent of tears until I was a safe distance away.

Rounding the corner and passing by the restaurant's main window, I glanced through to see if he was watching me go, but his ugly face was illuminated by his mobile screen. Probably messaging his new spiritual advisor, Jessyka, now that he was finally free of his unsympathetic girlfriend and could live life as his true self. Or perhaps he was just making plans to meet up with her when he got back from Thailand and have sex after pushing a tire around or something.

I made it to the car before my tears arrived in a long, steady stream, interrupted only by my noisy and unglamorous nose blows. I sat for a long time staring at the rain on the windshield, trying to figure out what had just happened.

Oh God, what have I done? I just broke up with someone who, up until a few hours earlier, I had planned to spend the rest of my life with.

Chapter

3

I SAT IN THE CAR and indulged my tears, wondering where the line between my relationship expectations and Paul's feelings had gotten so skewed; wondering how I'd wasted close to a decade dating a guy who could so easily tell me that he was leaving me to go and "find himself." For a few seconds I contemplated calling Mum to tell her that Paul and I had broken up, but then decided against it, fearing the complicated discussion that would follow.

Where did I go so wrong?

I thought back to when I met Paul. It was eight years earlier on a European summer tour. I was young and wide-eyed and so was he, but while I was trying to see and experience the world—having been backpacking around Thailand, Vietnam, and China for a month beforehand—Paul had flown into Paris directly with four of his college friends, and it was obvious they were only there for a good time.

I'd fallen in love with Paris the second I stepped out of the train station at Gare de Lyon; the river, the buildings, Parisians—everything seemed so old and romantic. I walked the streets for hours, getting lost in my admiration of the city, strolling into galleries and eating crêpes whenever I got tired or hungry. I was mystified by the grandeur of the parks and gardens, tempted by the windows full of pastries and cheese, and enchanted by the city's inhabitants, whose main preoccupation seemed to be enjoying life.

Falling in love with Paul had taken a little longer. With the tour group, we set off on our ten-day extravaganza around western Europe. The standard tour revolved around oohing and ahhing at historic monuments during the day, and then desecrating whatever beautiful city we found ourselves in with nights of drunken debauchery. After nearly two weeks of this, we ended up back in Paris with a couple of mostly free days before everyone went their separate ways.

It wasn't until a few days in—our first night out, in fact—that I even spoke more than a few sentences to Paul and his friends. And on the penultimate night of the tour, after returning from a boozy night out in a club on the Seine, he pulled me aside, finally finding the guts to ask me if I wanted to spend our last evening together, with a picnic in the Champ de Mars overlooking the Eiffel Tower.

Paul was different from the rest of his group of friends; he seemed to care a little less about drinking and was more serious about life in general. I liked how discreet he was when asking me out, how sweet it was that he waited until the last minute to do so. He reminded me of a Labrador with big, adorable eyes, desperate for affection. Of course I jumped at the offer, thinking to myself, *a love affair beginning in Paris . . . could the story get any better?*

So later that afternoon, we'd strolled off to an *épicerie* to buy picnic food and loaded our backpacks with bread, cheese, and fresh fruit. It was summer in Europe and everything delicious was in season. Figs were ready to explode with their sweet juice at the merest touch, the summery smell of peaches infused the sidewalks, and the baskets of strawberries lining the fruit stands screamed for attention in a flurry of luscious red temptation.

Paul wandered around the cheese section and picked up a slice of Comté. He began telling me that it was one of France's finest cheeses. He seemed so confident and sophisticated when I looked at him through my twenty-one-year-old eyes— especially compared to the other guys I'd just spent the past two weeks with—and I was impressed by his knowledge of French food. When we got to the cash register, Paul paid for the cheese and the baguette, and then added two bottles of champagne to our haul. He brushed my offer of cash away and slipped out his—parent-funded—credit card. It was such a small thing, but that impressed me, back then. He was such a *grown-up*.

On the Champ de Mars, we sat, drinking and reminiscing about our European adventures, edging closer together as the summer sun slowly set over the city. I cut myself a slice of Comté and mindlessly bit into it but was immediately overtaken by my senses. It was glorious. The light, slightly rubbery and slightly crumbly cheese was perfection: fruity and nutty, interspersed with salt crystals that popped like flavor explosions on my tongue. And as if by magic, during that bite, the Eiffel Tower lit up, flashing brilliantly in time with my chewing. I asked Paul how he'd known that this cheese was so delicious.

"A man never reveals his secrets," he replied. And I laughed because it sounded corny, but after a lot of champagne and under Paris's spell, I found Paul utterly charming.

Finally, after an involuntary shiver and just as I was about to suggest we go back to the hostel, Paul slid his arm around my shoulders. I remember in that moment feeling the safest yet most free I had ever felt in my life. We were having this amazing holiday over on the other side of the world without a worry or care between us. All that was in front of me was this gorgeous Australian man and the lights and intoxicating beauty of the city. And then he kissed me. A little awkwardly at first, with his perfectly straight white teeth clunking against mine, but once we'd found our rhythm, I felt like we were the force making the Eiffel Tower sparkle.

We must have been kissing for quite some time, because when we finally broke apart for air, the mass of other people who had been picnicking around us was nowhere to be seen. After realizing that we were more or less alone—there were a few other couples engaging in similar activities at a safe distance—Paul pulled me closer again. I felt dizzy with what seemed like love, but was more likely my raging twenty-something hormones.

When I told friends and family this story, I would generally stop around this moment, before Paul slid his hands up my top and, a little too expertly, undid my bra, keeping that part to myself. But lately, despite it being an entertaining tale to tell people when they'd ask how we met, it had begun to seem cliché, like I'd outgrown it. I'd reverted to telling people the short version: that we met when we were both students traveling through Europe.

A few years after we started dating, I asked Paul again how he'd known about the deliciousness of Comté, and he told me the real story. During university he'd been reading a series of British spy novels starring Jonathan Boons and one of the books in the series had been set in France. After defeating August Le Comté, a corrupt French aristocrat, Boons had finally managed to sleep with the elusive French agent, Fanny d'Amour.

Following a night of hot passion, they too had shared champagne and twenty-four-month-old Comté, but against a backdrop of the French Riviera.

"But hang on, had you even tried it before?" I asked as a follow-up.

"No, but I figured that if it was good enough for Boons and Fanny, it'd be good enough for us."

Maybe if I'd known this at the time, our relationship would have deteriorated sooner. *I mean, who learns about cheese in a spy novel and pretends to know anything about how it tastes?* It seemed absurd even thinking about it. I'd pegged Paul as a worldly food connoisseur, knowing about cheese and wine. And while a slice of cheese wasn't solely responsible for us dating, it'd certainly been a contributing factor to making that night in Paris, and Paul, seem perfect.

But that was Paul. Always jumping on a trend and believing it was the most important thing in the world. What was once cheese became CrossFit and had now morphed into meditation. Perhaps I should have guessed what would come next.

⌒

I checked my watch and even after half an hour of sitting miserably in the car, I realized I was probably still too drunk to drive home. I grabbed my phone and ordered an Uber. When the driver pulled up next to me, he looked me up and down carefully before letting me in. He must have spotted my red, puffy eyes a mile off.

I blew my nose loudly and the driver sighed, turned down the radio, and asked if I was all right.

"Yeah, I'm totally fine. Just another Friday night," I told him, trying to sound chipper.

"Thank God. I just had this customer who'd broken up with her boyfriend over dinner. Can you imagine? She was a total mess. It was a sad state of affairs. She was a real desperado. Didn't even see it coming."

A two-star rating seemed more than reasonable.

I reached Paul's apartment with frozen fingers and fumbled with the keys. Once inside, I slammed the door behind me, threw off my heels, and chucked my mobile on the kitchen table. I went immediately to bed, ripping off my dress as I stumbled down the stairs.

Chapter

4

I WOKE UP THE NEXT morning with sun streaming through the windows. The clouds from the night before had cleared and it was a gorgeous day.

Eugh, just my luck, I thought.

I got up to go to the bathroom, took one look at my puffy, mascara-stained face, and gasped in horror. I closed the curtains and got back in bed, thanking God it was Saturday and I didn't have to go to work. I let the tears flow again and eventually fell back to sleep, avoiding any thoughts of Paul, the breakup, and having to move out of his perfect apartment.

I spent most of the morning between sleep and tears. It was only after hearing a half dozen or so message alerts from my phone upstairs that I was pulled from the safety of my warm bed. My heart sank when I saw that there wasn't one from Paul. No message to say that it'd all been a big mistake and he was sorry. Instead, they were nearly all from my mother asking me how things had gone last night. I really didn't want to respond to her, but I knew she wouldn't stop bothering me if I didn't. I sent a quick message telling her that Paul hadn't proposed, avoiding any mention of the breakup, which would lead to an eventual interrogation over a long and arduous phone call.

There were also two messages from my good friend Billie—the first asking me if I was free for coffee, the second, precisely an hour later, making sure I wasn't dead. I called her immediately. I needed to talk to someone about what had happened and she was always good at giving advice. She'd be more sympathetic than Mum. Or at least she'd take my side.

"Hey," she shouted, and I turned down the volume on my phone. "How're things?"

"Not so great. Paul and I broke up last night." I fought back tears.

"You guys what?"

"Well, I broke up with him. But it was sort of an accident," I said.

"An accidental breakup? Tell me everything."

And so I gave Billie the extended version of what had happened, from the tight dress to Paul's desire to go on a retreat and find himself, and finally, the moment that instigated the breakup: his telling me that I could wait to see how *he* felt about our relationship when he got back. I didn't mention that I had gone to dinner expecting Paul to propose, because in the light of day, it felt too ridiculous to even say out loud.

How could I have been so blind?

"Well, good riddance. You'll be one hundred percent better off without him."

Billie's quick appraisal of my situation may or may not have been entirely truthful, but I didn't mind. She was dependable and sweet, and she certainly knew how to lie when she needed to, especially if it was to protect her friends.

When I didn't reply, she continued, filling the silence. "Don't you think? You were too good for him. You must be relieved."

"I haven't even really processed what happened. It was all so out of the blue. I mean, what am I going to do? I don't know how to be single. Where will I live?"

"You don't need to worry about any of that now," she said. "You have at least three weeks until Paul gets back."

"I guess I could go stay with Mum, but God, the shame of it all. After eight years with the same guy, moving home with my mother . . . I just feel like I've wasted so much time. What about my ovaries?" I couldn't hold back the tears any longer.

"Ella, seriously. Nobody expects you to figure all this out immediately." She paused briefly before saying, "I'm coming over. I'll bring supplies."

"No, I'm a mess."

"I don't care. You need me," she said, and hung up abruptly.

I heard the doorbell as I was applying a second layer of mascara to cover the mess I'd made of the first coat. I knew it was probably a bad idea to even bother putting on makeup but I considered it a preventative measure, an incentive not to cry. I opened the door to Billie's warm embrace and felt immediately relieved. I needed a hug more than I'd realized.

She unpacked the "supplies" she deemed appropriate for post-breakup consolation: a tub of salted-caramel ice cream, chocolate chip cookies—and cookie dough, in case the mood struck—a baguette, a wheel of Camembert, and a thick slice of Comté, which she knew was my favorite cheese, but had perhaps forgotten how I'd come to love it. She filled the table with food and then pulled out a bottle of red wine from her bag. It was only 2:00 p.m. but desperate times called for desperate measures, she told me.

I told Billie that I felt that Paul's retreat was an excuse, that maybe he wanted to leave me but didn't have the guts to actually say it out loud. I figured that I'd been fine as his girlfriend while he'd been working his way through pay grades, but when it came to a future with me, the idea of commitment sent him into a self-reflective spiral. Or perhaps in his efforts to emulate his boss and the CrossFit girl, I'd just gotten caught in the crossfire. *Was I being self-important, trying to figure out why Paul didn't consider including me on his journey*, I wondered. But, as Billie said, perhaps it was all for the best. *Did I really want to marry a guy who took advice from a girl named Jessyka?*

Billie let me talk. She sat sipping wine, perfectly composed while I rattled on with theory after theory, trying to justify Paul's behavior and questioning my own. But then she shushed me, as if she knew I needed to get it all out but now was the time to stop. The concerned look disappeared from her face as she told me, in a tone that made me feel like I was the naughty kid at the back of classroom, to stop with the self-doubt, that she'd worked it all out in her head. "Right. Ella. Let's get serious: Paul and you weren't meant to be. That much, at least, must be clear to you now."

I was about to counter, about to make another excuse for Paul but she stopped me before I could.

"Honestly, you're better off alone. Paul has always been a bit of an odd one and you guys *are* so different now. During university, you both lived to travel and loved gallivanting around the world, but since he graduated, he's been obsessed with his career and how much money he earns. It's always been Paul's ambition and desires in front of yours, you must see that. I know you're chilled out about these things, but—correct me if I'm wrong—you don't really love your current job and it doesn't seem to be going anywhere. Right?"

"You're not wrong."

"And has Paul ever asked you what you really want to do, or put your goals first?" she asked.

I shook my head.

"No, he encouraged you to settle down in Melbourne, and then when he decided he needed a change of scenery in order to 'find himself,' he didn't think twice about picking up and leaving you. Sorry to be harsh, but that's a dick move!"

Still fighting the need to defend my now-ex-boyfriend out of habit, I thought back over the past eight years. Paul hadn't always been so awful. There were even times when we'd been seriously happy: those days as students, basking in the sun and drinking coffee between classes. We'd go on holidays during semester breaks and when classes started up again, he'd take me for expensive lunches on his dad's credit card; I remember how good it felt to escape student life for a couple of hours. We'd talk about our lives post-graduation and make wine-fueled plans to travel back to Paris and find jobs there.

But while Paul's student lifestyle was family-funded, I worked part-time in cafés and restaurants, and had been relieved and grateful to land a job in a small independent publishing house after graduating. I'd done an internship there and they'd kept me on, mostly to do photocopying and get coffee. It wasn't a dream job, but I didn't know what else to do, and in the back of my head I believed it had the potential to go somewhere. The problem was that nobody ever left the company, so for years I'd essentially remained an intern, all while taking home minimum wage.

Meanwhile, before Paul had even finished his degree, he was offered a job at his father's hedge fund—nepotism at its finest—and since then had been steadily working his way up within the company. His colleagues were the type of guys who would go out after work on Friday nights and wouldn't return home until late Sunday morning, the type who bought new cars every time they got a bonus and upgraded their apartments every couple of years. But despite his frequent pay rises and the fact that we were in very different life stages, even despite an ego that seemed to grow with his salary, Paul had still been my Paul and our lives had remained solidly intertwined.

"Seriously, El, what kind of person lets a girl like you go? He's turned into one of those wanker bankers who thinks the world owes him something for existing." Billie was getting worked up now but I was beginning to see where she was coming from. Paul had encouraged me to settle down and I'd accepted this as a sort of sacrifice for our relationship. Sure, I'd felt nostalgic for the traveling we'd done while still at university and often felt the urge to up-and-go when I looked at the photos I'd posted around my cubicle at work, but who wouldn't rather escape to the beautiful white sands of Phuket, the hand-cut noodles of Lanzhou, or the colorful prayer flags of Lhasa, rather than stare at an ever-overflowing inbox? Of course I missed the adventures, but work and life were part of growing up, and I'd had Paul to fill the void.

Billie unwrapped the cheeses and we moved onto our second glass of wine. My tears had stopped and I was starting to feel a little brighter. The booze and Billie's good humor were helping.

"So what's the plan now?" she asked, which set my mind racing again.

The reality was that I was a few months away from entering my thirties and had just accidentally dumped the man I was expecting would propose. Already, I'd spent the last eleven months worrying about not really having achieved anything noteworthy by the end of my twenties—not having become the strong female with her shit together that I'd always pictured in my head growing up—and now after trying to instigate marriage and start a family, I found myself single and soon-to-be homeless.

"Well, first of all, I need to move out," I said, taking a large sip of wine.

"I can help with that. When are you thinking? Where will you go?"

"That I'm not sure of."

"You can stay with me," Billie offered.

"No, no. You're busy with work at the moment, and your place is far too tiny for the two of us."

"Ha, that's true, but still, we could squeeze in. It'd be cozy."

I looked at my friend, grateful for her generosity and not wanting to put her out. But I had told Paul that I'd be out of "his apartment" by the following weekend. And there was no way that I could bring myself to ask him for any more time. I wasn't even sure how to get in contact with him while he was on his retreat.

Billie's phone buzzed. She looked at me apologetically, mouthing "sorry," and rushed into the other room to take the call. She was a jewellery designer who had achieved sudden success with a range of beaded bracelets and, having grown in popularity much quicker than she could have planned for, she was constantly troubleshooting. I was used to her taking calls like these and it seemed that this time, something was causing a lot of grief. She spoke increasingly loudly and her tone felt foreign to me; she was all business and her comforting manner had turned professional.

Hanging up, she apologized again and told me she needed to go, asking if I would be OK on my own. To which I, of course, said yes. As much as I loved the fact she'd come over, I'd be relieved to have some time alone to think things through and try and figure out what the hell I was going to do. She'd given me a small but timely emotional boost.

After seeing her out, I topped my glass up to the rim—*classy, Ella*—and went back downstairs to bed. I grabbed a notepad and sat writing a list of things I needed to do: find apartment, pay rental deposit, get pay rise, buy car, move out, set up house. It was a short but seriously daunting accumulation of tasks, and breaking things down plunged me back into a state of dread. I didn't bother including finding a new boyfriend and having babies, but they were there, ever-present in the back of my mind, and the thought alone was enough to make me drain the rest of my glass and throw my notepad across the room. It hit the wall with a thud and fell on the floor near a pile of Paul's things.

I let a few more tears go on their merry way and willed myself to sleep.

Chapter

5

I DIDN'T LEAVE THE APARTMENT all weekend. Tissues littered the floor, giving off the impression that I'd come close to drowning in my own tears. By the time Sunday morning came, I had become fully cocooned in bed and an expert at ignoring my lingering hangover.

My phone started ringing and the sound made me wince with pain.

"Hi, Mum." I'd already ignored two of her calls that morning. Maybe it was time to come clean.

"Finally," she said. "Where have you been? Were you at the Sunday markets with Paul?"

I took a deep breath.

"Mum, I need you to listen carefully. Paul and I broke up. I know you'll have a lot of questions but I'm seriously not in the mood to talk about what happened."

"Oh," was all she said, which sent me into a panic.

"And I know you really like him, but it wasn't anything I did. He's decided to go on a soul-searching mission, which he doesn't want me to be a part of."

"So he broke up with you?"

"Not exactly."

"What do you mean by 'not exactly'?"

"Well, I sort of broke up with him." I heard Mum tutting quietly. "But he didn't leave me much choice. It was either that or wait around for him to come back from his 'journey of self-discovery,' whenever that might be."

She suggested that perhaps I was overreacting to things, and that maybe Paul was just going through a hard time. "I still think he's worth waiting for, that one," she said with a sigh.

That was typical Mum, always taking his side. I tried to explain to her that Paul and I had never been very well suited, but I struggled to translate my thoughts into words and suddenly, she was accusing me of being unreasonable. Apparently in Mum's day, you'd meet a man once at a dance and you were pretty much engaged after that. I desperately wanted to make fun of her for talking like a grandma, but thought better of it. I also contemplated asking her if my dad had been worth waiting for, but even in my frustrated state I knew that that would be too hurtful.

Mum paused and, in a rare moment between us, I couldn't tell what she was thinking. I walked over to the faux-vintage Smeg fridge and pulled out the dregs of the cheese that Billie had brought around the day before.

"Well, that's a real shame," she said finally. "I liked Paul."

"I know, Mum, but there's not much we can do about that."

"He was good for you," she said, somehow still not grasping the fact that he'd taken me out to dinner to tell me he was leaving.

"Well, obviously he wasn't *that* good for me . . ." I said, pausing to take a bite of the Comté before trying to explain what had happened in more detail.

"So what will you do now?" she interrupted.

I tried not to scream down the phone that I had no idea what

I would do. That I didn't have the money or desire to buy a car, pay the deposit on a rental apartment, or set up a house from scratch. I couldn't find the words to tell her that I was terrified of staying in the city where at any moment I could run into Paul. I was scared to see him enjoying his daily life without me, perhaps meditating in the park or cuddling up with a new girlfriend. I fought back tears and searched the objects around the room in a desperate attempt to find something concrete to tell Mum, and myself, about the future.

My eyes fell on the block of Comté. I couldn't help but think of Paris as I looked at the yellow sliver of cheese. I remembered how inspired I'd felt when I'd first arrived in the city, the joy of walking the streets for hours and feeling ensconced in an energy and passion that could only be described as French.

"Ella, talk to me."

And perhaps it was the lack of sleep, or maybe it was my newfound sense of freedom born out of fear, or even just a dehydrated brain struggling to function logically after too much wine and too many tears, but suddenly I had an idea.

"I thought I'd go away for a while," I told her.

"Oh, a little holiday will do you the world of good, make you see things more clearly."

I kept talking. "I need to move out of Paul's apartment by next weekend so I'm going to box up all my things and ask work if I can take some unpaid leave. I might have to quit, actually."

"Huh?" she said, sounding surprised. "Where are you going? For how long?"

It'd been a long while since I had packed up everything I owned and jumped on a plane on a whim. I started to feel excited, making up the details of my plan as I went. Paul wasn't the only one who could disappear at a moment's notice.

FROMAGE À TROIS

"I'm moving to France for a year. I'll live in Paris."

"A year! But what will you do there?"

"I'll drink wine, eat cheese, and go to galleries. It's summer there now. Maybe I'll take a trip through the countryside, find work—"

"You can't go to France to drink wine and eat cheese; that's ridiculous. What about your life here?"

"What about it, Mum? It'll be here when I get back."

"Ella, you told me you were finished with all this jetting about. Weren't you going to settle down? Try and get a promotion at work, try and . . ." She trailed off. I knew she wanted to mention Paul again.

"Mum, I did try and make it work here. And don't worry so much; it'll all be fine."

And for the first time since Paul left, I felt like things might actually work out. As Mum told me I was being completely irrational, a wave of freedom and adrenaline rushed through my body. It was high time I went back to doing things my way.

And what better place to do it than in Paris?

We hung up shortly after, Mum frustrated and conflicted as to whether or not I was acting crazed because of the breakup, and me feeling certain that moving to Paris was the best decision I'd made in a long time.

I grabbed my post-breakup to-do list, ripped the page into tiny segments, and started a new one: get boxes and pack belongings, drop boxes in Mum's garage, quit job, get working-holiday visa, pack backpack, book flight to Paris, LEAVE! It felt manageable, fun, exciting. And although I didn't have a huge amount of savings, I had some frequent flyer points that would help get me there. I also had a bit of cash set aside— mostly thanks to Paul insisting that I put a percentage of each paycheck in a savings account—that would keep me going for at least a few months. I didn't want to plan beyond that; a loose future felt good right now.

A couple of hours later, and after numerous cups of tea and as many chocolate chip cookies, I started to doubt myself. I called Billie to tell her my plan and ask her if I was being stupid.

If she had any qualms about me moving to France, she didn't let on. She actually seemed beyond excited and couldn't contain her enthusiasm for the idea. Going abroad would be the perfect antidote to breaking up with Paul, she said, and she was certain that I'd end up having the best year of my life. Her confidence gave me an additional boost and a necessary jolt of energy that I knew I'd need to get me through this dark period.

So it was decided. I would spend the next year of my life, and the first year of my thirties, in Paris. I'd relearn how to live life as a solo adventurer. I'd take things as they came and make up a plan on the way. I'd mourn my lost love—and the near-decade I'd lost to it—surrounded by wine, cheese, and the most beautiful city in the world. And after all, I did speak a little French. *Je parle un petit pois de français,* I thought confidently, not realising I was saying I speak a "little pea" of French, rather than a "little bit." Regardless, it all felt right.

Chapter

6

AND BEFORE I KNEW IT, I was in Paris. Driving through the streets so full of history, architecture, and—perhaps most importantly—chic boutiques and quaint restaurants, I knew I would be happy living here. I wanted all the city's beauty to be mine. I wanted to get lost among the streets and to wander the wide boulevards, drinking wine *en terrace* and eyeing up French men. Oddly, I felt immediately at home.

I arrived at the Hôtel du Petit Moulin in the glory of the evening light and was struck by the beauty of my new—sadly temporary—Parisian digs.

I'd stayed with Billie for a week before flying out, which had pepped me up and gotten me through any final moments of doubt that could have put a stop to this whole crazy plan. We'd had fun cooking, drinking wine, and planning out my adventure. We'd scanned blogs and Instagram, which was where we'd found this cute little boutique hotel in the Marais. Billie had convinced me to book it for the first week despite the room rate being well out of my price range, insisting that it was worth the splurge to start things off in Paris on the right foot. Her enthusiasm was contagious.

The hotel's reception area occupied a former bakery and the

view from the street looked like it had been lifted directly from a vintage black-and-white photo. The façade was decorated with murals of people in charming village settings and the word "Boulangerie" stood proudly in gold-and-black lettering above the window, vying for attention. Visible through the window was an array of perfect pink orchids and lush green ferns that brought the scene to life. The effect was like a little gateway to heaven, and it was to be my haven.

My room was only sixteen square meters but it was perfect. There was enough space for me, my luggage, and not much else really, but the best thing was that it was a big change from Paul's apartment back home and it already felt a hundred times more wonderful. When I looked out the window at the rows of Haussmann-inspired buildings spanning the long, straight Rue de Poitou, something in my heart surged back to life.

I fell asleep to the sound of French cars driving by and sirens blaring in the distance. I slept blissfully for the next eight hours, waking only when my phone started buzzing.

"Hello, *oui, bonjour*," I croaked, still not fully awake.

"It's just me, love. It's your mum. Are you OK?" She seemed thrown by me speaking French.

I stood up to try and get some blood running to my brain. "Mum, hi. How are things? God, I feel like I've been sleeping for days."

"I'm fine. Are you OK? I'm still very worried about you, taking off quite suddenly like this. It's very unsettling. And you leaving Paul, what a terrible shame. You two were perfect together."

"Mum, stop. Paul didn't give me much choice; we've been through this already. I'm fine. I'm in Paris. What could be wrong?"

"I don't know, love. What are you going to do for money? Do you need any money?" She sounded worried but I was too exhausted to indulge her concerns.

"Eugh. Mum. No, I don't need money. I'll start looking for a job and an apartment soon. Everything is going to be fine. Better than fine. Everything is coming up roses," I said, eyeing the jaunty floral wallpaper lining my room.

"OK, but promise me you'll call when everything goes pear-shaped?"

"Fine," I said, mostly to stop her from talking. "If anything goes wrong, I'll let you know."

I looked at the clock. It was already ten in the morning and the day was slipping by. "Mum, I've got to go," I said hurriedly. "I'm heading out for coffee and then lunch. Love you."

"You too, dear. Look after yourself."

I hung up, feeling disgruntled. Where was the faith? I jumped in the shower and got ready to hit the Parisian boulevards.

⌒

Although I was only leaving Melbourne for a year, one of the hardest things about this whole plan had been saying good-bye to my friends. On my final night, Billie had hosted an overly boozy and emotional dinner for our group. We were all in tears by the end of the meal and to postpone saying good-bye, we ended up going for celebratory cocktails until the early hours. Not a great idea, when I was flying the next day.

I'd arrived at the airport more than a little frazzled. But Billie, the friend who always drinks water before bed and never looks hungover, thankfully saw me through check-in and pushed me through the international departure door with a hug and a smile.

Once I was through security, I'd ordered an overpriced glass of champagne to pass the time and take the edge off my hangover. I sat bleary-eyed, watching the planes flying in and out, nervous but so happy to be hitting the road again.

I was in my own world, already relishing my own company and feeling empowered. So much so that I missed my boarding call and panicked when I heard my name being announced grumpily over the loudspeaker. *Shit, shit, shit! There is no way I am missing this plane*, I'd thought frantically, as I'd sprinted to the gate.

But here in Paris, leaving the hotel, I felt like a completely different person. I felt refreshed after a long shower and I was in a much more receptive state to enjoy my newfound sense of freedom than I had been the night before, jet-lagged, slightly anxious, and still wrestling a fairly painful hangover.

I turned onto Rue de Poitou and basked in the picturesque beauty of my immediate surroundings. The morning sun was already heating up the streets. Having flown in directly from winter in Melbourne, it was a delight to be out in a summer dress and strappy shoes. Despite being in the heart of Paris— only a stone's throw from Notre Dame where hordes of tourists would be snapping pictures and lining up to climb the towers in the hope of glimpsing Quasimodo—the Marais felt relatively quiet and peaceful. The buildings on either side of the road were home to envy-inducing apartments with vibrant planter boxes spilling over with flowers and foliage. Striking iron and glass street lamps amplified the feeling that I'd moved onto a movie set. My eyes devoured every unique detail. The straight lines of the almost-symmetrical apartment buildings were a sharp contrast to the hodgepodge of architecture that hugged the tram-ridden, wide streets of Melbourne.

Turning left, I found myself on Rue Vieille du Temple where a charming sign for an "École de Garçons" towered above a large green door. It was little things like this that had made me fall in love with Paris the first time around: snippets into a rich history that transported you into the past. The old boys school, which now looked like it had been converted into apartments, was only the width of one room and rose three stories high. It looked like something from a different era. I pictured the boys from the *école* walking up to the front doors and wondered if they had stopped to admire the beautiful street, or if for them, it was just life as usual. Perhaps after school they'd stop and pick up a chocolate croissant from the boulangerie next door.

Perhaps I should pick up a chocolate croissant from the boulangerie next door . . .

I nipped into the bakery and was immediately hit with the scent of flour and butter. The woman behind the counter handed me a still-warm *pain au chocolat,* the flaky pastry curling around the aromatic sticks of chocolate. "Heavenly," I murmured to the empty paper bag, which was now scattered with pastry crumbs.

Reaching Rue de Bretagne, I spied a very sweet little table for one on the terrace of a café called Le Progrès—The Progress—which seemed fitting for my first stop of the day. I did a quick mental calculation of how long it'd been between coffees. I'd crossed so many time zones in the past few days that after a few excruciating minutes of mental calculation, I settled on "too long" and took the chair with a view of the street.

Not really knowing what to order, I asked for a *café au lait.* What arrived was a really weak version of a latte, with a strong hint of burnt coffee and the lingering flavor of long-life milk. It wasn't particularly nice, but surrounded by Parisians at the cutest little French outdoor tables, it helped to bring my jet-lagged self back to life.

I was absolutely loving people-watching from my vantage point at the café, though I was still experiencing that wave of nausea that comes with swapping time zones and seasons. I thought back to the exasperatingly long flight that had brought me here and remembered the wave of relief that had flooded through me as soon as my feet had hit the airport corridor at Charles de Gaulle. "Sweet freedom," I'd said softly to myself as people rushed past me into the border control queue.

It had felt like an age ago that I'd made that same journey into Paris, flying in solo with stars in my eyes. I'd arrived with a steely determination both times, though for different reasons, and as people buzzed about, kissing each other on both cheeks and picking up their chic baggage from the carousel, I'd flung a scarf over my shoulders and headed towards the taxi stand.

I'd have to figure out the metro today, though, I thought to myself. Last night all I could focus on was getting to the hotel, getting a decent night's sleep, and downing a generously-sized glass of *vin rouge*. But now, looking at the café's price list hanging helpfully in the window, I wondered just how expensive Paris had become and how economical I'd need to be. When I was in Europe with Paul, I was still a student and everything felt expensive; but even now, as I sat and converted the prices for wine and coffee into Australian dollars, I began to feel a little nervous. I pulled out the rough Paris budget I'd done on the back of a sick bag on the plane. I'd calculated that with money for rent, food, wine, and the odd shopping splurge, I would run out of my life savings in eight weeks. Now it seemed like it'd be closer to six weeks.

What a grim prospect, I thought.

But then again, I was in Paris for the first time in years. And while I didn't want to fritter away all of my money swanning about the Marais eating and shopping for a month and a half—as lovely as that sounded—I did want to give myself a few days off before looking for a job and an apartment so I could acclimatize to my new home and get over everything that'd happened since dinner with Paul. I needed to defrost from life in Melbourne.

The butterflies that had skipped about in my stomach while I sat on the plane were finally calming down. Now, sitting here with my cup of rather average coffee, all I could think about was the fact that I had made it. I'd actually made it; I was now officially far away from Paul, far away from work, and far away from everything in Australia. My doubts about how I'd readjust to traveling after such a long hiatus were abating. I was *living* in Paris. I was doing it.

This is it, I thought, breathing in the lovely Parisian air and admiring my new surroundings.

I decided to sit a while longer and order another coffee. I checked out what my French comrades were drinking and followed suit. I wanted to feel like a local as quickly as possible. The espresso I ordered came quickly and I thought, *Ah, this is better. Still a little bitter, but better.* Despite the quality of the coffee not being what I was used to in Melbourne, I was in love with the fact that my *café* arrived with a tiny, individually-wrapped, chocolate-coated almond. What a fabulous addition to a caffeine hit. Why didn't every café around the world do this?

At noon, well-dressed business people started filling the tables, which were covered with red-and-white check tablecloths. They sat, laughing together, drinking carafes of rosé, scanning the roving blackboard and ordering *steak frites* and salads. I looked on quietly, surprised at how happy all these groups of colleagues and friends seemed to be as they lingered over lunch, drinking wine, then coffee; many having dessert. I thought back to how bleak Melbourne had been before I'd left, with the majority of my coworkers eating miserable-looking salads at their desks as rain pelted the office building. I felt a wave of gratitude for the *joie de vivre* that seemed abundant here.

After a while, I began to sense that the waiters wanted my table for the lunch trade, and although they'd never say so directly, their exasperated looks eventually clued me in. I got up to continue my promenade up Rue de Bretagne.

After having spent a couple of hours on a sunny terrace, it was lovely to walk under the shade of the tree-lined street, passing quaint little cafés, butchers, and bakers. My mouth watered at the smell of baking bread. By the time I walked past a chicken rotisserie and eyed the fat dripping onto a tray of very willing potatoes, I could barely contain my hunger. My stomach grumbled to life. *Where to have lunch on my first day in Paris?* I sang to myself in anticipation.

Chapter

7

I WAS LOOKING AT MENUS in restaurant windows when fate intervened and my eyes landed on a shop that stopped me in my tracks. The yellow sunshades drew me in like a homing beacon and my legs sped up in anticipation.

The "Fromagerie" sign above the store screamed out for me to pay it some attention, the word *fromagerie* a joyous blend of *fromage* and *rêverie*. I wondered if anyone else had ever noticed this before.

Oh yes, cheese is always the answer, I said to myself, and approached the window greedily, my surroundings blurring into insignificance as my eyes locked on the window display. It was cheese, real French cheese, in all its glory. The *fromagerie*— which was highly likely to become my new local—was one of those quintessential French stores that sells one product and does a damn fine job of it. The windows and cabinets were lined with dozens of cheeses, covering a huge array of shapes, colors, and textures. There was round cheese and long cheese, moldy cheese and gooey cheese. Some cheeses were thin and some were thick, and one of them had holes in it that would put cartoon drawings to shame. There were tiny cheeses covered in raisins, fluffy white cheeses in little wooden containers, and huge wheels bigger than my head. My mind flashed back to the deli section of my local supermarket in Australia and I laughed thinking about how exciting cheese shopping would be now that I *lived* in Paris.

I inhaled deeply, the smell of farm animals, mold, and other indescribable odors hitting me in a wild wave, even through the window. I stood staring for what felt like seconds but may have been hours, my mouth open in amazement. As I gazed farther into the shop, I spotted the salesman tending to his babies. He was tall with broad shoulders and looked different to how I pictured a French cheesemonger would (that is, as the spitting image of a young Gérard Depardieu). He was rugged, with a rough-cut beard and salt-and-pepper hair. His strong arms were visible under a striped blue-and-white top and his apron gave him an artisanal air. I instantly christened him Mr. Cheeseman.

He gave me a reserved smile.

I smiled back but hesitated before entering the store, tossing up whether to go in now, or wait until I'd learned a few more French words before embarking on my maiden voyage. I didn't want to embarrass myself by pointing wildly at a cheese and then having Mr. Cheeseman rattle off a bunch of incomprehensible sentences to me. My nerves were getting the better of me and I nearly turned away, until I thought about the end product—*cheese!*—the food that had coerced me into coming to France in the first place; an indulgence I'd enjoyed since my first visit to Paris with Paul, before things had gone south. Thoughts of everything that had happened in Melbourne further fueled my desire to create a new cheese memory: one that wouldn't be tainted by boyfriends or breakups.

Putting my fingers over the handle, I pushed the door.

And then I pushed, and pushed again.

Mr. Cheeseman looked at me sideways and tapped his watch. I kept trying to open the door until he came from around the back of the counter and turned a key on the other side.

"*Nous sommes fermé entre midi et deux,*" he said. I looked at him blankly and he followed up with, "Shut between midday and two."

"Oh, *pardon,*" I said, flustered.

"*Dix minutes,*" he said, shutting the door abruptly.

Maybe not so friendly after all . . .

I went to get a bottle of water and then returned, my cheeks still tinged red with embarrassment. *Don't mess with a French person's business hours*, I told myself for future reference. This time, I successfully navigated through the door and was met with a neutral look that made me wonder whether my earlier faux pas had already been forgotten.

I immediately launched into my schoolgirl French. "*Bonjour. Je voudrais . . . eh . . . a-chet-er fromage, s'il vous plaît, monsieur.*" I stuttered that I wanted to buy cheese, grateful that my embarrassing attempts to converse only fell on the ears of the cheese and the man selling it. My efforts, however, turned out to be futile, as Mr. Cheeseman replied to me in perfect English without pause or hesitation.

"Well, *mademoiselle*, you have come to the right place." His accent was glorious and thick, like the oozing wheel of Roquefort in the corner of the store.

"This is a beautiful cheese shop," I replied in English, still stilted despite being a native speaker myself. I'd come over all flustered again.

"*Merci*," he said, and then asked, "Are you American?"

"No, Australian."

"That's a long way to come to buy cheese. Are you visiting Paris?" He clearly wasn't rushing to get me out of the store like he had been earlier. His two-hour lunch break must have been a good one.

"Yes . . . I mean, no. Err . . . I'm thinking of moving here."

"Moving here?" he asked with raised eyebrows. "But you don't speak any French."

Ouch!

"I'm learning," I said, hurt by his all-too-accurate observation and promising myself I'd amp up my language efforts the next day.

"It's a very complicated language. Hard for foreigners to learn," he said, making me feel inept.

Mr. Cheeseman looked around thirty-five but had an air of a distinguished, older Frenchman about him that I found intimidating. If this was to become my local cheese shop, my efforts to start things off on the right foot weren't going so well. I tried to think of something clever to say.

The seconds passed slowly.

I only realized I'd been standing immobile for quite some time when Mr. Cheeseman asked me if I wanted to buy anything.

I announced confidently that I'd like a small piece of Comté.

He answered me with a blank stare and I pointed at one of the giant cheese wheels in the cabinet to make sure he'd understood.

"Ah, *Comté*," he said, a look of recognition crossing his face.

"Yes, Comté," I said.

"No, it's *Comté*, not Comté," he told me, repeating the two pronunciations exactly the same way—at least, *I* couldn't for the life of me differentiate between them. We moved on, thankfully.

"So what kind of Comté would you like?" he asked.

It hadn't occurred to me that there was more than one kind.

Before we fell into another awkward silence I blurted out "What do you have?"

"Well, I have young Comté and old Comté," he said.

I shrugged and he continued. "Young Comté is more rubbery with a lighter flavor. Old Comté has a deeper taste and is more expensive because it's been refined." He spoke with a passion for cheese that was so endearing I was tempted to order a slice of each. Instead, feeling overwhelmed, I asked him which he preferred.

"I prefer old Comté, but it depends on what you like and how refined your palate is. Children tend to like fruity Comté. But old Comté . . . it's very, how do you say, dynamic?"

I nodded, pretending to understand what he was saying, but I still felt confused. "I'll have a slice of that, then."

"Anything else?" he asked.

"What would you recommend?"

"Again, it depends on what you like," he said, seeming almost confused by the question. I got the impression that personal recommendations perhaps weren't as common in France as in Australia, where sales assistants are always armed with suggestions on how you should spend your money.

"Maybe a Brie or a Camembert," I said quickly, embarrassed that I couldn't bring a more niche French cheese to mind in the heat of the moment.

He nodded, obviously not aware, or perhaps not caring, that I felt like a walking tourist cliché.

"This Brie is perfect for today or tomorrow. When will you be eating it?" he asked.

"As soon as possible after leaving the store," I said with a giggle, trying to make him laugh.

"OK, that settles it," he replied seriously. "How many people are you going to share the cheese with?"

"Just me," I replied.

He looked at me like he was about to say something, but then said, "*D'accord*. Then you won't need very much." He cut me off a chunk that looked large enough for four people, but that suited me perfectly.

Then, as he was jotting down the names and origins of each cheese onto the wax paper they were wrapped in, he laughed and told me an anecdote about how the man who made this Brie sang to his cheese in the morning, giving it an extra *je ne sais quoi*.

"*Merci*," I said, taking my beautifully-wrapped cheeses. "By the way, I'm Ella. I'll be back again for more cheese soon, Monsieur . . . Monsieur . . ."

My hunt for his name hung heavily in the air. I guess he wasn't ready to share that very personal detail with me yet. Feeling myself starting to blush again, I hurried out of the store yelling thank you and cradling my cheese as I might a newborn baby.

Despite the multiple blushing outbreaks, my first cheese-buying mission had been a success! I felt elated that I'd managed to purchase both Comté and Brie and not make too much of a fool of myself. Yes, Mr. Cheeseman hadn't been as soft and cuddly in person as I'd hoped when I'd spotted him through the window, but he seemed to know his cheese, he spoke English, and I was sure I could get him to warm up with a few more visits. Perhaps I'd even make it my mission to try and get him to laugh at one of my *own* stories the next time I went in.

I kept up my shopping momentum and found a bakery to buy a baguette to go with my cheese—*oui, oui*—and headed towards a little park in the Marais to try my first post-Paul and post-Melbourne Comté.

The Square du Temple was quintessentially Parisian, mixing perfectly-manicured gardens with huge trees that shaded the rows of bench seats lining the off-white gravel paths. A large children's play area was overrun with kids wearing colorful shorts, round-rimmed glasses, and cravats. They buzzed about, screaming to one another with their high-pitched voices as they picked up insects and tortured them in a charming, inquisitive French way. Keeping a casual eye on these excitable terrors were chic Parisian mothers—or perhaps au pairs—who every now and then would trot after *les bébés* as they darted a little too close to the park gates or into the flower beds that were bright with pristine summer blooms.

Sitting down on an empty bench, I laid the carefully folded little parcels of cheese onto my handbag, using it as a makeshift table, and ripped into the baguette. I quickly realized that it was hard to cut cheese without a knife so I improvised, breaking off a couple of chunks of Comté and placing them on a generous hunk of bread. I bit into my one-ingredient sandwich and waited for my taste buds to wake up. And then they did, and I felt like I was melting, right then and there in the middle of Paris, and not from the heat of the early afternoon sun. I'd been right remembering that cheese tasted better in France. Slight hints of salt and just the right amount of sharpness and sweetness hit my taste buds in tandem.

When Mr. Cheeseman had been slicing the twenty-four-month-aged cheese, he'd told me that old Comté had a little more bite and a more intense flavor than its younger counter-parts. It was certainly richer than anything I'd been able to buy at home in Australia. It tasted more refined, more French. It was love at first bite. I practiced my French on my lunch. *Je t'aime, je t'aime, je t'aime*, I repeated over and over again to my cheese sandwich.

I watched as groups of friends and family congregated to-gether on a small patch of grass bathed in sunlight, disrobing in the warm summer sun to reveal bare chests and—for some incomprehensible reason—bikinis and bathers. Couples sprawled intertwined on rugs, sipping beers and kissing each other as though they were the only people in the park. *Ah, to be young and in love in Paris*, I thought.

As conviviality surrounded me, I felt a twinge of melancholy, my first since getting on the plane, and I couldn't help wishing I had someone to share my picnic with. I was desperate to talk in great detail about the magical flavor of the cheese, the fluffi-ness of the baguette, and the sweetness of feeling the summer sun on my pasty skin.

As fun as being on holiday was, I knew that eventually I would get lonely, and that sooner rather than later, I was going to start running out of cash to entertain myself during my long days off. It became clear that I needed a job, money, and friends if I were going to create a life for myself here. The blissful ex-istence of a happy Parisian was like a carrot dangling before me, and I felt like it was going to be hard to reach.

I started to get overwhelmed thinking about what I needed to do to set up in France and I was reminded of the horrible post-breakup to-do list that had helped spur on my move to Paris in the first place. Mum's instruction to call her when things went pear-shaped rung in my ears. It was as though she'd foreseen how my day would play out and saw it ending in a bout of homesickness. I headed back to the hotel, brushing off the unwelcome wave of sadness as jet lag. Whatever my current feelings were, I was desperate for an afternoon nap.

Chapter
8

I WOKE THE NEXT MORNING to the sound of cars beeping their way into the pre-work, rush-hour furore. Checking the time on my phone, I groggily realized I'd slept through the night. I must have been more jet-lagged than I'd thought. My stomach was grumbling loudly having been deprived of dinner, and I made a beeline for the tiny bar fridge where I'd stashed the Brie. For the second time since arriving in Paris, I was hit in the face with that unique farmyard aroma—not always pleasant but synonymous with delicious French cheese.

I ripped open the curtains and windows to let in the sunshine, which had been peeping brightly through the curtains and promising weather as glorious as the day before. A warm breeze gently filled the hotel room, helping disperse the cheese smell. My positivity had returned. As Mum used to say when I was small, a good night's sleep can sort out any bad mood.

Tearing open the packet of Brie, I dug out yesterday's leftover baguette from my bag. While I had originally thought the cheese was too generous a serving for one, I was now thankful that Mr. Cheeseman had given me such a large slice. I cut a segment and placed it directly in my mouth, abstaining from bread for the first taste, as the French do. I let it sit a moment, registering the flavor on my tongue. It was soft and creamy, flavorsome but at the same time mild. Perfection.

I remembered the poor representations of Brie I'd so often eaten in Australia, and how good the real thing was in comparison. The delicate and soft white crust, which I used to happily avoid back home, almost formed the best part of the cheese here, with the two textures working together harmoniously. I hardly touched the baguette, barely came up for air as I dreamily ate my way through my second cheese since arriving in France. I wondered how soon I could go back to the same cheese shop for more recommendations without looking greedy.

Hearing the happy sound of people filling the city's many terraces for coffee and brunch, I felt a pull to get out among the action. Thinking about Mr. Cheeseman's astonishment at me not speaking French, I downloaded some beginner language podcasts to kick-start my efforts before heading out the door.

On my way out, the receptionist asked me if I had any nice plans, perhaps meeting up with friends? Her assumptions brought back that pang of loneliness from the night before, but I couldn't be deterred. It was a new day, and armed with my language lessons, I'd get the hang of being French in no time.

I strolled around for hours as if in a dream, repeating phrases like *"Comment allez-vous?"* and *"Je voudrais un verre de vin rouge."*

I passed many old couples having a pre-lunch tipple—*don't let the fact it's only eleven in the morning put you off, dear French friends*—and in my distraction, almost walked straight past the entrance to a charming little market called "Le Marché des Enfants Rouges." The Red Children's Market was housed in a compact space, concealed just off Rue de Bretagne, but the cramped lanes and food stalls were humming with stallholders, shoppers, and visitors.

Entering through the gates, it was hard not to feel transported into a hidden French world, where food and beauty seemed to be the order of the day. I jostled between customers buying fruit and vegetables, wine and fresh-cut flowers. There were even tour groups with headsets to contend with, but thankfully they didn't detract from the magic. When I stumbled on a man making crêpes towards the back of the market, I couldn't help but stop and enjoy the show. He was singing and calling out to people as he expertly swirled the batter around his hot plate before adding Nutella, sugar and butter, or chestnut paste. I couldn't resist his charms and tried to order one in my best French. But then his attentions were on me as he sang and joked, and I laughed despite not understanding what was going on. I didn't mind, though. It was a nice moment of feeling lost.

I continued to walk around the market, ogling the seasonal vegetables and fantasizing about buying ingredients for future dinner parties with all my wonderful French friends. I made a note to come back to the Moroccan stall, whose line snaked well into the market; it was the perfect spot for lunch. I peeked behind those queuing and saw colorful cabinets filled with huge bowls brimming with couscous and tagine, and piles of shiny, sticky baklava screaming out to be eaten accompanied by a pot of sweet mint tea.

When I realized Nutella was oozing out of my crêpe and down my hand, I decided it was probably time to go before I embarrassed myself. But before I could dart out of the market, I suddenly found myself swept up in a tour group. It was such a busy day that extricating myself from the crowd was easier said than done. The group leader looked at me and nodded while speaking to me in *another* language I didn't understand and I desperately ducked behind a vegetable stand just to get away from him. Finally free, I looked down at my Nutella-soaked fingers and licked the mess away, rather indelicately; fortunately nobody was around to see my very unladylike behavior.

Or perhaps not . . .

I spotted him before I could even put a name to his face. It was Mr. Cheeseman, walking directly towards me. In that moment he was the epitome of the French cliché, still wearing his white apron and carrying a baguette and a bottle of red wine. He must have been on his way to lunch.

I was so excited to see someone I recognized in Paris that I started waving and sung out to say hello. He looked momentarily taken aback.

If he doesn't recognize me, at least please let him remember me.

When he drew near, I jumped right in and said, "Thank you again for the delicious cheese yesterday," hoping he wouldn't think I was some kind of Parisian crazy.

After what felt like an eternity, recognition flashed across his face and he smiled widely. I felt like we'd already made progress from yesterday's meeting.

"'ello, Ella," he said. I was surprised he remembered my name and quite impressed, despite still being embarrassed I didn't know his.

"*Bonjour. Comment allez-vous?*" I said, feeling smug that I was already putting my French phrases to good use.

"*Très bien*," he replied. "Are you staying locally?"

"Just around the corner—for now," I said, taking his cue to switch to English before things got too linguistically complicated.

His face opened, as though my living close to his store made me more interesting, more worthy of a chat. I couldn't help but notice his piercing blue eyes in the sunlight.

"So tell me, you liked the cheese?" he said, his brow furrowed and serious.

"It was perfect," I said.

"*Bien*," he said. "And the Comté, it wasn't too, how do you say, *piquant?*"

"No, in fact, it was the best I've ever had."

He nodded. "Ah, then, you'll have to come back and try some more." Another charming almost-grin.

Someone's in a good mood today, I thought.

"It would be my pleasure. I'll come by tomorrow afternoon."

"OK, *à demain alors*," he said, and I nodded along, hoping that I was translating correctly what I thought meant "see you tomorrow." His facial expression didn't suggest that I'd made a faux pas and as we went our separate ways, I couldn't help but feel excited at the idea of having made a French acquaintance, and a cheese-seller no less.

After leaving the market, I continued down to the Seine, past epic buildings and beautiful boutiques, all the while unable to wipe the smile off my face. I zipped past Notre-Dame, took a quick selfie, and then crossed the river into the busy Saint-Michel, walking past couscous restaurants, crêpe stalls, and bars promoting too-cheap happy hours. Arriving at the famed Shakespeare and Company bookstore, I stopped in to buy a new English-language book. *And yes, I should be reading in French,* I reprimanded myself, *but that can wait until next week at least.*

On previous trips to Paris, I'd always been disappointed to miss out on visiting the bookstore associated with Hemingway, Joyce, and Pound. Like most other tourists, I wanted to mull around the store, which I'd seen in the films *Midnight in Paris* and *Before Sunset*, and I was going to enjoy every last second there. Snapping another selfie, I thought about how traveling solo had its advantages when it came to doing things on your own schedule. After stalking the shelves, listening to a man playing the piano upstairs, and flipping through various old books, I finally settled on buying a copy of *Mastering the Art of French Cooking*, which I figured would stand me in good stead at any future dinner parties I might host.

Exhausted from the heat and the walking and keen to dip into my new book, I parked up on a bench in the shade overlooking the boats and the picnickers who had taken over the banks. Families walked by with multicolored ice cream cones from the famed Berthillon, savoring every last lick. And as the sun fell over the city, groups of dancers began to congregate and take over the mini amphitheaters that lined the river. The whole scene felt like a movie, but rather than being glued to a screen, I was sitting amongst the action.

No longer able to keep my eyes open, I left the river and began making my way back to the Marais. En route, I saw a café that looked cozy and welcoming, and totally different to the hundreds of other Parisian cafés that are unmistakably associated with the city thanks to their representation in films and photos. It was called "Flat White," clueing me in to the fact that maybe it wasn't French-owned at all.

But even more noteworthy than its obvious differences to other French coffee shops was a small job advertisement in the window for a barista.

While café work didn't really fit into my glamorous Paris career goals, I couldn't discount the fact that I needed money, and the ad was thankfully written in both English and French, which seemed like a good sign considering my current comprehension level of the latter. Plus, the thought of having colleagues who I could go for a drink with, coupled with the prospect of having constant access to good coffee, made me feel like perhaps this was just what I needed. I made a note to come back and check out the café's vibe the following day.

Chapter

9

IF MY FIRST TWO DAYS in Paris had been all about eating, strolling about, and appreciating the Parisian *joie de vivre*, the next few days needed to morph into business. *Come on, Ella, it's time for action!* I said quietly, coaxing myself out of bed.

My booking at the hotel was only for another four nights, so I needed to find somewhere permanent to live, and quickly. Securing accommodation was the order of the day and I spent the first few hours of magnificent sunshine holed up in my room wading through announcements for share houses, sublets, and short-term rentals. Prices were much more expensive than what I was used to paying in Melbourne, especially considering Paul and I used to split the mortgage repayments seventy-thirty. I did some sums and realized that I would have to rent a room in a share flat because I couldn't afford something to myself. If I wanted to live solo, I'd squander my savings even faster than my revised budget had accounted for. *Not ideal.*

Two hours in and I'd already sent some inquiries and emails. The prospects weren't overly exciting but I'd made a solid start, and given the smells of lunch and baking pastries and bread that continued wafting through my window, I decided I couldn't stay inside a minute longer.

I planned to go down to Flat White, the café I'd seen the day before, to get a decent cup of coffee and perhaps ask about the barista job if I could pluck up the nerve. After sleeping on the idea, I'd come to realize that getting a hospitality job, at least in the beginning, would quite literally buy me some time to apply for better opportunities.

The days following my resignation in Australia had passed in the sort of panic that involved a detailed visa application, a lot of cardboard boxes, packing tape, and stress. I really hadn't had time to think about what type of job I would be able to get in France and how much money I'd need. My mind had been too busy constantly swinging from terror to excitement: I'd doubted my plan when putting all my stuff into storage; then I'd felt positive about it as soon as I'd stepped out of Paul's apartment for the final time. I'd felt anxious about the finality of leaving Melbourne when I'd texted Paul to tell him where I'd left the keys, then I'd felt vindicated when he hadn't even bothered to reply. It was an emotional time.

My working-holiday visa had arrived the day before I was due to fly out and I'd had to stop myself from hugging the postman when I saw him with a large registered post bag in his hand. Instead, I'd hugged my passport close to my chest, thanking the universe for delivering my getaway pass just in time.

But now, here in Paris, I missed the comfort and familiarity of my job at the publishing house in Melbourne. I'd known that by coming to France on a working-holiday visa—and without being fluent in French—getting a similar job here would be pretty much impossible, but the dreamer inside me had hoped I'd eventually find something interesting to do.

I thought back to how great my old boss had been when I'd told her I was leaving. I'd walked decisively into the office the

Monday after breaking up with Paul, smiling, knowing that quitting my job was the first step of my new adventure. My head was held high and my heels were on. It was only my eyes—red, puffy, and still bloodshot—that gave me away. *You can't win them all,* I had told myself, as I'd tried to cover the mess up with mascara to no great effect.

After flinging my handbag on my desk, I'd walked directly into my boss's office and asked her if she had a minute to chat.

"Are you sure about this?" she'd asked. "I mean, I can pop this resignation letter into the shredder and pretend I never saw it; perhaps you'd like to take the rest of the week off."

After I'd told her about Paul though, she understood. She was surprisingly supportive of my decision to move to France. I wasn't sure what I'd expected, but I was almost hoping she'd beg me to stay, perhaps offer me a promotion and a pay rise that would be too good to turn down. Instead, she'd told me I didn't have to worry too much about serving my full notice period, I was free to finish whenever I felt ready.

Quitting my job had been an irreversible action point from my Paris to-do list, and with that ticked off, changing my mind about the move hadn't really been an option anymore. And now I had to make sure that running out of money in France didn't give me an easy excuse to move back to Australia. I needed that café job.

Nerves were already creeping in as I got out of the shower; by the time I arrived at Flat White with a copy of my résumé tucked into my handbag, I was shocked at how jittery I felt, especially considering I'd had a decent full-time job up until a week before.

"*Bonjour,*" I said to the barista, who was wearing a flannel shirt and ripped jeans.

"Hey," he replied immediately in English, obviously clocking my hideous French accent. "You fancy a coffee?" His Australian accent was unmistakeable. What were the odds?

I was initially taken aback by his surfer look, with his sandy-blond hair, bright-blue eyes, and ridiculously tanned arms. I wondered how he even managed to get a tan in Paris.

"I'll have a long macchiato," I said determinedly. Normally I was the type to go for a flat white, but I thought changing up my order might help me stand out, like I knew a thing or two about coffee.

"Here or to go?" he asked.

"To have here, thanks."

"Grab a seat," he said, and I laughed because I felt like I could be back in Melbourne.

I was very momentarily hit with a surge of guilt for cheating on the traditional French cafés, but I'd been craving a decent coffee since I'd left Australia, and if an Australian barista was to make that happen, I could come to terms with any niggling sense of remorse.

I sat drinking my long mac—sort of wishing it were a flat white—and checked out the clientele. I got a feel for how the coffee counter and the kitchen worked, and the food coming out looked good: avocado on toast, fancy and unusual granola flavors, a variety of biscuits and cakes—*all dishes I'd gladly eat on a lunch break*, I thought to myself. And the coffee was perfect. I saw myself fitting happily into the fold at Flat White and started planning how to casually ask the barista about the job vacancy.

All thoughts of charming my way through the application, however, were thwarted by the arrival of the most handsome man I'd ever seen. If love at first sight existed, I'd just become a casualty.

He was the stereotypical tall, dark, and handsome, with well-manicured stubble contrasting a crisp white shirt and a dashing blue cotton scarf. He looked around the café with his dark-brown eyes and a slight, upturned smile and I genuinely thought I might be sick. He swept towards the coffee machine, leaving a wave of weak knees (perhaps just mine) in his wake, shook the barista's hand and said with a deep, sexy voice, *"Salut, Chris. Un espresso, s'il te plaît."*

"Coming up, mate," the barista replied, emptying the porta-filter and grinding some fresh beans.

If I hadn't made up my mind about applying for the job based on the quality of the coffee alone, picturing myself behind the counter shaking mystery Frenchman's hand sealed the deal.

I watched the two men interacting and got lost in thinking about how we're often most attracted to those who are different to what we know. Although I could acknowledge that the barista was a conventionally handsome Australian, completely embodying the relaxed-surfer look, he did very little for me. Perhaps because I'd grown up surrounded by "dudes," so to me they lacked any international charm. The Frenchman, however, had an air of mystery that lit something inside me. My first impression was that he had a bit of a wild side that would keep things interesting.

After quickly drinking his espresso, he waltzed out of the café, and after a few minutes—giving myself just enough time to collect my jaw from the floor—I finally mustered up the courage to ask the barista about the job.

"Great coffee," I said to him.

"Right!" he replied. Obviously modesty wasn't his key strength.

"So, I saw the advert for a barista in the window," I said.

"Can I drop off an application?" I fished about in my bag for my résumé.

"Sure. You got any coffee-making experience?"

"Well, up until recently I was in publishing, but I worked in hospitality during my time at university. So yes, I've made coffee before."

"Coffee isn't a part-time job. It's a lifestyle."

I stifled a laugh. *Typical Australian barista, thinking coffee is life.*

"Oh, totally," I said, adding unconvincingly, "and it's a lifestyle I want."

He looked at me as he was steaming a jug of milk and, over the sound of the machine, he said, "All right then, why don't you come in for a trial and we'll see what you can do. You from Melbourne or Sydney?"

"Melbourne."

"Good," he replied with the slightest raise of his eyebrows.

Thankfully, I'd had the good sense to be born in Australia's coffee capital. It seemed to have scored me some points.

"So when shall I come in?" I asked.

"How about tomorrow morning? Eleven a.m., after the morning rush."

"Sure. I'll see you then."

"See you tomorrow. And don't worry about dressing up," he said, eyeing my green leaf-print summer dress. "We're pretty casual here."

Who could have predicted that I'd be overdressed applying for a job? Or maybe I'm just not hip enough in his Melbourne-hipster eyes?

"I'm Ella, by the way. It's nice to meet a fellow Australian."

"Right," he said again, this time uninterestedly. "I'm Chris."

I left the café unsure of whether I liked or hated Chris. He seemed easy to get along with, but was a bit of a douche when it came to coffee. Regardless, it'd been a relief to drink a good cup of joe and speak freely in English.

And the memory of that Frenchman was enough to make me glad I'd gone in and applied for the job. I hoped I'd see him again when I returned tomorrow.

Chapter

10

I WAS FEELING PRETTY POSITIVE about getting the coffee job and the good vibes continued as I checked my emails. It was a relief to see that one of the better-looking share houses I'd emailed that morning had responded, asking if I could come check out the room. I replied that I could, and Mike, my potential new housemate, sent me the address.

I headed towards the Latin Quarter, where the potential room for rent was waiting, and grabbed a sandwich to eat in the nearby Luxembourg Gardens. *The perfect location*, I thought as I strolled through the epic gardens with their flawlessly-maintained flowerbeds and imposing lines of identical trees. I sat on one of the iconic green Paris park chairs by the central fountain where children were playing with toy boats and squealing with joy. It was fun watching them dip their hands into the water and wait patiently, and sometimes not so patiently, for their boats to float ashore.

I met American Mike off Rue Mouffetard. Between the café and my potential new home, I pondered whether I'd be able to create a life in Paris in which I wasn't required to speak French at all. Mike was tall, well-built, blond, and handsome. He carried himself with an unmistakably American-prep-school sense of self-assuredness.

As we walked up to the apartment, he was all business, telling me about the setup. "So there are four bedrooms. The new tenant will take the vacant room and will share all the communal spaces with me, a good friend of mine, and our app's other co-founder. We're all pretty entrepreneurial and sometimes we'll be working from home; I hope you don't mind watching people create magic."

I looked at Mike to see if he was joking. He wasn't. "So what's the app you're working on?" I asked.

"It's a coworking congregation app. You know. For people like us who are breaking down the barriers of traditional work environments in Paris."

"It sounds like it'll be a great resource for expats here," I said.

"Yeah, I guess," he said. "But it'll be more than that."

I didn't know how to reply so I nodded awkwardly.

We climbed the five flights of stairs—no elevator—in silence and entered to find the other two housemates waiting on the couch. Mike gave me a tour of the apartment, saving my "room" until last. I say room, but it was really no bigger than a cupboard.

"This is it?" I said, surprised. "For eight hundred euros a month?"

"Yep. This is Paris. Doesn't get much cheaper. Oh, but bills are included in that."

Again, I checked his face to see if he was joking. Again, he wasn't.

I walked around, wondering if the room could even fit a single bed. I tried to remain positive. Perhaps I could ditch the frame and squeeze in a mattress. Maybe I could even get a min-imalist roll-out bed, Japanese style.

"Well, let's get to the interview then," Mike said. "I've got another candidate coming in half an hour."

"The interview?" I asked.

"Come through to the lounge room."

I sat on an upright dining chair as the three housemates eyed me from the couch. I got the feeling I was about to be interro-gated.

Mike said, "This is Ella, another Australian," without both-ering to introduce his two housemates to me.

The girl started things off. "So what do you think you can bring to this share house?" she asked.

"What can I bring?" I repeated. "Well, to be honest, I just moved here so I don't have much in the way of furniture or household items."

The trio gave me completely blank stares.

"I do know a great cheese shop in the Marais. I could bring some cheese. And toilet paper is always handy," I said.

"Ha, you're funny!" she said, not looking at all amused. "But seriously now. We're creators, we make things. This is a collab-orative, creative space. What energy will you bring to the apartment? What ideas?"

"Huh?" I asked.

The guy next to Mike looked at me and half rolled his eyes. "You know, what projects are you currently working on? What's your next big thing?" he said, as if that would clear things up.

"Well, my plan was to move to France without a plan. I'm starting fresh, so to speak. I've got a job trial at a café tomor-row. So I guess I might be making coffee soon."

"Oh cool. Yeah, that could work," the girl said.

The guy sniggered before launching into a five-minute monologue on the importance of living in creative spaces and making the most of your downtime to be your up time.

I tuned out, weighing up the pros and cons of living here. Yes, I needed a room, but they were all completely insufferable. Without a Plan B, though, I decided to give it one last shot.

"So how about you guys? Are you all working on the app?" I asked when he finally paused for a breath. My enthusiasm, however, was short-lived.

"We can't actually talk much about it right now. We've just finished this huge funding application and we should find out next week if we've got it. So until then, it's super top secret. You understand, right?" the girl said.

"Totally," I replied, not really understanding, or giving a damn, what she was talking about. At this stage I think we'd all made up our minds about whether or not I'd be a good fit for the apartment.

"Great, well, I think we have everything we need," Mike said. "Let me show you out."

"That's OK," I replied, relieved to be getting away from him. "I remember the way."

Shutting the front door, I heard their hushed voices discussing the lack of expat entrepreneurs in Paris. I couldn't help a huge eye roll myself thinking about how ridiculous that'd all been. As I clumped down the stairs, I wondered if all share houses in Paris were going to be like this one.

Checking my phone, I saw that it was already after five and remembered that I'd said I'd visit Mr. Cheeseman's shop that afternoon. Although I was excited to discover all the other Parisian *fromageries* I could frequent, there was something about Mr. Cheeseman's demeanor that I liked and I wanted try to build a good relationship with him. Maybe this visit I might even find out his name!

Arriving in the Marais, I began to feel more at home as I recognized the street names and was able to orient myself directly to the *fromagerie*. I stood outside momentarily to admire all the different types of cheese again and check the open hours before walking casually through the door.

Mr. Cheeseman wasn't behind the counter, so I pretended to be engrossed in the cabinets while another lady, who I didn't recognize, finished serving a group of people. When all the other customers had left the store and I had nobody left to hide behind, she looked at me impatiently and said, "*Je peux vous aider?*" Or, in my off-the-cuff translation, "Can I help you?"

"Ah, *je* . . . I'm just looking," I managed to finally get out. Given the shop's location, I was sure they were used to tourists sticking their heads in to have a look.

After an excruciating silence, with Mr. Cheeseman's colleague huffing about the store, I asked, "I'm sorry, I was hoping to talk to the man who works here. Is he in today?" I felt desperate asking after someone I hardly knew, but then again, I was really keen to pursue his cheese mentorship.

"*Qui?* Serge? *Ah, bien, non. Desolée.* He had to go out on some very important business. Did you have a cheese order to pick up?" she said, her patience growing thin as more customers entered the store.

So he's called Serge! I thought, excited at finally being able to attach a name to his face.

"No, I don't have an order. But I'd like to buy something delicious." I smiled, trying to get her to warm up a bit.

"But what cheese?" she snapped.

"Maybe you can recommend something," I blurted out, remembering too late that the French often found personal taste too subjective to make recommendations.

"OK, no problem," she said, shuffling about behind the counter and wrapping up a small wheel of cheese. A few seconds later she handed it to me without another word, no notes on the flavors or where the cheese came from; just the bare white packet. My forte clearly didn't lie in charming French sales staff.

"Can you please write the name of the cheese and where it came from on a piece of paper for me?" I asked. "I'm interested in learning more about French cheese."

She looked up at me with contempt, her irritation becoming evident as her forehead wrinkled above her beady, dark eyes.

"*D'accord*," she said, scribbling illegibly on a piece of card and handing it over to me. I think it read "Camembert." "That'll be ten euros."

"Ah . . ." I hesitated.

"Is there a problem with the price, *madame*?"

"Oh, *non*," I fumbled, handing over the money. I didn't want to cross this woman. Prior to this conversation, I'd assumed that anyone who worked in a cheese shop would be happy. I mean, who wouldn't enjoy a job where they were surrounded by so much delectability? Maybe the smell was getting to her.

Once outside again, I wondered why Serge had agreed to me stopping by when he wasn't going to be there. *And who was the lady who served me in the store? Was it Mr. Cheeseman's wife, or maybe his girlfriend? Maybe she was nasty because she thought that I was trying to muscle in on her relationship with Serge? More importantly, why do I care what she thought?* At any rate, I didn't think we were destined to be friends.

After picking up a bottle of Chenin blanc wine, plus a baguette and a *tarte aux fraises* (because they looked too good to resist), I headed back to the hotel, exhausted from what had turned out to be a very strange day filled with headstrong expats, bizarre interviews, and a frosty cheese-shop interaction. I snuck my bag of goodies past the receptionist who bid me goodnight and told me to sleep well, even though it was only seven thirty.

"You too," I replied, not knowing what else to say, and then willed the elevator to hurry up so I could escape her pitying gaze.

I opened the bottle of crisp, grassy white wine and poured a generous glass. I was happy to be alone for the evening and raised a little toast to myself for getting out there, despite the fact I hadn't made much concrete progress. Setting up in a new place certainly was difficult, but I figured that it was better to be doing so in Paris rather than having to start again in Melbourne. At least in Paris, memories of Paul weren't lurking around every corner. I just needed to keep avoiding the Eiffel Tower for now.

I unwrapped my cheese for one and felt that increasingly familiar twinge of loneliness . . . *Welcome back again, old friend*, I thought. I'd read somewhere that Camembert had originally been made in large rounds, and the smaller round had only been created so solo diners wouldn't waste anything. And while at first I found this story interesting, after a glass of wine on an empty stomach, it made me feel somewhat melancholic. It was as though all those years ago, the makers of the cheese had known that I would move to Paris to mourn a breakup. It was as though they'd anticipated that I would start to fill the void in my broken heart with French cheese.

Cutting a chunk, I smelled its barn-like perfume. The off-white, shiny shell was slightly sticky and the bubbles inside the cheese reminded me of those that occasionally line the top of a chocolate mousse. The flavor was a tiny bit sweet and floral, even slightly citric. It was good, but still I couldn't help feeling that it should have been better. Then again, maybe that was my frame of mind.

As I poured myself another glass of wine, a big, fat, hot tear escaped down my cheek. This was the first time since arriving in Paris, and since the horrible weekend post-breakup with Paul, that I'd shed an actual tear.

Dammit, this isn't meant to happen, I thought.

I looked out the window, reminding myself that I was in Paris and that I was happy. But, given the day I'd had, I couldn't help feeling a little blue, and a nagging voice in my head kept asking: *Did I do the right thing by coming here?*

Two

"You have to be a romantic to invest yourself, your money, and your time in cheese."

—ANTHONY BOURDAIN

Chapter

11

I'D ONLY BEEN IN PARIS for a few days when I woke up in a puddle of drool with my phone smooshed against my face and a half-written email to Billie on the screen.

As I lay in bed, I ran through the whole spectrum of emotions I'd felt since arriving in France: the relief of escaping Paul—and winter—in Melbourne, the empowerment of finally traveling solo again, and then the unexpected loneliness that accompanied it.

Realizing I must be cutting a pretty sad picture of a singleton in the City of Light and Love, I leaped out of bed to turn my day around before spiraling too far into despair.

I deleted most of my despondent ramblings to Billie and instead sent her a quick message saying that the weather was wonderful and that the hotel was gorgeous, a great find—*positive vibes only*, I told myself. I told her about my job trial at the café and recounted the cringeworthy share-flat interview I'd had the day before, which I knew would give her a good laugh. My still-somewhat-miserable self couldn't help adding that the hunt for accommodation wasn't going so well, and that I'd probably need an interim place to stay, maybe a cheaper hotel, if I wasn't able to find a permanent solution soon.

By the time I got out of the shower, she'd written back. "Glad to hear you're giving everything a go, El. Regarding accommodation, did you check Airbnb? Just a thought. Now, go get that job!"

I threw on jeans and a black T-shirt—although it was already thirty degrees outside, I figured this was probably my "coolest" outfit—and walked down to Flat White. As soon as I entered the café I looked around for my mystery man. I couldn't help but feel a little disheartened when I didn't see him there, but told myself it was probably a good thing given I was about to go through a trial for a hospitality job and it'd been more than a few years since I'd made coffee.

Chris welcomed me more warmly than he had the day before, handed me an apron, and said, "Right, Ella, let's see what you can do. Why don't you make me some coffee? Let's start with two identical lattes and then we'll do two identical flat whites."

I felt slightly panicked. It was one thing to remember correct coffee-to-milk ratios, but re-creating them in real time was another thing altogether. Not wanting Chris to smell my fear, I smiled as I pulled the espresso shots and then poured the steamed milk. There was some panache to my style, but I failed to produce anything near identical.

"Hmmm. Not great," Chris said. "You wanna try again? I'm guessing you haven't used this machine before, right?" He was being generous.

"Sure, totally," I said.

This time, my flat whites looked identical, much to my own surprise, but the lattes were still wildly different. Chris nodded and got us to taste them.

"Bitter," was his first remark. "The milk is a little burnt," was his second.

"Ah . . ." I was about to launch into an excuse but Chris cut me off asking, "Where did you say you'd worked again?"

"Just a small café on Brunswick Street. It's not around anymore."

"I thought you said you'd worked at ST. ALi?"

"No, never."

"Ah shoot, that must have been someone else. Never mind . . ." He paused. "Look, it's great you're keen on the job, but your coffee tastes like shit."

"I can learn," I said, disappointed that I hadn't done better. Perhaps it'd been too long between coffee-making jobs. Obviously standards, even in Paris, had gone up.

"Look Ella, I kinda think you've either got it or you don't. And I'm not sure you do," he said.

"I understand," I told him, devastated that I wasn't going to walk out of the café with a job.

Thankfully, Chris wasn't finished with me yet. "The good news is, if you're still after a job, we do need someone to help out in the kitchen on weekends. We get slammed pretty much from open until close, so it'd be good to have an extra set of hands on deck. And we can pay you cash too. Sound good?"

"So I'd be cooking?" I perked up at the thought.

"Mostly washing dishes, maybe helping with some prep; it depends. It's probably not your bag, though. You're more a corporate gal, right?"

I paused for a moment, resenting being boxed into a specific job type, but also wanting to hurl at the thought of washing dishes. It was hardly the glamorous job I'd envisaged getting in Paris; but then again, the whole point of leaving Melbourne was to try new things and get out of my rut. And I quite liked the café. The idea of hanging out and doing something free of responsibility was liberating. Anyway, I didn't have anything else lined up, so why not?

"Chris, I'd absolutely love to wash dishes here," I told him, and we arranged for me to start the next day.

"And sorry about the coffee," I said as we were wrapping things up.

"Yeah, not good. How about I make you one for the road?"

Relief flooded over me that a) Chris wasn't pissed off that I'd wasted his time, b) I'd gotten a paying job, even if I'd be working as a dish pig, and c) I was about to get a decent flat white. I wouldn't say the trial had been a raging success, but a small victory nonetheless, and it was a concrete start towards establishing my life in Paris.

En route back to the hotel, I felt drawn in the direction of Mr. Cheeseman's shop. I wasn't sure that I wanted, or needed, to buy more cheese given I'd already indulged pretty heavily since arriving in Paris, but I couldn't help passing by to see if my new acquaintance was working.

When I looked through the window, I was delighted to see he was back—and a little more than pleased that his female friend was nowhere to be seen.

He waved me in.

"*Bonjour,*" he said jovially as I walked in the door.

"*Bonjour,*" I replied dutifully. The French were always so formal in their greetings. "I came by to see you yesterday but you were out."

"Ah yes, an emergency, I'm afraid," he said. I wondered how often he encountered cheese emergencies in this area of Paris.

"No problem." I tried to sound casual. "Your colleague gave me some cheese."

"Ah good, so Fanny looked after you."

I suppressed a chuckle at her name.

"Yes, your girlfriend was very kind and helpful," I lied, wanting to keep him in good spirits.

"Fanny? Kind?" he questioned. "She certainly knows a lot about cheese but I wouldn't say she is particularly friendly. Oh, and she is only a colleague."

It made sense that they were not an item. Where Serge gushed with adoration for cheese, and, I assumed, everything in life, Fanny had treated it as a job.

I couldn't think of anything to say to brush over the fact that I'd just indirectly asked if he was dating his not-so-friendly co-worker, so I said a long, "Hmmm," while turning a vibrant shade of red.

"So what cheese did Fanny give you to try?" he asked.

"Oh, a Camembert. Perhaps she thought I was just another tourist and would only want to eat an iconic French cheese. It was nice, but it seemed a little hard . . . I thought Camembert was meant to be softer, more gooey." Google had taught me this when I was noshing down my wheel at the hotel.

"Did you tell her it was for eating immediately?" he asked. The serious expression that he seemed to reserve for intense cheese discussions was suddenly back.

"No, I didn't. Was I meant to?"

"Well, it helps us to choose the ripest wheel with the best flavor."

"Oh," I said, embarrassed.

"Not to worry. There's plenty more Camembert in the sea,"

Serge said, laughing at his own joke. His face softened, and I found myself once again captivated by his blue eyes. I tittered so as not to be rude.

"Anyway, it's lucky you came back because I have a cheese I think you'll be interested in. Not all foreigners like it because it can smell a little strong, but it's something I'm sure you can't get in Australia."

"Great," I said, glad he was finally on board for recommending different types of cheese. I was also keen to dispel his impression that foreigners don't like stinky cheese. "So what is it?"

"Roquefort."

"Oh, I've tried Roquefort before," I told him, feeling proud of myself.

"But I'm sure it wasn't the real Roquefort. At least not the best Roquefort."

Man, this guy is hung up on the "realness" of cheese.

"What's the difference?" I asked, slightly annoyed.

"Real Roquefort has to be aged in the Combalou caves in Roquefort-sur-Soulzon. Anything else is just a poor imitation. Would you like to try some?"

Putting my frustration aside, I eagerly agreed to sample this famous Roquefort, happy to be getting the star treatment and feeling like my patronage at the store was already starting to pay off.

He handed over a slice and it felt wet and slippery between my fingers. I ate it quickly, surprised by the sharp, salty flavor I found when my tongue hit the vein of blue mold puncturing the cheese.

"Wow," I said, buying myself time to figure out if I liked the taste or if I was going to have to rush outside and spit it out. I let the cheese linger in my mouth a little longer, nodding along as I chewed, then forcing a wide grin. I decided to buy a small chunk to take home and investigate further, this time with some bread to soften the force.

Serge hummed along to himself as he wrapped up my order, clearly happy he'd taught me something about real French blue cheese. His change in demeanor since our first meeting was dramatic. He was sweet and unpretentious, kind in a goofy way.

"By the way, *je m'appelle* Serge, Serge Marais," he said, his French words spilling into the air, smooth as cream.

I replied in a garble of French. I'd practiced saying, "Pleased to meet you" many a time walking the streets of Paris waiting for this moment, but as it came out I knew that I'd bungled it. But Serge didn't let it show; he smiled, handed me my cheese, and wished me a pleasant evening.

As I walked out, the little bell tinkling over the door as I did so, I swear I heard him chuckle.

⁓

Back at the hotel I started to scroll through options on Airbnb. Even with my new source of income, it didn't take me long to realize that the price per night was still too high for solo apartments in the areas I wanted to live in, and that those I could afford were all in far-flung locations. I moved my search to private rooms in share houses and tried to remain as open-minded as possible. After so many years of living with Paul—and after the pretentious share-house interview I'd just sat through—I wasn't sure I could go back to living with a stranger, or strangers, again: having to learn and preempt their rhythms, their whimsies, and factor in the time they spend in the bathroom getting ready. But then I figured I had to compromise. *There's no point being in Paris if you can't live in the heart of the action, or at least within one of the twenty arrondissements that make up the snail within the ring road.*

I unwrapped the Roquefort in an attempt to help me concentrate. It had the opposite effect; the smell was almost overpowering in the tiny hotel room. I opened the windows and hoped it wouldn't permeate into the walls. I ate and scrolled, surprised at how moreish the cheese was, and soon I found myself wishing I'd gotten a bigger slice.

Long after my cheese had run out, and exhausted from trying to find somewhere to live that didn't sound too bizarre or intimidating, I came across a listing for a gorgeous apartment in Saint-Germain, sharing with a mother and her adult son. According to the description, they were "socialites" and "hardly ever home." The thought of living with a mother and son would normally have been a deal-breaker for me, but as I looked through the pictures of the apartment, I was shamelessly lured by its grandeur.

I wouldn't leave home either if my mum lived here, I thought. The apartment was luxury beyond what I could have imagined, and there was a great discount for monthly bookings. I sent them a message and crossed my fingers that the room was available. I didn't have any other very promising leads.

I went to bed with my head full of images of ornate and overpriced apartments, big hunks of Roquefort, and a blossoming friendship with a French cheesemonger. I couldn't believe how quickly my fortunes had changed in this magical city. *Why was I even upset this morning?* I asked myself.

Considering I'd been in Paris less than a week, things were actually going rather well. I had a job, a constant stream of delicious cheese, and I'd even learned Mr. Cheeseman's name.

Chapter

12

WHEN ACCEPTING THE KITCHEN JOB at Flat White, I didn't realize I'd get to see my handsome French mystery man the very next day. And I certainly didn't count on being exhausted, sweaty, and disheveled when I did.

Thankfully, my first shift had gone so much better than I could have expected. I found not being confined to an office desk really refreshing and I enjoyed the freedom of being able to move around the kitchen, despite its tiny size. The constant access to good coffee was a huge bonus. When I considered how much money I'd save on my weekend cups of joe, it made the kitchen work all the more worthwhile.

My not-so-positive initial impressions of Chris were thankfully quickly dispelled as I got to know him better. Behind the front that I'd mistaken for arrogance, I found that he was sweet, funny, and just ridiculously earnest when it came to talking about coffee. During the lulls in service, we stood around shooting the breeze.

"So what brought you to Paris?" Chris asked what I would come to know as the standard expat question.

"Change," I told him. "I needed a change of scenery."

"Yeah,.I get that. Melbourne can seem small sometimes, hey?"

"Oh my God, can't it?"

"Remind me what you were doing back home before you came to Paris? You were working a corporate job, right?"

"Book publishing."

"You're a writer?"

"Not quite. I've always enjoyed writing but somehow ended up on the business side of things, as an assistant. I guess that's part of the reason it was so easy to pack up life back home and move here."

Chris nodded.

"And what brought you to Paris?" I asked. "The pursuit of good coffee?"

"No, the pursuit of French women. I came to seek them out, to date them, and to love them."

I laughed but Chris wasn't trying to make a joke. His shameless obsession with *les femmes françaises* was surprisingly endearing.

"I'm head over heels for them, Ella. I'm obsessed with this country's Brigittes, Charlottes, and Marions."

I admired his honesty. I decided I'd try a similar approach next time somebody asked me what I was doing in Paris: *I decided to come to France because I didn't know what else to do after breaking up with my boyfriend. A slice of Comté convinced me it was a good idea.* Might be hard to pull off without sounding completely crazy.

I was just about to head home, feeling ragged after my first day back at work, when the handsome French mystery man walked through the door.

Shit, I thought, smoothing down my hair.

I froze, torn between rushing out the door and wanting to hang around and see if I could find out anything else about my espresso-drinking dream guy.

I told Chris that on second thought, I might just grab a coffee before I go.

"The usual flat white?" he asked, raising his eyebrows. He must have understood my game.

"Actually, I'll get an espresso," I said quietly.

I could feel the Frenchman's presence behind me. It was like his eyes were burning a hole through my head. I was desperate to turn around and look at him but I wanted to maintain some sense of composure. Feeling flustered, I collected my coffee cup and, steadying my hands, took it to the bench outside. I sat and concentrated on inhaling and exhaling, feeling my heartbeat gradually slow back down.

I closed my eyes for a second.

"*Je peux?*" a deep, sexy voice asked.

My eyes flung open to see him towering over me, motioning at the empty spot next to me. "Ah. *Oui,*" I said, fumbling through the most basic of French words.

The handsome man sat, placed his espresso next to him on the bench, and pulled a packet of cigarettes out of his pocket. He lit one effortlessly, looking incredibly dashing in the process.

"*Vous-en-voulez une?*" he asked, probably wondering why I was staring at him.

"Oh. *Non, merci.*" After hunting for some more words in French and coming up trumps, I finally told him in English that I didn't smoke.

"You're English?" he asked.

"Australian. And you're French, I take it?" I don't know what hold this man had over me but it seemed I was incapable of saying anything intelligent in front of him.

"Yes. Why are you in Paris?" he asked.

"Oh, I'm taking a year working holiday," I told him. Faced with such a well-dressed Parisian, I chickened out of practicing my Chris-inspired honesty.

"And you like working here as a barista?" he asked, motioning back to the café where I could feel Chris watching us like a hawk.

"Sure, it's not bad. I'm looking for something more serious but this is fun for the time being." I didn't bother to correct him by admitting I was working in the kitchen. *Who cares about semantics*, I thought to myself.

Mystery man finished his coffee in two quick sips and checked his watch. I panicked that he was about to leave and felt disappointed that I hadn't had time to leave a better impression.

"What are you doing this evening?" I blurted out, trying to postpone his departure.

"I'm meeting friends in an hour or so. Perhaps you would like to join me for a quick drink before I do?" he suggested. "I want to find out more about Australia."

I was momentarily speechless, too busy blushing and squealing on the inside to respond immediately.

"Sure," I finally managed to say. "I'm meeting friends later too, so it's good timing."

Of course I was lying about my evening's social engagements, but the alluring Frenchman didn't need to know that.

I rushed our coffee cups inside while my date—*was it too early to call him that?*—waited for me outside.

"Everything OK?" Chris asked, looking confused.

"Yep! We're off for a drink," I said, fully aware that I was smiling like a maniac.

"You and Gaston?" Chris asked, sounding surprised.

"Yep. Me and Gaston."

Could he have a more French name? Just saying it aloud got me all hot and bothered.

Gaston popped his head around the door to see if I was ready.

"Find out if he's single," Chris whispered to me as I left the café.

Walking down the road, I was lost in thought trying to figure out what Chris had meant by this comment.

"I'm Ella, by the way," I said, breaking the silence.

"Gaston."

"I know," I said, probably coming across like a stalker.

We sat at a tiny table outside a French-style café in the Marais. Our chairs were so close together that I could smell Gaston's cologne and I had to rearrange my legs so they weren't obviously touching his. I felt self-conscious sitting so close to him, although I was thoroughly enjoying the view. His chiseled cheekbones and dark, broody eyes were making my stomach feel like it had a life of its own.

Gaston ordered two glasses of rosé and some ice.

"We call this a *piscine*," he said, slowing sliding two ice cubes into his glass.

"Like a swimming pool?" I asked.

"*Oui*," he replied.

"But I thought it was sacrilegious to add ice to wine," I said smugly.

"Ah, but it's summer and in France, this is what we do." He shrugged. "But you would never do it with good quality wine, you're quite right."

I felt like I'd been given a gold star.

The rosé was cold and refreshing, and after a long day at work, it was just screaming out to be drunk quickly. I took a deep sip to settle my nerves and give me time to think of something else to say. Babbling on about myself was the last thing I wanted to do when faced with such a good-looking man; there was so much room for error.

"And what do you do in Paris?" I asked.

"Oh, this and that," he said—so aloof. "But tell me about you. Tell me about Australia. What's the best way to cook a kangaroo?"

Was he joking? I wondered, thrown by his question. I laughed uncomfortably and told Gaston the basics of my life back home, glamorizing it as much as possible. I must have been doing quite a good job, too, because he seemed interested, asking a lot of questions and keeping me talking.

He was also completely relaxed, one leg crossed over the other, his shirt unbuttoned just low enough to give me a view of his tanned chest. He sipped his wine with gusto, like he'd been doing it his whole life.

I could see other women checking him out as they walked past; he was like a homing beacon for attention. I could almost feel the jealousy in their eyes when they realized he was sitting with me. But his gaze remained fixed on mine as he flirted with me. Hard. It'd been so long since I'd been the center of attention with a man that it went straight to my head. I felt giddy with what seemed like genuine adoration. I thanked God I'd hung around for that espresso after finishing work.

"So where are you living?" Gaston asked as we moved onto our second blissful glass of wine. *Angling for a booty call?* I wondered.

"I'm in this gorgeous little hotel down the road," I told him, grateful I was staying somewhere so chic. "But I'm hardly ever there," I continued, trying to give the impression that I had an exploding social calendar. "It's the perfect season for picnics by the Seine and in the Luxembourg Gardens."

I then detailed my obsession with the epic selection of gourmand ingredients from the French delis and supermarkets. I wasn't exaggerating when I told him I could spend entire days inspecting products and stalking the aisles. The overwhelming selection of yogurt and potted desserts alone was enough to keep me entertained for hours.

"So you like food?" he asked.

"I love it," I replied enthusiastically. "Especially French food. God, I found this cheese shop which has got me completely hooked . . ."

Despite my efforts to avoid it, I was now officially babbling on. I forced myself to stop talking about Serge's shop before I came across as cheese-obsessed.

"But tell me more about you. Do you live alone?" I asked, getting right to the point.

When he told me that he'd been in his solo apartment for close to a decade, I couldn't wipe the smile off my face.

In terms of additional intel I managed to gather between swooning over Gaston's good looks and charming personality, I learned that he was born in Paris and had never lived elsewhere. He went to school and university here, but like many wealthy Parisians, holidayed on the Côte d'Azur. He told me that for years he'd been longing to visit Australia. That he thought everyone there seemed laid-back and beautiful. *Perhaps I could help him get his fix?*

I'd forgotten that Gaston had plans that evening and I was

devastated when he suddenly checked the time and told me he had to go. He laid down a twenty-euro note, got up, and kissed both my cheeks. *Did he just linger slightly longer than required? Or was I getting ahead of myself?* Before he left, he asked for my phone number, which I gladly wrote down for him on a napkin, my hands shaking wildly.

As I watched his muscular arse walking off down the street, I remembered that Chris had wanted me to find out if Gaston was single. It certainly seemed like he was, but I didn't want to be presumptuous; I'd need to wait for a second date to be sure.

I went through the evening play-by-play. Despite being exhausted after a long day of washing dishes, I felt like I'd gotten back on the dating horse quite elegantly. Fingers crossed I hadn't blown it. The only thing I wasn't sure about was whether I'd written down the correct mobile number.

Shit!

I pulled out my phone to double-check and saw I had a message from the Airbnb hosts in Saint-Germain. The dates I had requested were available. I breathed a sigh of relief—I'd found an apartment to move into. Living with a mother-son duo wasn't the perfect solution, but at least it was a month of having somewhere to sleep sorted.

Feeling joyful but a little tipsy after the couple of glasses of wine Gaston and I had drunk in quick succession, I decided to take myself home. I strolled back to the hotel, picturing what life in Paris might be like if I ended up with Gaston—clearly the booze was talking—and felt jittery at the thought of walking the romantic streets arm-in-arm. It'd been a long time since I'd gotten any action and the thought of ripping off Gaston's perfectly tailored suit was almost too much for me to handle.

Chapter
13

"SO WHAT THE HELL HAPPENED between you and Gaston?" Chris asked, walking into the kitchen at Flat White the next day. There was a mix of nervousness and desperation in his voice that intrigued me—why was he suddenly so invested in my dating life?

"Nothing," I replied. "We just went for a couple glasses of wine. Why? What do you know about him?"

"Not too much, which is why I was surprised when you guys left together. He comes in a lot with this French girl who I'm sort of friendly with. Well, if I'm being honest—I want to ask this girl out, but I have no idea if the two of them are an item."

"You mean Gaston has a girlfriend?" I was shocked. "He definitely gave off single vibes."

"I don't know, it's complicated," he said, rubbing his temples.

While Chris appeared to walk so self-assuredly through life, his dalliances with French women seemed to make him slightly hysterical.

"Why don't you tell me what you *do* know?" I almost demanded. "Why do you think Gaston is dating somebody?"

Chris took a swig of water before launching into his—surprisingly detailed—knowledge of Gaston's love life. "So way back at the end of last year, probably before you'd even decided to come to Paris, we had a launch party here for this start-up called Food To Go Go. This Scottish guy that I know called Tim started it. Anyway, it's a food delivery app, pretty cool, actually. They're working on . . ."

"Chris, back to Gaston," I directed. He seemed to have a tendency to flesh out stories to the point where he forgot what he had initially been trying to say.

"Right. So anyway, at this launch party, I met this knockout French woman called Clotilde. I mean, there's beautiful and then there's Clotilde. She's next-level stuff. Legs up to my ears but I wouldn't let that stop me. God, even just thinking about her makes me hot."

"Yep . . ." I said. "And?"

"So Clotilde is gorgeous, and I thought she'd be a bitch, but she's actually really friendly, so I decided to ask her out the next time I saw her. Only catch is, the next time was when she came in here with Gaston for coffee. I didn't want to jump to any conclusions, but I got the impression they were dating—but I couldn't be one hundred percent sure. Perhaps they were just old friends. Regardless, they certainly looked very comfortable together. Anyway, after a few weeks of Clotilde coming in by herself, I was all prepped to finally ask her out, and then in she comes again with Gaston. So I'm just sort of biding my time. Every time she comes in solo, I try and get more information, but I'm at a loss."

"Why haven't I seen her before?" I asked.

"Well, it *is* only your second shift. But you might not, anyway—she mostly comes in on weekdays, and even then only about once a week. Her office is just down the road."

"Why would Gaston invite me for drinks if he has a gorgeous

girlfriend?" I voiced my concerns aloud, but Chris wasn't much help.

"That's what I was hoping you could tell me . . ." he said. "But you remain useless and the mystery lives on."

"Well, if she ever comes in while I'm here, come get me, yeah?" I said as Chris headed back out to the front of the café. "I want to see my potential competition."

⌒

Before I knew it, my stay at Hôtel du Petit Moulin was over. Although I regretted having to leave the comforts of my Marais digs— and the luxury of having someone make my bed every morning—the move to the Airbnb went seamlessly. And my new apartment was even more spectacular in person than it was in the photos online: high ceilings and large windows gave the rooms a regal feel, which was complemented by dark-wood antique furniture and intricate woollen rugs over parquetry floors. It felt like the kind of old-money home you'd see in French movies, where large families live together across one floor of the building and hilarious comedy and/or drama ensues.

As far as housemates go, my new ones were quite eclectic: There was the mature and rather glamorous French mother with silver hair and an air of importance, and her wispy-bearded, forty-year-old son, Jean-Pierre. We communicated through translation apps, my high-school French, and Jean-Pierre's high-school English. While always friendly to me, they spent a good portion of the day bickering with each other in French when they thought I wasn't listening. Neither of them had a job, so they mostly sat in the formal living room drinking tea and listening to classical music.

So much for them never being home!

To get out of the apartment one afternoon in my second week living there, I decided to head back to the Marais to pursue my budding friendship with Serge. I wasn't sure he actually wanted or needed a slightly unhinged Australian in his life, but he'd certainly warmed up since I'd first met him and I decided it was worth a shot. Even if our relationship never moved beyond the professional confines, I figured the worst that could happen if I became a daily visitor in his store would be getting offered more tasters and better cheese.

I'd hardly consider that a lost cause, I thought.

"Back so soon?" Serge said, eyebrows raised when I entered.

"It's been nearly two weeks," I protested. "And I can't help myself. I'm falling in love with cheese."

"You should be careful not to eat too much," he said seriously, looking at me over the counter.

Oh shit, he's already got me pegged as a cheese pig.

"Everything is better in moderation," he said.

Typical French mentality, I thought. *Leave me alone with a wheel of Brie and a whole baguette and then we'll see what's better.*

"Having said that, I just received a delivery that you might be interested in." Serge smiled.

Another recommendation? I was starting to feel cocky. Now I'd just need to work on my acting skills to pretend that my palate was French enough to handle it.

"Mmm," I said nervously, wondering if today's cheese would be more intense than the Roquefort I'd had last time.

"It's a goat cheese, a Sainte-Maure de Touraine. When it's young, it's pale, white, and soft, and then when it ages, it goes darker and the flavor gets more intense. This one is old now, and it must be tasted." He handed me a sliver.

"OK, let's do this," I said, slipping the slice into my mouth. Serge did the same in a tit-for-tat kind of motion. The cheese was, as built up by Serge, fruity but fresh, fluffy in the middle, oozing to a gooey exterior. I shut my eyes and tried to savor the multi-textural sensation but ended up devouring it greedily.

"I'll take some," I said, desperate to eat the whole log myself.

"*D'accord*," he said, busying himself wrapping up my cheese.

I racked my brain trying to think of a way to continue our conversation, to take it beyond the margins of the customer-seller relationship.

"You certainly have a lot of cheese here," was the best I could come up with.

"It wouldn't be a very good *fromagerie* without it," Serge said with a smile.

"You know what? I think I'm going to try every type of French cheese while I'm living here," I said offhandedly.

"You couldn't!" he replied, almost yelling.

"What do you mean, I 'couldn't'?"

"There are very many different types."

"Lucky, because I love cheese."

"No, but seriously. This is the idea of a crazy person." He looked concerned.

"Well, I think it's a great idea," I said, trying to impress him.

"Perhaps you don't know how many types of cheese there are in France."

"Nope. But I'd guess around one hundred. It should be easy to sample them all."

Serge laughed. "I would like to see you try. And it would be good business for me."

"OK then, why not? I've done harder things in life. It'll be a fun challenge." I was feeling assertive, and almost wanted to get a rise out of Serge. Getting a job and finding an apartment had given me the sense that I could do anything here, and Serge telling me otherwise seemed to just fuel that fire.

"It will be a *big* challenge," Serge said. "I'm really not sure you can do it."

"Do you bet I can't?" I asked, jokingly.

"Yes. And I think it would be impossible for you to win this bet."

"Where's your faith in my stamina, Serge?"

"*D'accord*," he said. "If you're sure: I bet you that you can't try all the types of French cheese in one year."

I laughed. "It can't be that hard. I mean, eating cheese a couple of times a week sounds like my idea of heaven. What do I win if I succeed? Will I enter a Cheese Eating Hall of Fame? Will you put my photo on your wall?"

"OK, Ella. In the highly unlikely scenario that you sample every variety of cheese in France, I'll take you to dinner at La Tour d'Argent. As well as having a fabulous cheese selection, it's one of the oldest restaurants in Paris. It's an institution."

Wow, that escalated quickly! It also has to be one of the city's most expensive restaurants.

"Sure," I said, not really thinking about what that implied. "It's a deal. I love dinner."

"So if you try every type of French cheese in one year, I'll take you to dinner. And when you don't manage to try them all, you'll take me for dinner?"

"Serge, you've got yourself a bet," I said, thrusting my hand over the counter to finalize our little wager. I felt a wave of electricity course through me; my excitement at the prospect of this cheese challenge made me feel high. I buzzed with an increased sense of purpose: eating cheese to win a very luxurious dinner with my new friend. I only thought to add after our handshake that—on the off-chance I lost—I'd take him to an authentic Australian pub for dinner. I certainly couldn't afford to treat anyone to dinner at La Tour d'Argent.

"I wish you luck, Ella. Either way, I think I'll be the winner," Serge said, winking.

Why was he suddenly looking so smug?

"So, exactly how many types of French cheese are there, then?" I asked, looking around the store, my brain finally kicking into action.

"There are *over* 365 types," he replied. "But for simplicity's sake, we can just call it one new cheese for every day of the year. You've never heard de Gaulle's famous line about the impossibility of governing a nation with so many different types of cheese?" He gave me a sly look, like he'd just tricked me into buying him dinner.

"Three hundred and sixty-five types? Seriously?" I said. "Tell me you're exaggerating."

"Three hundred and sixty-five, although you're down to three hundred and sixty-four now with the Sainte-Maure de Touraine," Serge said, and handed over my cheese.

Oh God, what did I just agree to?

Chapter

14

WHEN I ARRIVED HOME THAT evening, I found Jean-Pierre and his mother sitting on the sofas in the living room drinking tea. Again. The mother waved me over, poured me a cup, and motioned for me to join them. I begrudgingly accepted, but felt desperate to get back to my room and dive into my roll of Sainte-Maure.

With Jean-Pierre and his phone acting as interpreters, his mother asked me how my job was going and how I was enjoying Paris. In our weird three-way conversation—with an added technological margin of error—I told them that I loved the city and that work was going really well. She nodded and asked Jean-Pierre to translate something else, which, other than picking out the French word *amour*, I didn't understand. Jean-Pierre replied quickly and angrily to his mother and she hissed something back before getting up to go into the kitchen. I rose and grabbed my cup and she almost pushed me back onto the couch, telling me to sit as she walked out.

I asked Jean-Pierre how his day was and he gave me a short, one-word response. He avoided making eye contact with me so I only sat for a couple more minutes before standing up and going to my room. *Sure, it was a great apartment, but was it worth suffering these awkward family interactions?* I thought.

⌒

Ah, shit! I said to myself after confirming everything I'd feared on my laptop. Serge was right: There are over 365 types of French cheese. *Dammit!* The more I researched, the more I began to realize I'd bitten off more than I could chew. I started to feel sick at the thought of cheese, day in and day out.

I ran through the potential cons of following through with the challenge. All that cheese buying was going to put a strain on my personal finances. And my waistline as well, come to think of it. I wasn't even sure that my—so far—voracious appetite for cheese could withstand a daily dose. In any case, I hoped my overly-eager bravado wouldn't jeopardize my love of cheese, or my burgeoning status as Mr. Cheeseman's favorite customer.

I considered forgetting the whole wager ever happened and never showing my face at the *fromagerie* again. But a bet is a bet, and Serge was one of the few people in Paris who knew my name. I didn't want to give up on him. Or the cheese.

I stared at my roll of Sainte-Maure and *almost* couldn't face eating it.

But once my initial surprise at the expanse of the world of French cheese had worn off, I began to cut slivers of the rich, ash-rind goat cheese, pairing them with black figs that I'd picked up at the market. The combination felt summery and light, and each bite was like a burst of happiness that kept me wanting more.

As I ate, I began to picture myself trying a new type of

cheese every day for the rest of my year in Paris. Suddenly, the image brought a smile to my face.

At least one cheese for every day of the year . . . No big deal . . . I guess I could manage that. The intoxicating mix of figs and goat cheese filled me with confidence and I decided that there was no good reason I couldn't win the bet if I put my mind to it. *I can become a chic, cheese-eating Parisian while working in a café kitchen,* I told myself. *Why not?*

And the whole idea wasn't without some pros: It would give me additional purpose during my year in France, cement my friendship with Serge, and give me an amazing excuse to learn the ins and outs of one of the country's most famous foods. *My God, by the end of the year, I could be a specialist. I could export cheese back to Australia; I could write a book about cheese!*

It felt a little deranged to commit to such a challenge, but I figured it couldn't hurt to start and see how it went. Give it a few months at least. What was the worst that could happen?

365 types of cheese in 365 days. It was almost beginning to sound fun.

I poured myself a glass of wine from the emergency bottle I'd stashed under my bed.

"I accept the challenge," I said to myself, waving my wine around. "Let's do this." I kept going, dancing around the room, now fully aware that I was talking to myself, but not wanting to lose momentum. "I can do this. I'm going to do this! This is going to be wonderful!"

To commemorate the occasion, I arranged my wine glass, the goat cheese, and the figs on the windowsill, with the stunning view of the rooftops in the background. I took a picture on my phone and the result was quintessentially Parisian. I'd never been one to post food images on social media, but opened up my Instagram anyway. I hesitated and then decided to create a new account. With a couple of clicks, I'd set up *My 365 Days of Cheese: a photo diary of my year in Paris*. It'd be the perfect way to document my cheese-eating adventures and my year in this gorgeous city.

I posted the Sainte-Maure picture with the caption "Cheese number 1 in my challenge to eat 365 types of cheese in 365 days. Follow my adventures as I make my way through the smelliest, gooiest, and downright ugliest varieties of French cheese." I added a few food and Paris hashtags for good measure. I chuckled to myself and sent the account name to Billie, certain that I'd at least have one follower.

⁓

The next morning I opened up my Instagram account to see whether Billie had liked my cheese picture and nearly dropped my phone in shock.

I have forty new followers?

I was gobsmacked. Overnight, forty people had decided to follow my cheese adventure in Paris. I only had a hundred and twenty followers on my normal account and that had been active for years. I felt like photos of cheese would put that number to shame in a matter of days.

Maybe I'm onto something with this challenge, I thought.

I also had a message from Billie congratulating me on my social media prowess and telling me that she was planning a trip to Paris in October.

Only a couple of months away!

Everything was clicking into place. I was to be a fabulous, single, cheese-eating woman in France. I had a source of income—though not a particularly glamorous job—a start on some friendships, and now a purpose to my life in Paris: cheese. And the sun was shining, to top it all off.

~

Leaving work the following Sunday, after a disappointing lack of Gaston sightings over the weekend, I tried to avoid thinking about men by thinking about all things cheese. I didn't want to disappoint Serge—or let him take an early lead on our bet. Plus, my Instagram followers were hungry and waiting. *Hurrah!*

There wasn't a shortage of cheese in Paris, but finding cafés that offered an assortment beyond the standard varieties was a little more challenging. I'd earlier spied a nice-looking café a few blocks from work; I would celebrate the end of my working week in style.

Before sitting down, I did a careful visual scan to make sure Jean-Pierre was nowhere in sight. I'd already endured an uncomfortable run-in with him last week when leaving work. Surprised to even see him outside the apartment, I'd only recognized him at the last minute and hadn't had time to alter my course.

"Is that where you work?" he'd asked, pointing to the café.

He'd shifted about uncomfortably from foot to foot.

I'd ummed and ahhed, not really wanting to confirm where I worked in case he turned up for coffee one day, so I'd changed the subject. "So what are you doing over this side of the river?"

"Shopping. It's Mother's birthday soon."

I'd instinctively looked down at his hands, which were completely free of shopping bags. He didn't seem to notice the look of surprise I'd given him.

"I'm just on my way home," he'd continued. "What are you doing now?"

I'd panicked at the thought of walking home with him so I'd lied and told him I was meeting a friend. I said a speedy goodbye and walked off, doing a quick check to make sure he was heading in the opposite direction. I couldn't pinpoint what I found creepy about him, but I figured that as long as I kept my distance, he wouldn't ever be a problem.

Shaking Jean-Pierre from my thoughts, I ordered a glass of white wine and a Saint-Marcellin: a soft-rind cheese from the Rhône-Alpes. It looked small and manageable on the plate, almost lamentably so considering the decadent mood I was in, but thankfully it packed a punch. The potent ball of cow's milk had a yellowish tinge and looked as wrinkled as a hairless cat. Admittedly it was not attractive, but it *was* addictive, which seemed to be the way with a lot of French cheese.

I took a couple of quick photos of the Saint-Marcellin, made even more appetizing in the dusky sun's glow, and uploaded one to my Instagram account. I couldn't believe the traction that an account dedicated solely to cheese was getting. It'd somehow grown to two hundred followers since I'd started posting pictures of cheese and the comments were often quite serious. For every post uploaded, I'd receive a few questions asking about the flavor, the best time to eat it, and where to buy it. I'd research the different types of cheese as I ate them—of course, only when Serge wasn't on hand to provide the information for me—and I'd been adding more and more detailed captions to keep my followers happy.

Another cheese down, only 340 to go, I thought ominously, but joyously, to myself. I'd taken another bite when my phone started to ring. Blocked number. With Jean-Pierre still in the back of my mind, I panicked, thinking it might be him. But then I had an even scarier thought: *Could it be Gaston?*

It'd been about three weeks since I'd given him my phone number and I'd been desperately hoping he'd get in touch. I looked fretfully at the remains of the cheese in front of me, hoping it would give me some moral support. I awkwardly swallowed what was in my mouth and took a moment to mentally psych myself up before answering the call.

"*Bonjour*," I said in my best French accent.

"Ella, darling, I thought you must have fallen off the face of the earth. You haven't called in ages."

It was Mum.

"Mum, it's only been a couple of weeks since we last talked. And why are you calling from a blocked number?"

"Didn't you get my emails?"

"No." And while it was the perfect situation for a white lie, I actually meant it—I hadn't received anything from her. "What address did you send them to?"

"Oh, I don't know, it was EllaHotHotBooty at hotmail, or something crass like that."

I rolled my eyes. "God, Mum, I haven't used that address since I was thirteen."

"You should have told me," she said.

"I have. Countless times." Not wanting to let myself get irritated with her, I changed the topic and began telling her about my new apartment and café job. She replied with the anticipated "shouldn't you be looking for a proper job?" which annoyed me no end, but I had to remind myself of what I already knew: It was a stopgap.

"I'm really enjoying it," I assured her. "And I'm meeting some nice people." My mind went dreamily to Gaston.

"So you won't be home in time for Christmas then, if you're too busy working?"

"Probably not. Sorry, Mum."

"That's OK, I have a plan," she said.

"What—" I began to ask, before she cut me off.

"Ah, someone's at the door. Have to go, darling." She was giggling like a naughty teenage girl.

What's gotten into her?

Mum hung up, leaving me feeling a little miffed. She'd added a quick "good luck on the job search!" before saying bye, but still, I was disappointed that she wasn't more interested in hearing how well Paris was working out for me. I wondered who her mystery door knocker could have been, to be important enough to make her basically hang up on her only child. I could barely manage to get her off the phone at the best of times, especially now that we only had a short gap at the start and end of the day when the time difference meant we were both awake.

And what the hell is this Christmas plan?

Maybe she was thinking of coming over, which sounded wonderful. So what if I couldn't tell her about my new and successful Parisian life? Showing it off would be much more fun.

I finished my cheese and asked for the bill—or *l'addition*—one of my favorite words in French. Standing up, I thought I spied Jean-Pierre across the square.

No, it can't be! I found it hard to imagine he would stray this far from home twice.

I shrugged it off and by the time I'd gotten my change from the waiter, his doppelgänger had disappeared. It must have just been somebody who looked like him. There were plenty of dark-haired guys with wispy beards and glasses in Paris. Jean-Pierre certainly didn't own that typically French look by a long stretch.

Chapter

15

PERCHED ON A CAFÉ STOOL the next morning with a coffee in hand, I was enjoying an early start to the day. Who cared if it was my first day off after the weekend and I was back at Flat White? I quite enjoyed the fact that it was starting to feel like home.

Thankfully, it was relatively quiet, and I took the opportunity to tell Chris all about my troubling Jean-Pierre imaginings the previous evening.

"It's not like it's even just him. There's something off about his mother too. She's just very . . ." I reached for the word, knowing it was going to make me sound crazy, ". . . *controlling*. And why are they even renting out their spare room? It certainly doesn't seem like they need the money."

"Ella, you're so hard to please," Chris laughed, before turning sharply towards the door. "Psst!" he whispered, and motioned with his head in the direction of a woman who had just entered. His reaction, plus the woman's immediate allure, told me that this could only be Clotilde, his French crush. She was tall with blonde hair, and perfectly put-together in that gorgeous, effortless, French way, her piercing green eyes somehow exactly matching her delicate green silk dress. Her hair was tousled and her lips were flawlessly painted red. She looked younger than me—I put her at around twenty-five—but perhaps she just had an amazing skin-care routine.

"*Salut. Ça va?*" she said to Chris, who I could only imagine was in a pool of longing at her adorable French accent.

"*Ça va bien, merci. Et toi?*" Chris's thick Australian accent made me want to laugh, but I held it in as I knew he was trying. He rarely spoke French, but was obviously happy to make an effort for love's sake.

"Ella, you must meet Clotilde," he said, calling out to me.

Fuck! I thought. I hadn't been expecting to meet Gaston's potential girlfriend. If I had known, I would have at least made more of an effort before leaving the house. I smoothed down my curls and hopped down from my stool.

"Hi, Clotilde," I said, trying to sound casual. "Nice to meet you."

I wondered if she could smell my fear.

She opened her mouth to say something but then her phone started ringing and she held up her hand as if to hush me. She stepped aside and began speaking in very fast French.

I snuck a look at Chris, who seemed to read my mind. "Don't worry, she's really friendly. You'll see," he whispered.

"Sorry about that," Clotilde said as she tapped her phone and placed it delicately back in her bag. As she did, I noticed that her nails were, of course, also impeccable. "A supposedly urgent call." She raised her eyebrows. Her English was impressive.

"Chris, I'll sit with your friend," she announced, pulling over a stool. "Is that OK, Ella?"

"Of course," I said, feeling nervous. After all, she was "the competition."

Chris looked at us hopefully while I ordered another flat white and tried to communicate with a long stare that he needn't fret; I had this. He dawdled back to the coffee counter, clearly wanting to join in, or maybe eavesdrop, on our conversation. I turned back to Clotilde.

My projected confidence for Chris was an act, though. In truth, I didn't have a clue what to say to the glamazon sitting next to me. I was suddenly feeling conversationally-challenged, worrying that I would say something to indicate that I might have gone out for a drink with her boyfriend. I shifted in my seat and reached out to hold my empty coffee cup just to give my hands something to do. Thankfully, she broke the silence.

"So, you work here with Chris?" she asked.

"Yep," I answered, kicking myself for giving such a monosyllabic answer.

"And where do you live?"

"I'm in Saint-Germain."

She nodded approvingly. "It's nice over that side, isn't it? My father lives there too."

"The area is lovely, yes," I told her. "But I'm staying in an Airbnb for the moment and I don't think I'll be there much longer. I need to find something more permanent."

"Will you buy somewhere or will you be renting?"

Ha! I thought.

"I can't afford to buy a place," I said, adding, "nor rent by myself. I've mostly been looking at rooms in share flats."

I was readying myself for Clotilde to judge me. She seemed the sort to have owned property since she was a toddler.

"Probably wise," she said. "It's really hard for foreign people to get a lease in Paris. Are you finding anything good?"

I was surprised she seemed so interested. "No, everywhere is either too expensive or tiny, dark, and ugly," I confessed. "Or the housemates are strange, which is my current predicament."

"I know what you mean," she said. "Finding an apartment in Paris is like searching for a quality, vintage Chanel handbag in a secondhand store. You can hunt for ages, but never unearth exactly what you're looking for."

I looked down at my calico bag and nodded along, understanding what she was getting at without relating to the analogy.

We fell into another awkward silence and just as I was about to make up some excuse to head off, Clotilde continued the conversation as if there had been no pause at all. I was having trouble reading her. She seemed kind and carefree but also distant and snobbish at the same time. I couldn't tell if she was genuinely trying to be nice or if she had an ulterior motive.

Oh God, I really hope she doesn't know about me and Gaston, I thought dramatically.

"So you plan to live here for a while?" she asked.

"At least for a year," I said. She continued staring at me so I added, "Who wouldn't want to be in Paris?"

Clotilde nodded as though this was the only logical response I could have given.

Ah, Parisians. No matter how much they complain about Paris, they still think it's the only reasonable place in the world to live.

After Clotilde swanned out, Chris came over with my flat white and said, "Well?"

"Sorry. I still have no idea if she's single. I guess we'll have to find out next time she comes in."

For the rest of the afternoon, my anxiety levels were sky-high as I continued to stress about Clotilde and Gaston's relationship. Should I have mentioned him? Or did she already know that I'd gone for a drink with him and was trying to suss me out? The questions ran around my head and I couldn't get them to stop. Was she the reason why he hadn't called me yet?

The one good thing that had come out of my conversation with Clotilde was the reminder that I really couldn't live in the Airbnb forever. I pulled out my laptop and started looking for a new share house. Far from the most exciting thing I could think of to do in Paris, but it was a welcome distraction from the worry I was feeling over the Gaston situation.

When customers started filing in for lunch, I could feel my stomach beginning to gurgle in response.

Maybe it was time for some cheese?

I headed to Café de la Place, which had a great selection. I intended to while away the rest of the afternoon sitting there in the sun, alternating between watching the after-work crowd go by and incessantly staring at my phone, hoping that Gaston would ring, or text, or . . . I don't know, friend me on Facebook?

I ordered a trio of cheeses—all the better to get a move on with the cheese challenge—and when they arrived I snapped a picture for my Instagram. Morbier, Beaufort, and Saint-Nectaire: They looked delicious and I took a moment to wonder what Serge might think of my choices.

And then I saw Jean-Pierre. Seconds after I'd taken a huge bite of rubbery and slippery Morbier, with its distinct ash vein still vivid in my eye, I spotted him. And this time I was certain. He was sitting drinking an espresso in a café on the other side of the street.

I called out to him, we locked eyes, and I motioned for him to come over. I wanted to get to the bottom of why we suddenly kept running into each other. Instead, I saw him get up, fling some money on the table, and walk off quickly down a side alley.

I couldn't begin to describe the look he'd given me. It was a mix of anger, resentment, and something else I couldn't put my finger on. I was puzzled. I knew he'd seen me, but why did he scurry away?

Not wanting to go back home just yet, I gestured for the bill and set off back to Flat White. I wanted to give Chris an update on my most recent Jean-Pierre run-in. He'd know what to say, tell me whether I was overreacting. The multiple sightings could have just been coincidental, but deep down, something was telling me they weren't.

But when I arrived at the café, Chris was occupied, his jaw just millimeters off the coffee counter. I checked to see who had stolen his attention and recognized the green silk dress immediately. What was Clotilde doing back so soon?

My mind raced with hypothetical situations, each one more outlandish than the last. She *must* have found out about me and Gaston. She was here to retaliate.

My heart pounded as she turned around, but she greeted me with a dazzling smile that stopped me in my tracks. "Ah, Ella, just the woman I'm looking for."

"Clotilde." I edged towards her nervously.

"Look, I know this might seem sudden, and I hope you don't think I'm crazy . . ." She paused, and my eyes flicked to the door, wondering how quickly I could flee the scene. "But I was thinking about what you were saying earlier . . ." she said, followed by another pause.

What the hell had I been saying earlier? I wondered.

"Anyway, I might have the perfect solution. I have a spare room at my apartment because my housemate just moved back to London. I was planning on placing an ad but perhaps you'd like to take a look?"

"But you hardly know me," I squeaked, terrified she might be plotting to murder me with her Louboutins.

"Any friend of Chris's is a friend of mine. Why don't you come over for dinner tomorrow night? I can show you the apartment and we can talk about how things would work. It's in Le Marais."

"That's really nice of you, Clotilde," I said uncertainly. "Why not? What time should I come?"

We agreed I'd get there around eight, which would leave me all day to stew over whether she and Gaston were together, and whether this dinner was a complicated ruse so she could ambush me about trying to make a move on her boyfriend. *And if she doesn't already know, what if he's there and I have to explain that we went for drinks? Or what if I move in and then she finds out? What would she do to me?* She was model-thin but I got the feeling that she could pack a punch.

I was full of worry, relief, and concern. This was potentially an end to my house dramas, but perhaps the beginning of Gaston dramas.

"Can I bring something? Dessert? Cheese?" I asked.

"*Oui, pourquoi pas?* Cheese would be great."

As I left Flat White for the second time that day, I started contemplating what cheese to take to dinner. It was a daunting task for a non-French person. Thankfully, I had an affable cheese man who could come to my rescue. I smiled. That wasn't a prospect I could have ever imagined back in Australia.

Chapter
16

THE NEXT MORNING IN THE kitchen, I was making a cup of coffee when Jean-Pierre walked in. *It's now or never,* I thought, readying myself to confront him.

"Hey, what were you doing down near Café de la Place yesterday?" I asked.

He was clearly startled. "Nobody tells me where I can drink my coffee," he blurted out. "Anyway, that wasn't me." Without another word, or any indication of why he'd come into the kitchen, he walked off.

What was that all about?

Before I had time to decide whether to follow him and pursue the conversation or just leave it, his mother rushed in.

"*Bonjour,*" I said, as breezily as I could.

"*Bonjour,* Ella," she said with a strained voice: serious, yet maintaining her sense of composure, as always.

She told me she needed to talk to me about Jean-Pierre, but my French was still rudimentary at best and failed me—all I understood from her five-minute monologue was that I had to be nice to her son.

Grabbing my things and heading out for the day, I was feeling perplexed about what Jean-Pierre's mother had been trying to tell me. I wasn't sure if she knew I'd just been planning to grill him about tailing me the other day or if she was simply being an uber-protective mother.

And why did she even feel the need to tell me to be nice to Jean-Pierre? I thought angrily. *I have gone out of my way to be civil to him. I simply wanted to find out if, down the line, I might need to get a restraining order . . .*

I couldn't figure out how I'd gotten stuck in the middle of their family feud. Although the house looked like a film set, I was merely renting a room, and I was fed up with the drama. I was relieved that I had plans to visit Clotilde's apartment later that day. Even if I was potentially replacing one complicated house share setup for another—she was Gaston's maybe-girlfriend, after all!—it would be an improvement: living with a moody forty-year-old and his meddling mother was getting beyond weird.

I spent the day outside with one eye out for Jean-Pierre, agonizing about what kind of night I had in store with the elusive Clotilde. Judging her purely on looks, I guessed that she enjoyed the finer things and I wanted to take a cheese that would impress. I headed to Serge's store to pick up some of the good stuff. He would have to help me out with the finer details and give me some tasting notes I could use to show my potential new housemate that I, too, could be a classy Parisian.

Arriving at the *fromagerie*, I spied Serge's big hands in the cabinet before I could make out his face through the window. I hadn't been to see him in over a week and I was worried he'd start thinking I'd flaked on our bet. I needed to go in—first to get some wow-factor cheese for dinner, but also to tell him about the varieties I'd recently ticked off the list.

Serge smiled widely when he saw me. He seemed to get friendlier with each of my visits.

"Serge, *bonsoir*," I said, hoping that it was indeed the seemingly-arbitrary French moment of the day to switch over to wishing people good evening.

"*Bonjour*," he said in reply, stressing the "*jour*," meaning it was still day. I blushed but thankfully he continued. "How many cheeses have you eaten? Am I closer to winning dinner with you?"

"Ha! Not yet, Serge," I said, making light of the dinner comment.

"But you haven't been here in days. Where have you been getting cheese?" he asked, with a jovial smile. "Please tell me you haven't been buying that *merde* they sell in the supermarket."

My face went red. "I've been eating out in cafés mostly."

"So, what types of cheese have you been trying?" he asked.

"Let me think . . . I've had Mimolette and Perail, oh, and a Saint-Marcellin."

"And how can I be sure you're not making up these cheeses just to be taken out to dinner?"

I couldn't help thinking, *Don't flatter yourself too much, Serge.* But I did have cheese-eating evidence up my sleeve.

"I have Instagram proof."

"What do you mean, Instagram proof?" he asked.

"Well, I've been uploading photos of all the cheese I eat to Instagram."

"*Oh là là,* Ella, this won't do. Cheese is to be eaten and appreciated in the moment. It's not meant for your social media click photo things. Oh *non, non, non.*" He sounded perturbed.

"No, it's great," I countered. "You should check out the account at *My 365 Days of Cheese* if you don't believe me. I've actually got quite the following already. Does the store have an account? I can start tagging it. Cheese seems very *à la mode* at the moment."

"Cheese is always *à la mode* in France," he retorted.

"Oh, of course," I said quickly.

A customer walked in, interrupting the flow of our conversation and forcing Serge to ask me in a more professional tone what cheese I wanted.

I let the other lady go in front of me, thinking about his disapproval of my Instagram account. *Why's he such a Luddite?* I pondered, eyeing him across the cabinet. He'd trimmed his beard, which made him look younger. *He can't be more than thirty-five. That's young for such a technophobe.*

When the customer left, he looked at me seriously and said, "You should come to me for dining recommendations. I stock cheese at some local restaurants and bistros and I can assure you of their quality. None of that cheap produce that you see in a lot of places."

Serge's arrogance was annoying—but at the same time, I found it kind of endearing. They were really obsessed with their food, the French.

When he asked me what I was in the mood for, I told him that I was having dinner with a new friend. A part of me really delighted in telling him this. At least now he'd know that I did have a life outside of his *fromagerie.* And that I finally had friends to eat the cheese with.

"I need something delicate and delicious. Maybe that blue cheese?" I pointed at a particularly gooey and moldy slice in the cabinet.

"*Mon Dieu, non*," Serge started saying. "If this cheese is for a romantic dinner, it is too strong. Are you certain your date enjoys blue cheese?"

"Oh, it's not a date. It's just a new friend. I'm not actually sure what she likes," I admitted. I hardly knew anything about Clotilde. "What do you recommend, then? Maybe goat cheese?"

His eyes scanned the cabinet and widened when they reached the end. He moved a few steps to his left and picked up a goat's cheese that was fully black.

"This! This will be perfect. And it is ready to eat tonight."

"What is it?"

"It's Valençay, a goat cheese from a town with the same name: Valençay."

"Why is it black?" I asked, tempering my surprise.

"The mold is coated with charcoal. It's beautiful, don't you think?" he drifted off as if lost in thought. "And this one is aged to *perfection*," he purred.

"I guess," I said skeptically.

"So you are still not convinced? Then you must try some."

"Oh no, don't cut it open for me."

"Nonsense," he said. "I can always finish it tonight."

As Serge thrust his knife into the cheese and cut a tiny little piece of Valençay pie for me, he asked, "Do you know the story of how Valençay got its shape?"

I shook my head, looking at the cheese, which was in the form of a topless pyramid.

"It's a good story," he continued, obviously taking pleasure in drawing it out.

I was all ears as Serge launched into his version of *Cheese for Tourists: 101*.

"So it is rumored that, way back when, the people of Valençay used to make their cheese in the shape of a pyramid, including the point at the top." He held his hands up to demonstrate the point. "For years, they'd been crafting their cheese this way and they'd perfected the pyramid shape. It was a very popular cheese in France at the time, and visitors loved going to the town to taste the pyramid."

He handed me a slice of the cheese and encouraged me to eat it while he continued with his story. "Now, as time went on, on the other side of the world, Napoleon was getting himself into trouble in Egypt. After coming back to France, sadly defeated, he went through Valençay, and do you know what happened when he saw the pyramid cheese?"

I shook my head, still chewing. The cheese was delightful: nutty and smooth, with a hint of citrus. Surprisingly fresh, despite the mold and charcoal.

"It sent him into a fit of rage, reminding him of his recent humiliation in Egypt." Serge folded a piece of wax paper into a Napoleon-style hat and put it on.

"He felt like the cheese was mocking him so he drew his sword and chopped the top right off the pyramid," Serge said, taking his own imaginary sword to the cheese. "And ever since that day, Valençay has always appeared in this new shape."

"No . . ." I said. "That can't be true."

"And why not?" Serge shrugged his shoulders in that quintessentially French way. "Unfortunately, we could not be there to see it, so we will never know if it actually happened."

"I guess not," I laughed. "But you've convinced me. Wrap one up for me please."

"And what else would you like to try tonight?" he asked, just as another customer walked in the door.

"Oh, um, a hard cheese, perhaps some Cantal," I said, trying not to laugh as he sheepishly removed his paper hat.

"*D'accord,* I will give you a special type of Cantal. Not like the others. You can tell me what you think next time," he said, wrapping the cheese and giving a friendly *bonjour* to the other customer.

That's my cue to leave, then, I thought, slightly disappointed that our conversation was over.

I gathered my Napoleon cheese and my Cantal and wished Serge a pleasant evening. Heading to Clotilde's, I chuckled at the thought of him theatrically reenacting Napoleon taking his sword to the cheese.

With every visit, I felt like I was getting to know Serge a little more; he was kind, animated, and fast becoming one of my favorite people in Paris.

Chapter

17

JUST BEFORE I ARRIVED AT Clotilde's apartment, I heard my phone buzz. I still got excited whenever it made a noise, given what a rarity it was to have someone contact me here.

It was a message from Gaston. *How's his timing!* I thought, as my palms started to sweat. I hadn't heard from him since that evening drinking rosé and had come to terms with the possibility that he'd lost my number, or—more devastatingly—that he just wasn't interested.

He wanted to know if I could meet him later that night for a cocktail. I was already nervous about spending the next couple of hours with Clotilde, who I wasn't entirely sure I trusted, and I didn't think accepting an invitation from her possible boyfriend was a good idea. But it was Gaston, and I was itching to see him again.

I hastily replied, saying I had dinner with a friend but should be done later that night. Suddenly, the evening had an extra agenda: I needed to find out if Clotilde and Gaston were dating.

Arriving at the top of Clotilde's three flights of stairs, puffing loudly, I took a moment to compose myself, checked in my pocket mirror that I wasn't too disheveled, and rang her doorbell. I heard her cry out "Coming, coming!" before she got to the door. She sounded stressed and I feared I was about to walk into a setup.

"Welcome to your new home," Clotilde sang, flinging the door open and juggling two glasses of champagne and a tray of canapés. "But of course, only if you like it," she added as she kissed me hello. She motioned with her head for me to come in and handed me a glass.

As I looked around the lounge room, I felt a surge of relief fly through me. First, that Gaston was nowhere to be seen. Second, that it seemed as though Clotilde was genuinely looking for a housemate.

The apartment wasn't like any of the other non-renovated, damp rentals and sublets I'd already seen advertised. Marble fireplaces sat proudly in the corners of each room and the charming wooden floorboards creaked with the footsteps of inhabitants past. Double French doors led into the lounge, where large Moroccan floor cushions surrounded a low wooden coffee table, lending the room a sense of warmth and conviviality. Lining one wall were a dozen houseplants healthier than anything I'd ever managed to keep alive. Large, vibrant green leaves contrasted with the white walls, breathing life into the space. The overall effect was, like Clotilde, gorgeous and wonderfully Parisian.

My eyes darted around for any signs of weirdness, but all I could see were fashion magazines, DVDs, and a rather large collection of wine bottles. Big windows overlooked a small interior courtyard where flower boxes and more plants contributed to the overall ambiance. It was almost too easy to imagine myself living there; all that remained was to see if I could imagine myself living with Clotilde. And to make sure she'd be happy living with me.

My concern about her confronting me over Gaston was fading. Since our first encounter, she'd been nothing but kind. And in her own space, wearing some cozy-looking loungewear, she seemed almost like a different person than the one I'd met at Flat White. I don't know if it was my love for the apartment—and desire to stop looking at dark and dank share houses—that was influencing my point of view, but she seemed warmer now, more approachable, less terrifying. Between checking on the oven, washing dishes, and hunting for a specific bottle of red wine, she showed me the spare bedroom, which was huge for Paris, and told me the rent, which was—also for here—surprisingly reasonable.

When Clotilde finally sat down and invited me to do the same, we worked our way through the canapés and another glass of champagne as we talked about what I was doing in Australia before arriving in France. I didn't feel comfortable divulging too many details about my breakup with Paul so instead I told her about work and my friends, which led to talk about traveling and eating, which it turned out were two of Clotilde's favorite hobbies.

"By the way, you're a great cook," I said as we moved onto the main course of roast lamb and couscous salad.

"Ha! That's not a compliment I get every day."

"But everything is delicious."

"I can't take any credit for these creations. I bought everything except the salad leaves at Picard."

"What's Picard?" I asked.

"Let's just say, if you move in with me, you'll get to know it well."

By the time we got to our second bottle of red wine, I'd learned that Clotilde—an only child—had moved into the apartment with her parents when she was four, and that her father still owned it. When Clotilde had turned twenty-one, her parents had moved out, having bought a new apartment in Saint-Germain; the gesture was a sort of coming-of-age present for their baby girl.

"I pay Papa minimal rent and the only condition is a weekly invitation to lunch or dinner."

"That's so sweet. And your parents still come over?"

"Only my papa," said Clotilde. There were tears in her eyes.

"Oh, I'm sorry. Did something happen?"

"*Maman* passed away a few years ago. It was quite sudden. I'm not sure Papa has really recovered."

I wanted to reach across and hug her but didn't know if she was a touchy-feely person. She shook her head stoically and told me that her dad normally came over for lunch on the weekend. "I hope it won't be a problem," she said. "He's pretty cool."

"Of course it's not a problem." I couldn't help leaning over and patting her arm. "My father hasn't been around since I was a kid so it'll be nice."

"I'm sorry. What happened?" she asked.

I rarely talked about my dad to anyone. "He left a long time ago; it's a complicated story. Not exciting enough to get into now, but I'll tell you some other time." I even surprised myself with the ease at which I accepted that we were about to be housemates. *It must have been the red wine . . .*

I checked my watch and was shocked to see it was already 11 p.m.

Shit! What about Gaston?!

But suddenly, securing a friendship with Clotilde felt more important than a potential tryst with a man, no matter how sexy he was. Besides, there was one thing I still had to suss out: Clotilde's relationship status.

"So are you seeing anyone at the moment?" I blurted out awkwardly.

"Oh, nothing serious. I'm dating a little, but I'm pretty happy to keep my independence."

Hmm, I thought, *seems like a good sign. At least it's not a full-blown relationship.*

"And you?" Clotilde asked.

"I just got out of a fairly long-term relationship back in Melbourne so I'm not looking for anything serious either. There is this one guy who comes into Flat White who I sort of like but I don't know if he's even single . . ."

"Sounds very French!" she laughed.

Before I had the chance to delve further into the topic, Clotilde started to clear the plates and said, "So shall we try this cheese you brought?"

"I thought you'd never ask," I said, forgetting all about men and getting excited to taste the deliciousness Serge had set us up with.

"Wow, Ella, this Valençay looks wonderful. Do you know it's my favorite goat cheese? This one looks perfectly ripe," Clotilde yelled out from the kitchen.

I couldn't help beaming, pleased to receive a cheese compliment from a French person. Clotilde returned with a large board and we started cutting chunks of the goat cheese and the Cantal. It was fun to be able to taste different varieties with somebody, and it was made all the sweeter eating it comfortably ensconced in an apartment, rather than in a café or at the park.

Where I'd previously thought that the Cantal would be boring—like a less-interesting version of my beloved Comté—this slice had an intense nutty flavor, made more prominent by months of *raffinage*, or ripening. It was almost like aged Cheddar and I fancied it would go well with a square of quince paste, although I wasn't sure my new Parisian friend would approve of this serving suggestion. I was beginning to understand that French cheese made in large factories had very little to do with the varieties you could find in good cheese shops throughout France. Apparently, Serge's Cantal had been made at a high altitude, which gave it a richer flavor. He told me cow's milk tastes better when it comes from cows that graze at altitude, which in turn makes for better cheese. *Who knew?*

Clotilde seemed to enjoy the Cantal, as well, and asked me where I'd gotten it. When I told her I bought it from a *fromagerie* around the corner, she nodded, as if she knew which one I was referring to. In France, most people have a specific cheese person who they know and trust, and the relationship is built over the years and then treasured for life. I felt that by taking quality cheese to Clotilde's that evening, she somehow trusted me more.

As we finished off our wine, I stifled a yawn and decided it was best to head back to my Airbnb. I was feeling a little tipsy by this point and didn't want to ruin my good impression by drinking one glass too many and falling asleep on the couch.

"So what do you think?" Clotilde asked as we stood by the front door. "Would you like to live here?"

I smiled warmly and told her I adored the apartment and would love to. Kissing me good-bye, she told me that the room was ready to go and I could move in this weekend.

What a relief! I thought, a lump forming unexpectedly in my throat. I was feeling emotional having made my first female friend in Paris, and I was beyond excited at the prospect of a more normal living arrangement *sans* mother and creepy son.

I was also looking forward to getting to know Clotilde

better, and desperately hoped that she was being honest when she'd said she wasn't serious about dating anyone. Which reminded me about my pending drinks invitation. I sent Gaston a quick text to apologize: "*Salut, desolée*, my dinner ran quite late. Perhaps another time soon?"

"*Peut-être*," was his succinct reply.

Maybe? What the hell does that mean? I thought, getting upset.

I talked myself down: *Perhaps given my new living arrangement, it is wise to just leave things with Gaston at that.*

When I got back to the Airbnb, I found Jean-Pierre's mother sitting in the dark staring at the wall. It was late and I wondered what she was doing still awake. I couldn't help feeling like I was about to get in trouble.

"*T'étais où?*" she asked, which I understood meant, "Where were you?"

"With a friend," I told her in French, heading to my bedroom. It was none of her business where I'd been and I didn't like the atmosphere in the room. "Oh," I added, before reaching the door. "*Je vais partir ce weekend*." I thought it was only fair to let her know I'd be moving out early.

She grabbed a piece of paper from the table and pointed to it somewhat aggressively. It was the booking receipt showing my departure date, originally scheduled for the following Wednesday. I nodded and told her in broken French that I would still be leaving on Saturday and I didn't want a refund.

She had tears in her eyes and looked at me imploringly. Suddenly, I was glad that my gut instinct had told me to find somewhere else. There was something off about this woman. She stood in front of me and took my hands in hers.

"You can't leave," she said in French. And then, probably after seeing the confusion on my face, switched to English, speaking with a slow and thick accent. "Jean-Pierre is in love with you."

"He's what?"

"He loves you," she repeated, and moved to block the path to my bedroom. "You cannot leave."

Three

> "*Wine and cheese are ageless companions, like aspirin and aches, or June and moon, or good people and noble ventures.*"

—M. F. K. FISHER

Chapter

18

THE START OF AUTUMN SIGNALED a change in fortunes for my life in Paris. I'd been living with Clotilde for a few weeks and couldn't have been happier with how things were working out in our apartment.

While I still had very little going on outside of daily cheese consumption and my weekend work at the café, Clotilde's schedule was fairly manic. On top of working at the food start-up where she'd met Chris, she modeled, juggled a nonstop social calendar, and was constantly at the gym—despite her innate French abhorrence of such an activity. We crossed paths mostly in the mornings over French-style bowls of coffee or occasionally in the evenings over large glasses of wine.

Our friendship had developed organically as she translated things and helped explain the French bureaucracy system when I was lost in piles of paperwork. I often asked if she minded helping her hapless housemate, but she always insisted that she didn't, saying she understood how it felt to move to a new country, having been shipped off to English boarding school when she was sixteen.

When I considered Clotilde's glamorous Parisian existence, I couldn't figure out why she'd taken me under her long, slender wing and offered me a room. And, despite her kindness, I still didn't know where she stood with Gaston. Or where I stood with him, for that matter—if, indeed, anywhere. I hadn't seen him in the café, or heard from him since his last dismissive late-night text, and I hoped I hadn't shot my chances of another rendezvous. I nearly mentioned him to Clotilde a couple of times but ended up chickening out, deciding that a few glasses of rosé with the guy were hardly worth potentially unsettling the status quo of our apartment.

Even though Clotilde and I had become quite friendly since I'd moved in, she was still a little reserved when it came to her love life. The only other time I'd asked her about it, she'd merely laughed and said she didn't want a serious relationship: "*Les mecs compliquent la vie.*" And didn't I know it. *Guys do complicate life.* After Jean-Pierre's mother declared his love for me, leaving the Airbnb early had been the best thing I could have done.

As she'd blocked my path, I'd said anything and everything I could think of that might make her move out of my way. The look on her face was intense and I worried that I'd underestimated what kind of woman she was and what she was capable of. I'd been genuinely scared.

"I'm sorry, I'm just not, *at all*, in love with your son," I'd told her definitively.

But she hadn't seemed to want to believe me.

"Honestly, I'm really happy being single," I'd insisted, this time perhaps a little harshly. Her face crumpled.

Seeing this well-poised woman tear up made me feel guilty for having been so blunt, so I'd ended up consoling her.

Through the hour-long conversation that had followed, the majority of which was conducted through the translation app on my phone, I found out that all the poor woman wanted was for Jean-Pierre to find a nice girl and move out of her apartment. She wanted to enjoy living alone for a while before she died.

"I can understand that," I'd empathized, wishing I too were living alone rather than with her and her son.

She'd then explained how Jean-Pierre would often interrogate her friends, to the point of them feeling uncomfortable when they came over.

I'd nodded vigorously.

"He's very protective of me," she'd said.

I'd kept nodding.

"Particularly with any gentlemen who drop by late in the evening," she'd continued with a loaded look.

It took a moment for me to register what was going on.

Jean-Pierre's mother wanted to make room in the apartment for her nighttime companions. I would never have guessed that behind her elegant exterior was a woman in the prime of her sexual life!

I'd assured her that Jean-Pierre would find a nice woman eventually. I'd even suggested she try setting her son up with a Tinder account. After a long explanation of the swiping process from my end, she'd seemed surprisingly amenable to the idea.

I'd then gently mentioned that she should encourage Jean-Pierre not to follow his love interests around town.

She'd looked sheepish.

I'd pressed further and she'd admitted that she'd told him to pursue me. This had been the last straw. *How had this woman manipulated me into feeling sorry for her?* Before I knew what I was saying, I'd lied and told her that I was moving to Madrid.

As soon as the sun came up the next morning, I made a hasty exit in order to avoid any further blockades. I holed myself up in a café until a reasonable time so I could contact Clotilde without seeming too eager or desperate. At eight o'clock, with her OK that I could move in a few days early, I was on the metro to my new apartment, a bulging suitcase in hand and bloodshot eyes from a sleepless night.

Clotilde didn't mince her words when she saw what state I was in. "What the hell happened to you between midnight and now?"

"It's a long story," I said, rubbing my temples.

"We've got time. It looks like you've had quite the night!"

I told her everything. She listened attentively, chipping in with exclamations of "You didn't!" and "What a commotion!" every so often. When my tale came full circle, she said, "A little drama never killed us. Anyway, it's a wonderful story. Now how about *un café*?"

And so began our routine of drinking coffee together in the apartment.

One morning, when I was settled on the sofa by the window and feeling particularly proud that I had understood a whole paragraph in French *Vogue*, Clotilde waltzed out of her bedroom and told me that she'd had an idea. She stood there with bare legs wearing an oversized T-shirt, looking like she'd jumped out of the magazine I was reading. She made me guess what it was. I joked—somewhat fretfully—that she was going to kick me out and move to Madrid herself.

"Ella, I'm throwing you a party. I want to mark your moving in with a celebration. I'm inviting my closest friends, and of course my papa, but hopefully he'll bring plenty of champagne and then leave early. What do you think? Doesn't it sound divine?"

Clotilde didn't do things by halves.

"Please say yes!" she pleaded when I took a moment to respond. "Please say you'll be the . . . how do you say . . . guest of honor."

"Of course, that sounds wonderful. It'll be like a house-warming," I said.

"Exactly! It's settled then. Is Saturday night OK with you?"

"It's perfect; I actually have this Sunday off. And speaking of work, should I invite Chris along?" I asked, testing the waters to gauge if she was keen to hang out with him outside of the café.

"Of course! And invite that guy you're seeing too!" Clotilde said.

I panicked. "Oh, I don't think it was ever even a thing. I haven't heard from him in weeks."

"Oh, what a shame," Clotilde said. If only she knew we were talking about Gaston.

"Can I buy anything for the party?" I said, changing the topic.

"*Non, non, non.* Leave it all to me," she squealed. "I'll even cook."

"Clotilde, I'm not sure shopping at Picard counts as cooking," I replied.

"No, Ella. I'll cook for real."

I tried to remember if I'd ever seen Clotilde make anything that hadn't come from Picard, the all-frozen supermarket chain that sold surprisingly elaborate ready-made meals. I was pretty sure I hadn't.

"Are you sure?" I asked nervously. "Maybe I could just get some cheese to add to the spread."

"Wonderful idea. You can never have too much cheese at a party!"

Saturday after work, I went in to see Serge and get a party wheel. I wanted a show-stopping cheese and was prepared to spend my weekend's paycheck to get it. After the requisite "*Bonsoir*" to Serge and his lone customer—an older gentleman lacking any sense of urgency—I started scanning the cabinets.

"Serge, I'm in a bit of a rush. I need a large wheel of cheese."

"No problem. Which one?"

"Something that will suit a party. Something fun." My eyes landed on a wheel of Brie as big as my head. And although it was already ticked off my list, I figured an Instagram shot of a giant cheese wheel was bound to be a crowd pleaser. "That'll do perfectly," I said, pointing to it.

Serge pulled the wheel out of the cabinet carefully.

"Ella, this is more than your usual order. Have you finally found someone to have dinner with? Perhaps a man?" he added with a wink.

"Ha! Not quite," I replied, glad that Serge felt comfortable enough to ask me such a personal question. "There was a potential candidate—this handsome French guy—but he seems to have completely vanished from the scene. It was getting a little complicated anyway, so I guess it's a good outcome."

"So you are now alone?"

Alone? How sad, I thought.

"You mean, am I single?" I asked.

"Yes, single. Sorry." He laughed warmly and I joined him, quietly hoping my life wasn't actually destined to be spent alone.

"I guess so, Serge. Anyway, this wheel is for a party my new housemate is throwing. She's the one I bought the Valençay and Cantal for."

"Ah, yes. And did she like them?"

"So much so that she asked where I shopped for cheese," I told him.

"Then she has good taste. Both in cheese and housemates," he said with a grin.

Holding my big wheel of cheese, I walked out of Serge's feeling victorious. Where only months earlier I had eaten my tiny wheel of Camembert-for-one feeling desperately sorry for myself, now I was buying a wheel of Brie big enough for a room full of people. It was as though my increasingly grand cheese purchases mirrored my expanding life in Paris. I couldn't think of a more appropriate way to show off my success.

It was only after leaving Serge's that I wondered if I should have invited him along to the party. He'd been so kind to me since I'd arrived in Paris, and we were becoming increasingly friendly, moving beyond just cheese discussions and into conversations about our personal lives. I felt that perhaps I should have. But I was running late and didn't have time to go back and ask. *Next time*, I thought to myself as I sped home to get ready.

Chapter

19

ARRIVING AT OUR APARTMENT, I was overflowing with excitement at the prospect of getting dressed up and meeting new people. I blow-dried my hair, carefully applied a coat of vibrant red lipstick à la Française and put on some ridiculously high heels.

I was flying solo because Chris bizarrely chose to keep a rendezvous with another French woman over spending time with Clotilde. "Good things come to those who wait," Chris had said. "She has long-game potential. I'll bide my time until the moment is right."

While normally I would have been intimidated by such a crowd, Clotilde had told everyone that this was my party, and I was reveling in my role as co-host and guest of honor. I helped pour drinks and got to know Clotilde's good-looking friends, the champagne helping to shake off any remaining anxiety.

While chatting to Clotilde's university friend Julie—and discovering that growing up in Bordeaux apparently didn't involve drinking a lot of Bordeaux—I noticed an immaculately dressed and well-coiffed older man walk in. Clotilde rushed over and embraced him. She dragged him over, introduced him as Papa Jean, and, despite him not speaking any English and me speaking moderate-to-bad French, we managed to have a short conversation. He apologized for the size of the apartment before laughing a very formal laugh. I joined him, thinking, *If only he'd seen some of the other share houses I'd looked at, he probably wouldn't even manage a chuckle.* This place was a palace in comparison.

I was midway through trying to explain to him how I'd met Clotilde when I was stopped in my tracks.

Gaston had just walked in. *Shit! What the hell is he doing here?*

I watched closely as Clotilde rushed over to him; he tenderly kissed her on both cheeks. *Did he linger longer than after drinks with me? Was he veering a little close to her mouth?* I couldn't help but notice that once again, he looked gloriously French, with slightly tousled hair and a green scarf wrapped around his tanned neck.

"*Ah, c'est Gaston,*" said Papa Jean.

My heart sank. If Papa Jean knew Gaston, maybe there was something more to his relationship with Clotilde after all. I watched, devastated, as Clotilde whisked him into the kitchen and I was left wondering how I could avoid him.

I turned back to Papa Jean and attempted to ask how he knew Gaston but was met with a puzzled look.

"Ah, Gaston? *Il est mon neveu. Excusez-moi, Ella,*" Papa Jean politely excused himself, heading into the kitchen.

I almost stopped him to ask what "*mon neveu*" meant but instead hunted out someone else who could fill me in.

Thankfully, Julie was still around to help. "I think in English you say 'nephew.'"

"Nephew? As in, the son of your brother or sister?" I asked. I couldn't really afford to get this wrong.

"Yes, is that the correct pronunciation?"

"It's perfect," I squealed.

So if Gaston is Jean's nephew, I thought to myself, *that means he's Clotilde's cousin!* I smiled at the prospect and felt a flutter of excitement in my stomach.

It turned out I'd been worrying for nothing all this time. I excused myself and headed towards the buffet, whipping out my phone to text Chris: "Turns out there is a God! Clotilde and Gaston are cousins."

Just as I was helping myself to an extra-large portion of mini quiches to celebrate, I heard a man's voice that I immediately recognized. "These are no good. I wouldn't eat so many if I were you."

I turned to look at Gaston and grinned. "I think they look delightful," I retorted playfully, piling a few extra onto my plate to annoy him.

"Yes, they do," he said. "But wait until you try one."

"I'll be the judge of that," I said, slipping a whole quiche into my mouth and chewing thoughtfully. "Ah, delicious," I lied.

As much as I loved Clotilde, unless she was shopping at Picard, her food really wasn't particularly edible. *Perhaps that's how she remains so slim . . .* I mused.

"So I hear you and Clotilde are cousins," I said.

"Yes, and I hear you're her new housemate," he said. "What a coincidence."

I blushed.

"So . . ." I said, changing the subject. "You don't like Clotilde's cooking?"

"*Non.* I have tried to teach her a few simple dishes, but she's too impatient in the kitchen. She always prefers eating out somewhere fun, letting someone else do the hard work."

"Well, I don't blame her. The food in Paris is so good; who doesn't want to eat out every night in this city?"

"You like eating out?" he asked.

"Sure, as much as anyone else, I guess."

He nodded, letting out a restrained laugh. "Me too."

"I never had a chance to ask over drinks, what do you do?" I asked, wanting to keep the conversation going.

"I'm a journalist," he said.

"Oh, cool," I said meekly, and kicked myself for not saying something better.

"And how is your coffee-making job?"

"Oh, it's fine," I said, thinking that I should probably get around to telling him that I wasn't actually a barista. "Speaking of which, I haven't seen you at Flat White in a while."

"It's a busy time of year."

"Even more reason for coffee," I said, with a cheeky smile.

But before I had the chance to flirt a little more, Papa Jean hurried over and interrupted us, taking Gaston away to deal with a kitchen emergency.

Oh dear, what's Clotilde done now? I wondered.

I checked my phone and Chris had replied: "Good luck with Monsieur! Keep Clotilde safe for me."

⌒

Gaston reappeared later in the evening holding a large tray of perfectly-crafted canapés. After very little edible food, the crowd descended on them like a pack of hungry dogs. I was trying to nudge my way towards what looked like a little cheese tart when Gaston grabbed my shoulder and pulled me back.

Why doesn't this man want me to eat? I thought.

"Ella, come with me. I have something for you," he whispered in my ear.

I followed him, discreetly checking out his arse in his well-tailored trousers. "Not bad," I said under my breath.

In the kitchen, my gaze swept across the rest of the food that Gaston had managed to create or salvage from the remaining ingredients that were strewn on the bench tops.

"I thought that you deserved this after eating so many of those terrible quiches."

I picked up a little prune wrapped in prosciutto and placed it into my mouth. As the meat-wrapped parcel hit my taste buds and began to melt, the salty sweet flavors made my heart sing. I hadn't realized I was so hungry and I chewed the delicious parcel greedily.

"Gaston, these are amazing," I admitted. Next, I tried a little goat cheese tart, which was the perfect balance of creaminess from the cheese and crunchiness from the warm pastry casing. The combination worked magic on my tongue.

"What kind of goat cheese is this?" I asked, and he glanced at me sideways, perhaps surprised I might be able to distinguish between France's many different varieties.

"It's a little Crottin de Chavignol from La Loire. Do you like it?"

I described the flavors elaborately, having drunk the perfect amount of champagne to sound wonderfully elegant and intelligent. That, or Serge's influence was rubbing off on me and I was finally thinking about cheese more critically.

"You need to try the foie gras next," said Gaston, motioning to a brown glob on a slice of fruit bread, which was not nearly as visually appealing as what I'd just eaten.

"OK," I replied, trying to sound enthusiastic.

"It's liver," he said slowly, reading my expression. "It's not meant to be handsome."

I laughed and shook my head, embarrassed that he'd sensed my apprehension. He lifted the foie gras toast to my mouth rather sensually. I could feel myself salivating, and I wasn't sure it was even for the food.

That's when Clotilde burst into the kitchen. "What's going on here?" she demanded.

I spun around, mortified, knocking Gaston's arm and causing him to drop the foie gras canapé down my top. The warm toast and slimy liver nestled cozily into my cleavage.

"Shit," I yelped, standing there, arms out, helpless.

Gaston tried to grab the runaway canapé but only succeeded in pushing it farther between my boobs. My face went stoplight red and I wanted to launch myself directly off the balcony; it was the only way I could think of to redeem myself in the current situation. Luckily, before that could happen, Clotilde ran over and pushed Gaston out of the way.

"Don't worry, my friend. We'll get you fixed up in no time. Come with me."

I breathed a sigh of relief as she pulled me towards her room. Thankfully, Clotilde didn't ask what I'd been doing in the kitchen with her cousin, and I didn't mention that I'd already met Gaston before at Flat White. I couldn't say why, but I wanted to make sure that what I had going on with him wasn't just some innocent flirtation before I introduced this potential complication into my home life.

"How about this one?" Clotilde asked, pulling out a dress from her huge wardrobe.

"Clotilde, I have dresses in my own room," I protested, though I couldn't help being wooed by the gorgeous fabrics and textures that filled hers. The prospect of redeeming myself in front of Gaston with a sexy plunging neckline might have also crossed my mind.

"I know, but you need a party dress. This is your night," she said. "Maybe this one?" she asked, handing me a bright-red one.

"I don't think it's going to fit, Clotilde." I was on the brink of hating my body for all eternity, but comforted myself by thinking that most people standing next to Clotilde would probably feel the same way.

"Give it a try," she said. "It's meant to be a free size. Meaning there is no size limit."

I tried the dress on, and to my surprise, it fit. It was much tighter than I would have expected from a "free size," but it covered all the necessary parts. It was also much shorter than I'd normally wear; thankfully, I had on my high heels and my legs were wonderfully tanned from the Paris summer.

"Welcome back our guest of honor," Clotilde announced, clapping as we reentered the living room. My face blushed once again, this time almost matching the color of my new dress. "She's had a wardrobe change so we can go out and hit the clubs," she sang in a gorgeous high-pitched voice. "OK, *on y va,* it's time to go!"

She stopped the music, kissed Papa Jean good-night and grabbed her purse. Within seconds she had managed to persuade the fifteen remaining partygoers to join us, and we were out the door, down the multiple flights of stairs and into the Parisian night.

It was only when we were halfway down the street that I realized Gaston wasn't with us.

"Where is Gaston? Is he not coming out?" I asked Clotilde.

"Oh no," she giggled. "Gaston wouldn't be seen dead in the clubs with us."

I laughed at her use of the expression "Wouldn't be seen dead." I'd gotten used to her almost-flawless English, but her knack for pulling out the perfect phrase at an opportune moment still surprised me.

"He's much too refined for the establishments we frequent. Why do you ask? Do you like him?"

"Oh, um, no. His loss, I guess."

I was disappointed that Gaston hadn't wanted to join us but figured it was probably for the best considering the embarrassing canapé incident I'd just inflicted on him. I also needed some time and headspace to come up with a game plan now that I was certain Clotilde was out of the picture romantically.

Chapter
20

THE NEXT MORNING AFTER A raucous night of drinking and dancing I was excited to see a message from Gaston on my phone saying he was looking forward to catching up again soon. I'd clearly received it while out, but thankfully I'd had the good sense not to attempt a long reply and in my inebriated state had simply sent a casual "*Oui, oui*" and a winky face.

It's back on! I thought, smiling widely. But now wasn't the time to get caught up daydreaming about another date with Gaston.

Billie's flight from Australia was due to arrive that morning, and while it was a shame that she hadn't made it to Paris in time for Clotilde's and my housewarming party, I was looking forward to seeing her immensely. Since I'd moved in with Clotilde, I'd hardly had a free moment to message her and I was excited to find out what had been going on in Melbourne and to show her my new Parisian life.

Ignoring my pounding head, I stumbled into the kitchen, turned on the coffee machine, and watched the restorative liquid drip slowly into the pot. Debris and glasses covered the bench tops from the party and I started to clean up quietly. I wanted Billie to see our apartment at its best. As I went, I avoided counting the empty bottles of wine and kept telling myself that things could have been worse. But when I saw and smelled the heaving ashtray, I was overcome by nausea. Turns out, it isn't a stereotype—the French still love to smoke. A lot. Even more so when drinking.

Hearing a man's muffled voice coming from Clotilde's room, I grabbed my coffee and went to hide in the shower, hoping to scrub away my hangover, or at least some of my leftover eye makeup. I tried to remember if there'd been anyone else in our Uber on the way home, but the details—all except me begging the driver to turn up the tunes—were hazy.

Emerging hot and red from the steamy bathroom, I ran into Clotilde and the sexy French dude that belonged to the voice I'd heard. I exchanged *les bises* with her midnight mystery man— awkward in a towel—and offered them coffee. Clotilde refused on her new beau's behalf and shuffled him out the door quickly. We listened carefully to his footsteps descend the stairs before we started giggling and discussing what had happened the night before. Hugo was a photographer from a shoot she'd been at a few weeks earlier who—unbeknownst to me—she'd had a massive crush on. She'd run into him last night and the rest was history.

"Then why did you chuck him out so fast?" I asked.

"He couldn't stay a minute longer," she said seriously. "Papa and Gaston are arriving soon to take me to brunch."

"Where are you going?" I asked, trying to sound calm despite feeling my heart flutter.

"Eggs and Co. Why don't you come?"

"I can't," I said, cursing the bad timing. "Billie is flying in today. I'm heading to the airport to meet her."

"Of course, I forgot. I'm sure he'll be sad you can't make it," she said.

"Who will?" I squeaked.

"Papa, of course. He said he'd like to get to know you better."

Phew! I thought, taking a deep breath.

"Yes, well, tell him I'd love to catch up soon."

Clotilde nodded, adding, "Though, thinking about it, Gaston will probably be sad that you can't make it too. He might have tried to drop a croissant down your top."

"Next time I see him, I'll wear a turtleneck," I said.

She gave me a smug look that seemed to say, *Bien sûr!*

Billie came bouncing out of customs at Charles de Gaulle airport and gave me a huge hug. After weeks of kissing everybody hello, I'd missed hugs between good friends and held on for perhaps longer than would have been considered normal.

"Hey," she said, pulling back. "Is everything OK?"

"Now that you're here, yes," I said, hugging her again.

"Good. Because I'm here for a good time, not a long time. Let's go make the most of being in Paris."

"Perfect," I said, helping her with her baggage. "Small disclaimer: I'm feeling a little fragile today. We went out last night and I danced a lot. I'm sorry!"

"Don't be sorry, El. I'll look after you. I'm excited to hear you've found your dancing shoes again." She wrapped her arm around my shoulder and gave me a squeeze.

Billie was passing through Paris for two days on her way to a friend's wedding in London, and sadly, because of work commitments back in Australia, she was on a tight schedule—not that that would stop her from loving every last minute of her visit.

As we jumped on the metro and chugged our way into the city, we discussed options for what to do. I ran through the list of tourist destinations that I thought she might be keen to check out—the Eiffel Tower, Pompidou, Le Louvre, Versailles—but she cut me off. "Ella, none of this tourist malarkey. I want to see *your* Paris this weekend."

"OK, then. How about we drop off your bags, drink too much coffee *en terrace*, and then go for a picnic by the Seine? It's supposed to be a beautiful sunny afternoon."

"Perfect. Wine, cheese, a baguette, what could be better?"

"Sounds great! Clotilde might join us too," I said.

"Good, I want to check out your new housemate. Make sure I approve."

───

Billie's first impression of my apartment was all I could have hoped for; she oohed and ahhed just like I would have if our roles had been reversed. Clotilde had managed to finish cleaning the kitchen before her brunch and it was sparkling; I felt a wave of gratitude. I offered Billie a coffee and a shower but she insisted she was ready to go exploring. We went to find a *terrace* in the sun, which in my neighborhood was as easy as gaining weight in France.

Over two espressos, with conversation topics flying left, right, and center, I finally started to feel like we were close to being properly caught up. Billie ran through everything that had been going on back home, with her business expanding into other states and, most excitingly, receiving a huge bump in orders after a cast member from our favorite Australian soap opera, *Neighbours*, wore one of her bracelets. When she casually mentioned this, I ordered two glasses of champagne to celebrate and reprimanded her for not telling me sooner.

I reciprocated by telling Billie how much I'd come to love life in Paris. I admitted that yes, things had gotten off to a bit of a rocky start, with the search for a dream job not going exactly as planned and the hunt for accommodation being less than easy-sailing, but I was happy to report that I was finally starting to feel settled.

From the moment I'd arrived in France, I'd been so scared that I'd fail at everything and have to move back to Australia that I hadn't really considered what my life would look like if I succeeded. Chatting to Billie made me realize that things were actually pretty peachy. It was exciting to consider how many adventures I'd had in such a short period of time, especially thinking back over the past eight years I'd spent with Paul and everything I'd missed out on while being "settled."

"So what's next in conquering Paris?" Billie asked.

"Ha! Well, I need to find another job to supplement my increasingly expensive lifestyle. Preferably something that doesn't involve dirty dishes."

"And what's with the Instagram account? Have you fallen in love with cheese or something?"

I hadn't told Billie about my dinner bet with Serge yet and she must have assumed I was tasting and Instagramming cheese for fun—not that it wasn't. The idea of telling her about Serge and trying to explain the cheese bet made me a little nervous. I didn't want her to dismiss something that had, at some point along the way, become quite important to me. But her support meant a lot so I came clean.

"I made a bet to try 365 types of cheese over the next year."

"You did what? With whom? But why? You're joking, right?"

"Well . . ." I started.

"Oh, God! You're not joking. What made you think you could eat so much cheese?"

"I sort of have this cheese guy," I said.

"You have a guy in your life and you didn't think to mention it until now?"

"It's not like that. He's just the guy I buy my cheese from," I said.

Billie seemed disappointed.

"Not long after I arrived in Paris, we made a bet that I couldn't try all the varieties of French cheese in one year," I explained.

"I think you've been had, my dear friend. It sounds like he's sucking business from you." She looked at me sympathetically.

"No, no. It's not that," I said. "I don't buy *all* my cheese from him. Just most of it."

"But why do you need to eat so much?" she asked.

I explained to Billie how when I'd first arrived, I'd felt a little aimless, and the cheese had provided comfort, which had led to me consuming a lot of it. "I think I was looking for something concrete to occupy my days and give my life here some purpose, which is when I sort of accidentally made the bet. To be honest, I didn't quite realize how many varieties there were . . ."

Billie nodded.

"Anyway," I continued, "the stakes were only dinner, so I figured it didn't really matter if I lost, but for some reason I've become rather attached to winning. I'd love to succeed. The Instagram account has become a sort of cheese diary."

Billie was quiet.

"You don't think I'm crazy, do you?" I asked.

"Well, it's never going to be a bad experience trying all the cheeses of France, but it does seem a little excessive. Couldn't you just try a hundred or something? Also, the stakes are *dinner*? What's the real deal with you and this cheese guy? Are you sure you're not into him?" Her tendency to persist was both admirable and irritating.

"No, seriously. It's not about that," I said, wishing that it could be as clear to Billie as it was to me. Serge was my first friend here and the bet was a big part of that. "He's got me really interested in cheese and has been teaching me about the different varieties and their origins."

"So this really has nothing to do with sex?" Billie raised her eyebrows at me skeptically.

I almost choked on my drink. "God, no. We're just friends. Why don't we go check out his store later and you can see how amazing it is. When you see all his cheese hopefully things will start to make a little more sense."

Billie twirled her hair, something she often did when lost in thought.

"So what is it with you, Paris and cheese?" she finally asked.

"What do you mean?"

"Well, it's ironic that you were in Paris when Paul wooed you with Comté, and now you're back after breaking up with him and you've made a bet with some guy to try a different type of cheese every day."

I shrugged, not really knowing how to respond. I'd never linked my first night in Paris with Paul to the cheese challenge. *Perhaps cheese has become my rebound guy!*

"Have you heard from him?" Billie asked gently.

"Who? Paul?" I shook my head. "I'm glad, to be honest. With

everything that's been going on here, I haven't even had time to think about him."

"You haven't seen any updates online either?"

"Nope, I deleted him wherever possible to avoid it."

"So perhaps you don't want me to tell you I ran into him in Melbourne a few weeks ago?" she said frowning.

I gulped.

"Or that he was with a girl."

My mind immediately went to Jessyka. "Did she look like a CrossFit girl?" I asked, intrigued despite myself.

"I have no idea what that means, El. I guess she looked fit, but I'm not sure if that's the same thing."

"It doesn't matter anyway," I said, trying to convince myself that it didn't, despite the golf ball that had magically lodged itself in my throat. Although I knew that breaking up with Paul had been for the best, I still didn't want him to be happy with anyone else.

Seeing tears welling in my eyes, Billie asked me when I was going to start dating French men. I told her about my "sort-of date" with Gaston, and our run-in at Clotilde's party the night before.

"I'm just not sure he's into me," I said.

"I'll be the judge of that. Tell me all about him."

I told Billie what I knew about Gaston and went into detail about our awkward canapé moment. She stopped me early on.

"Ella, I'm all for you dating, but this guy sounds kind of pre-tentious."

"No, he's just very Parisian. He's suave and sophisticated. He's a journalist," I said in his defense.

"What type of journalist?" she asked.

"I'm not exactly sure," I admitted.

"All that glitters isn't gold, Ella."

"Billie, don't be so dramatic," I said with a laugh. "And don't worry about me; nothing could be worse than dating Paul."

"I'm certainly not advising you to get into another long-term relationship. Just date and see who's out there. Perhaps try going out with someone you wouldn't normally consider."

"Seriously, there's nothing to worry about," I told her. "I hardly have a lineup of men offering to take me out. Sadly, the drought continues."

Billie rubbed her stomach dramatically.

"Where's this cheese shop then? I'm starving! Shall we go make a dint in your challenge?" she asked.

"Let's do it," I said, motioning for the bill.

"So can you eat multiple cheeses in one day?"

"Of course. I think it's going to be a requirement to stockpile and then take a few days off," I said seriously.

"Probably better for your health too."

"Well, it's hard to say if any configuration of mass cheese consumption is really that healthy," I replied.

With hoarse voices and caffeine pumping through our bodies, we set off towards Serge's.

No sooner had Billie and I walked into the *fromagerie* than Serge poked his head around the storeroom door, theatrically singing, "Hello, is it Brie you're looking for?" to the tune of Lionel Richie's "Hello."

I wondered how often Serge used that line on foreigners and whether he was this friendly with all his other customers. I hoped not, thinking back to how serious he'd been on our first meeting.

"Gouda one, Serge." He wasn't the only one who knew a cheese pun or two.

He slapped his thigh, laughing and nodding in approval. Billie tittered and gave me a loaded look.

"Serge, this is Billie," I said, before she could say anything that would embarrass me. "She's just arrived from Australia and is going to help me eat cheese over the next couple of days."

Serge offered his hand over the counter and said a rather charming "*Bonjour.*"

"Do you think she's as crazy as I do for making this bet?" Billie asked immediately. I dug my fingers into her ribs.

"Oh, *non, non, non*. I think learning about French cheese is an enchanting thing for a foreigner to do. It shows commitment to this beautiful country. It's very patriotic."

"Would you say the same about a foreigner coming here to learn French history?" Billie probed.

"Ah, you see, the history of this great country is often best told through the story of its cheese—Napoleon, religion, and revolution—it's all there," Serge replied wistfully before looking at me, beaming. He was hardly helping me convince Billie that he was just my cheese guy.

"So what cheese shall we take to our picnic tonight?" I interrupted.

"Would you like to try something new? Or maybe you'd like your friend to taste one of your favorites. Comté, perhaps? Or Sainte-Maure? Valençay?" Serge continued to rattle off my favorite types of cheese and Billie turned to me.

"Yes, Ella. What shall we try? You certainly seem to have a *lot* of favorites."

Thankfully, the nuances of Billie's teasing, which would have been ridiculously obvious to a native English speaker, turned out to be subtle enough for Serge to miss completely.

"She does have a lot of favorites," Serge chimed in. "Very good ones, I must add."

I fake laughed, desperate to get out of the store before Billie could implicate me any further. "Serge, why don't you wrap us up a selection of cheeses that are good for a picnic and would pair well with a bottle of rosé."

"*Parfait,*" he said, pulling out a few cheeses enthusiastically.

With Serge's back turned, Billie leaned over the counter and eyed him up and down. Turning to me, she raised her eyebrows as if to say, *Not bad*. I shook my head dismissively, but from where we were standing, I had to admit that Serge did look pretty good. I tried to see him through Billie's eyes: Although I'd previously considered him a little too stocky, today he'd tied his apron tighter and I saw that he was taller, and better built, than I'd realized. His T-shirt was showing off some pretty enticing arm muscles and I wondered if he was the type of guy who worked out. I definitely didn't take him for the CrossFit type, thank God.

Serge turned around and busted both of us staring at him, so I made a joke about Billie being in a jet-lagged daze and hastily paid for the cheese.

The minute we were out of the store, Billie turned to me and said, "Ella, he fancies you. It's clear as day."

"It's not like that. It's an innocent cheesemonger-customer relationship. I think he just really cares about cheese."

"It definitely seems like more than that," she said. "When he asked you to visit him again soon, the longing was palpable!"

"Not for me, though. You know I prefer my men clean-cut and suave, a little more modern."

"Oh, Ella! Don't be so square. He's really good-looking, and he's totally rocking that beard.

"I admit he has a certain *je ne sais quoi*, but he's still not my type."

"You're right. He seems nothing like Paul," she said, and we both fell quiet.

⁓

With more cheese than two people could consume in a week, I messaged Chris and Clotilde to ask if they wanted to join us for an *apéro* by the Seine. Chris had been asking so much about Clotilde that it felt like I'd be killing two birds with one stone.

We went down to the banks of the river with our cheese, picking up the requisite wine and baguette en route. The packs of dancers were back and we settled at a spot near the tango area.

Chris joined us as the sun was setting and I introduced him to Billie—my two Australian friends who lived on different sides of the globe coming together. They spoke about Melbourne and figured out that they had friends in common. They got along as if they'd known each other for years.

"So, how is Ella at washing dishes?" Billie joked.

"She's the best I've ever seen," he said, laughing. "She's much better at washing up than making coffee. But just between us, I think her brain is being wasted in the café. It's probably time she started looking for a real job . . ."

I blushed. Chris had never suggested this to me before and I wondered if I'd given off a vibe that I was unhappy at Flat White. Of course, I loved working at the café and it'd been great to have an immediate source of income so soon after arriving in Paris, but it was getting to the point where I could see myself doing something more challenging. Chris must have sensed it.

Starting to feel uncomfortable, I asked him to tell Billie why he moved to Paris. He unabashedly told her that he'd moved here because he was madly in love with French women. I'd thought perhaps he'd try and spin it differently in front of a complete stranger, but he was resolute, as always. He was half-way through a story about being chased naked out of a married woman's apartment by her irate husband when Clotilde showed up to join us. She was wearing a short leather skirt and a white T-shirt and looked generally divine. She shimmied into a sitting position between Chris and Billie, and I was sure I could see stars in Chris's eyes. Despite being the only French native at our picnic, Clotilde slotted into our group perfectly, and after a few glasses of wine, I was bursting with love being surrounded by old and new friends.

Well into our second bottle, the conversation turned to me and my life in Paris.

"So, do you both eat as much cheese as Ella?" Billie asked. I turned the color of my rosé.

Chris shook his head. "Impossible."

Clotilde smiled. "Of course. It's a very important food group for the French."

"Personally, I can think of better things to spend my cash on," Chris added. "El, how are you even paying for all this cheese? I can't imagine your pay from Flat White would cover it."

"I have some savings left too," I admitted. "But you're right, I should probably start looking for another job soon."

Chris winked at me.

"I didn't realize you needed more work," Clotilde said. "What do you want to do?"

"She's a good writer," Billie chipped in.

"She's certainly got a way with words," Chris added. "You should hear her running commentary at the café some days."

Clotilde nodded thoughtfully.

As the dancers and picnickers began packing up, Clotilde checked her watch and said she had to go. We all rose to say good-bye and Chris managed to successfully convince her that they just so happened to be heading in the same direction. This was the first time he'd seen her since finding out she was related to Gaston and he appeared to be a man on a mission. I raised my eyebrows at him and he shrugged his shoulders. I wasn't sure she felt the same spark he did, and I hoped she'd be gentle with my lovestruck friend.

Billie and I stayed to finish the bottle of wine and devour the remnants of the cheese. It got late, and we got drunk and emotional, hugging each other under the stars. It felt good to have her with me in Paris. It felt normal. I wished she could stay.

As we walked home, she asked me what type of modeling Clotilde did, and I admitted that I had no idea.

"I think there's something odd going on there," she whispered. "When I asked her about it she said it was a little complicated and that she only did it to help out a friend."

"I wouldn't read too much into it," I said, remembering my early interactions with Clotilde. "She can be a bit aloof with new people."

"I just felt like maybe she was hiding something. It's hard to explain."

"How many glasses of wine in were you?" I asked.

Billie laughed. "Quite a few," she admitted.

"Besides, her modeling is only a side job. She mostly works for a food app."

"You're right, it was probably nothing," Billie said, linking her arm through mine.

⌒⌐

After another wonderful day of reconnecting, the time came to say good-bye to Billie at Gare du Nord where she was catching the Eurostar to London. As we parted ways, she handed me a gift.

I'd planned to wait until I got home to open it—make a real moment of it—but as soon as I got on the metro I couldn't resist taking a peek. Beyond the layers of red wrapping paper was a leather-bound journal. I admired its weight and texture in my hands before flipping it open and reading the inscription:

Ma belle, Ella.
For all your cheese-tasting adventures, which should be recorded and shared. In particular, don't skimp on the details of any potential cheese-shop interactions.
Love, Billie xx

The gesture was thoughtful and encouraging, although her reference to Serge was as see-through as the holes in a slice of Swiss cheese. Regardless, I couldn't help smiling. In a few short days, Billie was already rooting more for Serge than she ever had for Paul.

Thinking about Mr. Cheeseman's laugh and his goofy face when he was deep into a cheese origin story did make me consider how wonderful it would be to date the owner of a *fromagerie. It would be perfect for my challenge too*, I thought.

But, despite all the superficial benefits, I still couldn't conjure up any romantic feelings for Serge.

Chapter

21

AFTER THE BILLIE WHIRLWIND BLEW out of Paris, I fell into quite a comfortable routine. The hangovers were abating, I stopped worrying about running into Jean-Pierre and I was getting used to working all weekend and being a French *flâneur* from Monday to Friday.

For the first time in weeks, I had a moment to slow down. The peace was temporary, however, because as soon as I caught my breath, I began to feel a little low, suffering what the French called a *coup de blues*.

It'd been so great having a close friend visit and I'd adored sharing my new life with somebody who knew me well. But Billie's visit had also stirred up a lot of thoughts and feelings about Melbourne—mostly relating to my failed relationship with Paul—that I'd blissfully ignored since leaving.

To help brighten my mood, I dragged myself out of bed and pulled on my running shoes. Having dined and imbibed to excess since arriving in Paris, I figured it was probably time for some well-overdue exercise. I puffed my way over to the Canal Saint-Martin and tried to evoke some of Audrey Tautou's stone-skimming elegance from the dreamy film *Amélie* in my running style. Instead, I broke into a fit of heavy breathing as I clomped along the cobblestones, my body adjusting to its first non-cheese-related strain in months.

After a good twenty-ish minutes, I stopped and stretched, which mostly involved putting my head between my legs and trying not to be ill. Mid-wheeze, my phone started ringing. The number was blocked, which was normally a free pass to ignore the call, but international numbers often didn't show up and I hadn't heard from Mum in a while, so I answered.

"*Oui*, hello."

"Hello, is this Ella? *C'est Gaston* . . ."

Gasp!

"*Salut*, Gaston," I replied between inhales. "Can you wait one minute, *s'il te plaît?*" I put my hand over the microphone. *Oh, mon Dieu!* I was breathing like a ninety-year-old man who'd just run for the bus.

"Are you still there?" he asked.

"Yes. Hi. *Desolée*, I was in the middle of something *très important*. Were you hoping to speak to Clotilde? She's not in Paris this week," I said, playing it cool.

"Actually, I was hoping to talk to you," he said. "Shall I take you out for dinner tonight?"

My heart stopped momentarily and it wasn't because of my abominable fitness level. My interactions with Gaston to date had been hot and cold, and other than his text and the canapé moment (which quickly—and literally—went south), I'd wondered if our appreciation of each other wasn't a little one-sided.

"Of course, let me check my schedule . . ." I said, and waited a few seconds to give the impression that I was indeed looking at a calendar. "Yes, I'm free. I just have a few appointments this morning." *Rushing to buy an outfit and shave my legs.*

"OK, great. I'll come and pick you up at Clotilde's around eight, *ça va?*"

"*Oui, d'accord*," I replied.

"*Super, à tout à l'heure.*"

I raced home as fast as I could after my "marathon" exercise attempt and leaped in the shower. Sweat washed away, I went out to hunt down a chic and cheap outfit. I was sick of the summer wardrobe that I'd arrived with, and besides, I felt like my first official date in Paris deserved something new. Gaston hadn't mentioned where we'd be going, but his tastes, like Clotilde's, seemed expensive. *God, I hope it's not too pricey, and if it is, I hope he's paying.*

A few hours later, after more than a few stressful moments trying to zip things up in various changing rooms across the city, I was home, ready and waiting for the door to buzz. I was wearing a black dress—slimming—and a pair of red heels to jazz things up a little. When I opened the door, Gaston looked me up and down. I felt a little self-conscious, sucking in my tummy and pulling back my shoulders.

"*Oh là là*," he said after a few seconds of appraisal, and I stood at ease. The lust brewing in Gaston's eyes felt a world away from anything I'd registered in Paul's in the last few months of our relationship. It was invigorating.

As we walked to the restaurant, Gaston told me it was a new opening and that the chef had trained at some three-Michelin-starred place that I'd never heard of. He said it was a big deal and there was plenty of hype about the food. I was excited.

We skipped past the queue—where I heard someone murmur that it was an hour wait to even get on the list for a table—and Gaston waltzed up to the first server he saw and said something in a low voice. She nodded and motioned for us to follow. The dining room was dark and broody, with ornate red wallpaper standing out against the wooden floors and dark velvet curtains. Lights hung low from the ceiling and nestled snugly above the tables. It was modern, almost too cool, and felt like the antithesis to a classic French dining room.

As we were led to our table, Gaston put his hand on the small of my back. His touch was warm and after so many years with Paul, followed by a few months of being single, it was enough to make me want to rip my dress off and get down to business. Thankfully for my modesty, and for the rest of the diners, my outfit stayed firmly in place and I managed to maintain a sense of Parisian-style composure.

"How did you skip the waiting list?" I asked when we were seated, craning my neck to look at the full dining room.

"I called ahead," he replied, very matter-of-factly, his tone almost businesslike.

"But it's so busy. I'm surprised you could get in," I said.

"I arranged it through work; it was no problem."

"That's right, you're a journalist, aren't you? What exactly do you write?" I asked, now even more curious.

"I'm a food critic. I write restaurant reviews."

Gaston being judgmental of Clotilde's cooking suddenly made more sense. He was used to eating at Paris's finest restaurants and obviously had oversensitive taste buds. I could forgive the man that.

"That's my dream job," I said.

"It's OK, but maybe not as fun as it sounds. Paris has its share of terrible restaurants that also need reviewing, *n'est pas?*"

He then spent the next half hour telling me about the endless free restaurant tastings and the daily eating out that his job entailed. It sounded brilliant and I was enthralled. *The perfect Parisian guy with the perfect job!*

My lusting over all things Gaston was only interrupted by the stealthy appearance of a waiter next to our table.

"*Bonsoir,*" he said coolly, smoothing down his chic denim and leather apron.

"*Bonsoir,*" I replied, trying my best to sound as French as possible.

"Oh, good evening," the waiter replied in English, not skipping a beat. "Would you like me to explain the menu?" He looked at us both as if we were wasting his time.

"*En Français, s'il vous plaît,*" Gaston said abruptly.

"*D'accord,*" said the waiter, launching into telling us about God knows what. I understood next to nothing. Gaston responded and the waiter left.

Gaston looked at me and smiled. I asked him why he'd told the waiter to describe the menu and specials in French rather than English.

"It's important for the review," he said quickly. "And also, I wanted him to leave us alone so we could get to know each other better. I've ordered us a bottle of wine; I hope that's OK." He looked deep into my eyes and I melted. I relaxed back into my chair.

"So I'm helping you review this place?" I asked.

"In a way," he replied. "I hope you don't mind sharing food." I assured him that I didn't.

"So, how do you like living with Clotilde?" Gaston asked.

"Oh my God, I love it," I replied honestly.

"Isn't she such a dork, though? When we were kids, she'd always get teased. I'd be so embarrassed. She never really fit into her own body."

I felt immediately defensive and said, "Look at her now, though. She's a model."

"Of sorts," Gaston said with a snigger.

What's that supposed to mean? I wondered, but I didn't feel like I should pursue it.

When the waiter came back to our table with the wine, Gaston ordered for us both. He told me there were three dishes we had to try: the pigeon, the pie, and the chocolate tart. I'd never eaten pigeon before, and I imagined Paris's flying street rats being dished up in the kitchen. The thought cut my appetite, but this was Gaston's domain and he seemed to know what he was doing.

The dining experience was very matter of fact: no amuse-bouche or palate cleanser that I'd normally associate with fancy French restaurants. This place was chic beyond measure and clearly wasn't into offering any free thrills. When the food arrived, Gaston snapped pictures of everything, making sure to get the look from various angles, whilst I indulged in the bread-basket with a little more gusto than I'd hoped to display. *I've been on a run, thank you very much!* I thought when the waiter grumpily asked if we "needed" more bread.

"So, what do you think, *ma belle?*" Gaston asked as I took a bite of pigeon.

"It's not bad," I said, trying not to gag. Despite my best efforts, I couldn't get past the image of the filthy birds.

Gaston spent a lot of the meal explaining Paris's dining scene while I listened, captivated by his in-depth knowledge. He told me in great detail how it had evolved drastically over the past decade. Where kitchens had lacked any exciting innovation for a long time, since the days of Paul Bocuse and "*sa nouvelle cuisine*," the city had once again become home to some of the most exciting restaurants in the world. Gaston disliked traditional French dining—the red-checked tablecloths and the older, portly waiters—in favor of the new, modern style. He rattled off the names of the young chefs who were leading the French food renaissance.

I wasn't brave enough to say that I loved everything about the traditional brasseries and bistros of Paris, even the stereotypical tablecloths. I felt terribly unqualified to argue about food trends so I nodded along, occasionally getting blissfully distracted by Gaston's chiseled cheekbones and defined jaw. I wondered whether he'd be a good kisser.

The waiter arrived to clear our mains and hand us a dessert menu. I asked Gaston whether we should have cheese, eagerly awaiting the right moment to show off my own food knowledge and tell him all about my challenge.

"But, Ella, anyone can buy good cheese in Paris. Let's get that chocolate tart I mentioned and another dessert of your choosing and see what the kitchen is truly capable of."

I shrunk back in my seat and didn't dare mention my bet with Serge. Instead, I ordered the mystifyingly named "apple in apple" and Gaston the "*Oops, ma tarte.*" By the time dessert arrived, we were emptying the last few drops of our bottle. My tolerance to wine was still nowhere akin to that of the French and I was feeling delightfully uninhibited.

Gaston broke off a piece of what turned out to be a deconstructed chocolate tart and fed it to me. I licked it suggestively and he asked how I liked it. I told him it was divine, despite the fact that I'd barely registered the taste in my attempt to eat sexily. I was in another world, one where we had already finished dinner and were getting naked together. It was steamy there. I completely ignored my own plate of dehydrated apple spirals exploding out of what looked like a meringue volcano on a bed of apple puree.

I felt Gaston's foot gently caressing the inside of my thigh. The date had been going well up until now, but this was still an unexpected advance. *A shoe up my dress*, I thought. *Is this a normal seduction technique?* I knew that the French were more sexually forward than many other cultures, but still, *Oh là là!* It'd been nearly a decade since my last "first date," and perhaps too many years with Paul had stinted my understanding of the requisite etiquette.

I looked around self-consciously but realized that no one was paying any attention to us, not even the nonchalant waiters who were now too busy standing around looking hip to be effective. I went with the flow, sunk deeper into my chair, and let Gaston's foot slide up higher.

"Do you have plans after dinner?" he asked, and I stifled a laugh, hiding the fact that I never really had plans these days.

"Nothing concrete," I said nonchalantly. Then I threw caution to the wind and suggested we get another drink.

"Perfect idea. I have a bottle of champagne at my house if you'd like to come over?"

That's some forward thinking right there, I thought, thanking the gods he'd made the first move.

"Champagne sounds great."

The next thing I knew, Gaston whipped out a black American Express card and settled *l'addition*. After signing the credit card receipt without even glancing at it—I hated to think how much it might have come to—he thanked the waiter and whisked me into an Uber I didn't even realize he'd ordered.

We sped through the streets of Paris and arrived at Gaston's building in Saint-Germain, on a street that I recognized from when I'd lived in the sixth *arrondissement* with Jean-Pierre and his mother. I quickly shook the image of them sipping tea in their formal living room out of my head.

After tottering up the carpet-clad wooden stairs to Gaston's apartment, I did a double take when he turned on the lights, shocked at how beautiful everything was. He'd decorated the generous space with an elegant mix of modern and antique furniture that looked like it'd been taken straight from the pages of *Vogue Living*. I didn't have long to admire the view, however, because seconds after shutting the door, Gaston pulled me closer and kissed me hard on the lips. He had my full attention.

The rest of the night was a blur of sex, champagne, and finally, some petits fours that Gaston just had "laying about" in his fridge. I hadn't realized how much I'd needed to feel desired again, and it felt good to be back in somebody's arms.

By the time we eventually fell asleep, my body was exhausted. The post-Paul drought was officially over.

Chapter

22

AS THE SUN SHONE THROUGH the windows of Gaston's apartment the next morning, I slid out of bed, pulled on a fluffy, gray bathrobe, and walked over to check out the view. His apartment was on the fourth floor of a Haussmann-style building overlooking a quiet residential street. It had high ceilings, ornate cornices, and a thin, wrought-iron balcony that screamed Parisian. I wondered if it belonged to his family, like Clotilde's did, but regardless, I couldn't help thinking I'd snagged a winner.

My night with Gaston had felt like a real turning point between the tears I'd shed over Paul back in Melbourne and my reentrance into the dating game, with a gorgeous Frenchman, no less.

Gaston appeared behind me and wrapped his arms around my waist. I remained fixated on the cars zipping past below, tracing invisible lines over the city, my city.

"Ella," he said in a husky morning voice, thick with his French accent. "Come back to bed. I don't need to work today. There's no point getting up early."

"Oh, I don't know," I said, trying to sound coquettish. "If you insist." With that, he spun me around and kissed me wildly. After nearly a decade with the same guy, I was unaccustomed to the wild and unexpected sex that was born out of lust. I pulled away momentarily and took in the sight—Gaston standing naked in the late morning light, his bronzed shoulders tapering down to his muscular abs—before moving in for more.

Everything felt new and exciting, and after last night, a little tender and sore. Still, I rallied. I was lightheaded with pleasure and the beginning of a champagne hangover. Running back to bed with Gaston made me feel free. With Paul, I'd been aware of my faults and had been plagued by teenage hang-ups and insecurities from the beginning of our relationship. As the years went on, I began to accept and love my body for what it was—slightly thick legs, a too-long torso, and narrow shoulders—but it wasn't until sleeping with Gaston that I finally felt sexy. I liked to think of it as the Paris effect.

The early-autumn day slipped away dreamily. After hours in bed, polishing off a bottle of rosé and finishing some leftover chocolates and mini éclairs, I thought about heading home. I was craving a shower and some decent sleep. Midnight romps were exhausting.

As I hunted for my clothes that were irresponsibly strewn about the apartment, Gaston's phone buzzed. I found my knickers and my dress and had just started pulling them on when he said, "Join me for dinner tonight." It was more of a command than a question, but it was sexy. I was exhilarated at the thought of going out again with the gorgeous Gaston and eating more glorious French food, but then I looked at my crumpled dress. There was no way I could respectably go out in yesterday's clothes without hating myself.

"I should probably go home," I said.

"But you need to come. It's a tasting and I don't want to go by myself," he pleaded.

"Which restaurant?"

"Le Bistro. I'll have you home before midnight."

I desperately flattened my dress with my hands. "But Gaston, I have nothing to wear. Isn't there someone else you can ask?"

"No, everyone is away," he said. "Besides, I only want to go with you."

I was flattered. A food critic had me lined up for two dinners in a row. Maybe my taste buds, as well as my company, had met Gaston's standards last night. And anyway, a bistro dinner sounded fun.

After a few minutes mulling over what to do, torn between wanting to spend more time with Gaston, but also feeling exhausted and disheveled, I told him that I'd love to join him but had to go home and throw on jeans and a T-shirt first. He grumbled, saying he was hungry and that the booking was for eight.

It was 7:40.

"*Oh là là*," I said, lightening the mood.

He smiled. "I have an idea. There's a shop down on the corner of my street; let me buy you something to wear. I promise I have good taste."

I considered the offer for at least one second before my excitement got the better of me. Two dinners, champagne, the Parisian apartment I'd always dreamed of, and now an offer to buy me clothes. *Was it too early to declare my love?*

"OK, *pourquoi pas!*" I said. "As long as you don't mind."

"For the dress, of course not; I'd rather you be naked, but maybe we can get something close to that. Oh, and we pronounce it *pourquoi pas,* you need to emphasize the *pooourrr,*" he said, rolling the "r" and pinching my cheeks.

Downstairs in the clothing boutique, I was eyeing a casual printed maxi dress when Gaston appeared beside me saying, "How about this one?" He pulled the dress—which could easily have been mistaken for a negligee—from a hanger and held it up to my shoulders. It was fire-engine red, extremely low cut, and also rather short. It wasn't an article of clothing I would ever have picked out for a "casual bistro dinner," but I figured, *When in Paris, why not?*

"It will look perfect on you," Gaston whispered in my ear.

"OK," I replied. "I'll try it on."

Gaston gently pushed me towards the changing room with a grin.

I stood in front of the mirror examining the girl I saw before me and was reminded of getting ready for that fateful dinner with Paul. I felt far away from that version of myself, and it was comforting; somehow the risqué dress seemed appropriate. Gaston beckoned me from behind the curtain before pulling it back and peeking in. I turned to him gingerly and asked, "It's not too short, or low, or thin . . .?" I ran my hand self-consciously over my cheese belly.

Gaston wolf whistled in approval and walked over to the counter with his credit card. It was by far the quickest shopping trip I'd ever been on.

With my new dress on, we left the boutique and began walking quickly down the street. I noticed the air had suddenly turned fresh. Autumn was well underway and the leaves were changing color, gradually making the trees look naked. I sympathized, feeling a little exposed myself.

As if on cue, I noticed an old man sipping red wine outside a café staring at my chest. I looked down and gasped. The cold wind and my lack of a bra meant my nipples were burning into everyone's field of vision like headlights on a dark night. I brought my arms up to cover my chest. Thankfully, Gaston was oblivious to my discomfort.

"You look incredible," he said. "Do you see how everyone is turning to look at you?"

No wonder, I thought, *I'm half-naked.*

He slapped me lightly on the arse and asked me if I liked the dress.

"I love it," I said, giving him a little kiss on the cheek.

I was already envisioning getting home and putting on sweat-pants and a hoodie.

⁓

When I set eyes on the "bistro," I was surprised. While I'd en-visaged wooden tables, hearty food, and maybe a poet sand-wiched in the corner writing in a Moleskine, I saw low lighting, a well-equipped open kitchen, and stools lining a fully-stocked cocktail bar.

Gaston's choice of dress suddenly made more sense. Regardless of how naked I'd felt during the walk over, I was now grateful to be wearing the slinky nightgown; it was as though it'd come back into its natural habitat.

"This is a bistro?" I asked.

"*Oh non,* Ella . . . This place is called 'Le Bistro.' It's very hot right now."

As we were shown to our table, I looked around and saw that Le Bistro was home to some seriously well-dressed people, most of whom were sashaying about, chatting to one another while sipping champagne. *What is this life?* I asked myself.

Despite the relatively small space, the tables inside the restaurant were spread quite far apart, giving it a rather exclusive and unique feel. Normally in Paris, space was of the essence and guests were squeezed in together to make the most of every square centimeter. At Le Bistro, maximizing potential covers was obviously not a pressing concern.

A waitress recognized Gaston and came over immediately, giving him a delicate air kiss on each cheek.

"I didn't know you worked here," Gaston said.

"It's a great place to be seen at the moment," she replied, winking. "Heaps of agents and talent scouts are dining here."

Gaston translated for me, and I looked around and noticed that the waiters were all exceptionally beautiful, most of them looking fresh out of high school. They flaunted their flawless baby skin with tight clothes and deep V necks.

Gaston introduced me to Camille, who, despite the fact that she was in Chanel ballet flats, towered over me with legs that seemed to stretch up to my neck. A pang of jealousy ripped through me.

"Hello, Camille," I said in English, forcing my accent a little, trying to sound aloof, foreign, and cool, but coming off as faux-British and vocally challenged.

"Hello, so pleased to meet any *friend* of Gaston's," she replied with a perfect, posh English accent. "Let me get you some menus." She swept away gracefully, leaving an air of mystique in her wake.

Before Gaston could tell me how he knew Camille, she came back carrying two glasses of champagne and the smallest menus I'd ever seen. I glanced at the list of dish names—all three words—delicately embossed on the paper and Camille asked us if we needed her to explain anything. I was about to tell her that my menu didn't make any sense but Gaston replied in French and she nodded and walked away.

"I've ordered, OK?" he said. Again, I wasn't sure if it was a question or a statement.

"Of course. You're the professional," I said smiling.

Feeling frisky after my glass of champagne, I reached for Gaston's leg under the table.

"Not here, Ella," he said sharply. "Someone might see us."

"Sorry," I said, slinking back into my seat.

We fell into a slightly awkward silence.

Artfully presented dishes began to arrive as Gaston was wrapping up a story about the worst restaurant he'd ever reviewed. Despite my best intentions to concentrate, I couldn't stop thinking about him naked.

Seconds later, Camille arrived by Gaston's side, checking if we were "loving" dinner. With my mouth full, I told her that everything was delicious, and despite Gaston also reassuring her that he was happy with the food and service, she lingered, asking him how work had been lately. He replied very quickly, too quickly for me to understand. But then, I finally understood something.

"How is your modeling?" Gaston asked. I unintentionally rolled my eyes, thinking, *Of course she's a model. I should have guessed when I saw her legs.*

She replied, "*C'est magnifique,*" and then said something I understood to mean that she'd signed with some kind of agency. *Humph,* I thought, readjusting the strap of my dress. *Is she the reason Gaston didn't want me touching his leg?*

The food continued with a few additional dishes sent out from the kitchen, just for Gaston's eating pleasure. Pumpkin velouté with hazelnut goat cheese foam, monkfish in a buttery and citric sauce, and duck breast in a red wine jus paired with wild asparagus. The delightfully balanced portions left me feeling satiated, but thankfully not so full as to stretch the seams of my dress.

Over a dessert of fresh raspberries, meringue, and bursts of pop rocks, I began to understand Gaston's adoration of this style of French cooking. It was sensual and satisfying, and certainly more elevated than the *croque-monsieurs* I'd been eating since arriving in Paris.

I couldn't help noticing, though, that aside from the goat cheese that had adorned the soup, there was no sign of cheese in the building, especially not in my preferred form of large hunks on a board . . . *What was one meant to eat before dessert?*

After dinner Gaston escorted me back to my apartment.

"Would you like to come up?" I asked. "Clotilde is still away."

"*Oh, non, non,*" he said hastily. "I have to be up early tomorrow morning to get to Bordeaux for a wine tasting."

"Ooh, how glamorous," I said.

"Not really. It's a pain to take the TGV early. Sometimes I wish I could just work full-time in an office."

"No, your job is amazing," I said.

"Sometimes." He smiled. "It's not always easy though."

What's so hard about going on a wine tasting trip? I thought to myself, but held my tongue.

"Well, thank you for the most amazing couple of days," I said, gathering up my purse. "It's been so—"

Before I could finish my sentence, Gaston kissed me intensely on the lips.

"*Allez, ma belle*," he said, almost pushing me out of the cab. "I'll give you a call and we can do it again some time."

I climbed the stairs to the apartment feeling elated but also slightly confused at the same time. Was I just exhausted or had Gaston been doling out mixed signals all evening? On the one hand, he had bought me an incredibly sexy new dress, and on the other, he hadn't wanted to come upstairs and take it off. He'd taken me to a new restaurant where he was sure to run into industry people, but then he'd brushed off my hand when I'd tried to touch his leg. *Maybe it had been stupid to sleep with him on the first date . . .*

For perhaps the first time in my life, I tried not to overthink things. Gaston was probably tetchy during dinner because he was on the job. Eating was his life, and if he was anything like me he must have been feeling pretty depleted from all the sex the night before. But then again, judging by the state of his abs, I'm guessing he had some kind of fitness regime sorted.

I fell asleep quickly that night despite the excitement of new romance bubbling inside me. When I set out for Paris, I never imagined that I would end up dating a food critic and dining in Paris's hippest restaurants. I was well and truly swept up in the moment. *Quel rêve!*

Chapter

23

THE NEXT MORNING, FEELING REFRESHED from a good night's sleep and full of endorphins from my recent romp, I got out of the house early for a walk around the Marais. I stopped for coffee and breakfast and as I sat, elbows deep in a flaky croissant, I heard my phone ringing in my bag.

Could it be Gaston again? So soon? I wondered, wiping my hands on my jeans and distributing crumbs over all my belongings. I didn't recognize the number but still remained hopeful.

"*Oui, bonjour,*" I said.

"Hello, is this Ella?" a man asked in a heavy Scottish accent.

Did I know any Scotsmen?

"Yes, this is Ella."

"Ah, perfect, this is Tim from Food To Go Go." He sounded flustered. Car horns were blaring in the background. It took me a second to recognize the name of the app where Clotilde also worked.

"Hi . . ." I said, trying to piece together what was going on.

"You're the writer, correct?"

"Not exactly. I mean, I can write, but I've been working in publishing," I admitted, having a vague recollection of Clotilde telling me her boss was hoping to expand the team.

"But you're the one with the cheese Instagram, yes?" he asked.

"I am," I said, trying to hide my surprise that he knew about the account.

"Great, that'll do. We need someone to write our social media content. We're trying to flesh out the app to help with a new round of funding applications."

Oh God, funding for an app. This sounds familiar, I thought, having a flashback to the awkward share house interview I'd gone to just after arriving in Paris. I wasn't quite sure if I was cool enough for this, but still, it was a proper job. Not that I didn't love washing dishes at Flat White.

"Can you start next week?" he asked, interrupting my train of thought.

"Shouldn't we have an interview first?" I asked, before kicking myself.

"Ah, I guess. Why don't you come by the office tomorrow?"

"OK, sure," I said.

What the hell just happened? I thought, hanging up and feeling perplexed. *Did I just get another job?*

I assumed Clotilde must have suggested me for the role after our chat at the picnic on the Seine when Billie had been visiting; she'd just forgotten to mention it to me. She'd been away for the past few days on a midweek getaway in Ibiza, which was perhaps why it had slipped her mind.

I ordered another coffee to help me concentrate and formulate a plan. My empty day ahead had just gotten busy. I'd need to figure out what Clotilde had already told Tim about me—although given the posts I'd seen of her dancing at sunrise this morning, I could assume that getting ahold of her might prove troublesome. I also needed to shop. *But what to wear to a meeting—or was it an interview?—at a start-up?*

⟋⟋⟋

Feeling overwhelmed, I decided to call Mum. I hadn't spoken to her for a couple months—we'd mostly been emailing—and our last call had ended abruptly. I planned to tell her about my meeting with Tim tomorrow, but also, more selfishly, I was desperate to talk to someone about my gorgeous new Frenchman. I knew it was too early for declarations of love, but I could at least let Mum think I was getting serious about someone; she didn't need to know that Gaston and I had only been on a couple of dates. I also thought that by telling her about my new romance, it'd help her—and maybe me on some subconscious level—believe that I was truly over Paul.

"Isn't it too soon? Poor Paul . . ." was the first thing she said when I told her.

I instantly regretted calling.

"Mum, it's been months. And once again, to reiterate the painful truth, Paul was the one who decided to leave me."

"But he was so nice, so dependable." There was an indulgent dash of melancholy in her voice. She still somehow thought we were perfect together.

"I know how you felt about him," I snapped. "Perhaps you should call him for a chat. See how he's getting along now that he's found himself."

She ignored my suggestion. "So who is this new man, then? Where did you two meet?" she asked.

I told her about the coffee shop run-in and then our most recent dates.

"Your housemate's cousin? That seems like a bad idea, Ella. Even for you," she scolded.

"God, Mum. What is that supposed to mean? Can't you just be happy for me?"

"Of course I am happy for you, darling, but I don't want you rushing into anything. I don't want you doing something that you can't take back."

Too late for that, I thought.

"Anyway, Mum. Enough about men, I have a job interview tomorrow morning."

"What is it this time? Babysitting?" she asked.

I rolled my eyes. Her disapproval of me leaving my job in Melbourne to come and wash dishes in Paris seeped through the phone line and I had to stop myself from hanging up.

"No, a proper job. Writing the social media content for a new food app here," I said.

"Well, I guess it's a step up from the café."

"Don't simplify things, Mum," I said.

"Why? Because you can never do anything simply?"

She really had a knack for rubbing me the wrong way. I hated fighting during one of our infrequent phone calls so I took a calming breath and said in a bright voice, "So what's this plan you have for Christmas, then?"

"Well, I was going to surprise you with some good news, but seeing as you can't seem to wait for anything these days . . ." She paused. "I'm coming to visit you!"

"Oh, good," I said, not really taking in the weight of what she was saying.

"Don't sound so excited."

"Of course I'm excited," I said, still trying to shake my frustration from the Paul/Gaston/job conversation. My mum was coming to Paris to see me. This was wonderful news. "I can't wait to show you my life. And take you around Paris. There are so many great things we can do—" I was about to start listing all the attractions but Mum cut me off.

"Well, if you're planning on booking anything make sure you get three tickets because I'm coming with Ray." Her tone was matter-of-fact, and I had to take a moment to decipher what she was telling me.

"Who's Ray?" I asked cautiously.

"You know Ray, from down the street."

"No, I don't know Ray from down the street."

"You met him once when he was doing the whipper-snipper thingy in my garden."

"Oh, *Ray* Ray!" I exclaimed, the memory of our dorky neighbor springing to mind. His head full of shaggy, graying hair popping up over our fence before his lumbering limbs came into view. Oddly, no matter the weather, I'd only ever seen him wearing flannel shirts.

This was a very weird development indeed.

"Why would you be coming to Paris with Ray? Some kind of charity project?"

"Ella, don't be a brat! I'm coming to Paris with Ray because I want you to meet him," she said plainly.

"I have met him, and I certainly didn't take him for much of a traveler. Anyway, wouldn't you prefer some mother-daughter time, just the two of us?"

"Ella, there's something I should tell you."

"Sure, what's up?"

"Ray and I are engaged."

I dropped my phone.

"What was that noise, Ella? Are you OK?"

"Sorry, my phone slipped. You're engaged?"

"That's what I said. Maybe if you try listening—"

"Oh no, Mum. I heard. Now who's moving too fast?" I asked, more viciously than I intended.

"We've been seeing each other for nearly a year, darling. You've just been too busy changing boyfriends and moving overseas to notice. You never ask about my life anymore. Anyway, it's important to me that you get to know Ray before the wedding."

"The wedding . . . ?" I asked, half yelping.

I was trying to process what was going on. I was in shock. *Mum is getting married!*

"Well, congratulations," I said, trying not to come off as a narcissistic only child.

"He's very funny when you get to know him," she said lightly.

"I'm sure."

"And he's been very supportive since you left me all alone."

"Mmm," I said.

"He's very good for me, Ella."

I'd already started to feel sorry for myself—it'd no longer be just Mum and me. Now it would be us, plus whipper-snipper Ray from down the street. I felt teary.

"I've got to go, Mum," I said. "I'll call you next week."

Whenever I'd traveled overseas before, I'd been amazed at how much life back home hadn't changed while I'd been away. My friends would mostly remain the same and our relationships would fall back into place as soon as we were back together. Any news they had was almost always predictable: someone got engaged, there was a baby on the way, etc., etc. Most of these developments could be spotted a mile off, which was comforting. What wasn't comforting, and what I hadn't been prepared for, was a change so big that it reminded me that I was far away in a foreign country. I didn't even know Mum was seeing anyone, let alone planning a wedding. I wasn't ready for this bombshell, or for the guilt that accompanied it. *Am I a terrible daughter?* I wondered.

I desperately wanted to tell someone the news and ask if what I was feeling was normal, but I had to prepare for tomorrow's meeting with Tim. I didn't have time for any indulgent emotional introspection. I put all thoughts of getting a new stepfather aside for the time being. Clotilde was getting back late the following evening, so discussions about my family, and her family—namely about my recent sex-capade with her cousin—would have to wait until then.

<hr>

The next morning, I was still finding it hard to believe that I was going for my second job interview in Paris. *Me, with potentially two jobs in a city where I hardly speak the language!* Granted, it really hadn't been that difficult to get the first job—terrible coffee-making trial aside—and the second, which sounded a lot more stimulating than washing dishes, seemed to have fallen into my lap.

Tim and I met outside the office and we walked to a café a few doors down. He was tall with red hair, wearing dark pants and a somewhat creased shirt. For once, I felt like I was appropriately dressed for an interview in my new—heavily-discounted—black pencil skirt and green blouse, which I had picked up on sale at Zara the previous day.

Once we sat with espressos in hand, Tim asked about my publishing experience and arts degree. He was from Glasgow and spoke frantically, fast and loud. I worked hard to keep up with him. He seemed to me like a good-time guy who had recently decided to get serious about work. Either that or he'd had a great idea for an app that had suddenly taken off and had forced him to become a responsible adult. He explained the Food To Go Go concept—a carefully-curated food delivery app—and told me about the current team, and lastly, about the pay, which was terrible. Currently, they could only afford to hire me for two days a week, but he hoped funding would come through so they could move the role full-time. He explained that the job was straightforward: managing the social media accounts and writing content for new listings, weekly promotions, and newsletters.

"It's not rocket science," he said. "I just need someone who'll fit in well with the team. And who can start immediately . . ."

"Sounds good to me," I said.

And with that, the "formal" part of the interview was apparently over and Tim asked me the dreaded, "So why did you move to Paris?"

This time, thanks to Chris, I came prepared—although I'd tweaked it slightly to brush over the advice-giving slice of Comté. "Well, I felt bogged down by life back home. I enjoyed my job, but felt like it wasn't moving fast enough," I launched into my rehearsed spiel. "Life in Australia seems to move much slower, you know? I wanted to come to Europe and be inspired. I wanted to try new things, which is how I ended up in the café."

I was surprised how easily all of this rolled off the tongue. "And now I'm aiming to try every type of cheese in France, with the help of a cheese man in the Marais," I ad-libbed. *Why of all times should I start talking about Serge now?* I wondered.

"Ah, so that's the story behind the Instagram account. It has quite the cult following in our office, you know?" Tim said.

I blushed, knowing that Clotilde had most likely strong-armed all her colleagues into following it.

"In any case, it sounds like quite the undertaking. You know France has more cheese than there are days in the year?" he continued.

How was this common knowledge to everyone except me? I lamented.

"I do now," I replied. "But lucky for me, this brilliant cheese seller is guiding me through the list."

"Well, you must have some serious stamina," he said.

"I guess I do . . . And what brought *you* to Paris?" I asked, eager to turn the focus off me.

"My girlfriend is Parisian. We're expecting a baby this winter," he said with a smile, and I wondered if the rush for funding had anything to do with supporting his new family.

"Sounds like you have stamina too, then," I said, and he laughed. I was pleased to be making a good first impression.

"So you can start first thing next week?" he asked suddenly, getting out his wallet to pay for our espressos.

"Of course. Whatever you need. I'm at the café Saturday and Sunday, and other than cheese eating, I'm totally free."

"Done. See you Monday."

I skipped down the road beaming. Here I was, in Paris, with two jobs, a cheese guy, a great apartment, and a dreamy French love interest. I crossed my fingers and hoped that my run of fabulous luck would continue.

Chapter
24

I DIDN'T HEAR CLOTILDE ARRIVE home late that evening but the following morning, I spotted a note from her on the counter.

> Ella, I hope you've had a nice week. I didn't want to wake you, but we need to talk. I'll meet you at Le Progrès at 6. C xx

I wasn't sure if she'd spoken to Gaston since our date. *Merde! Does she know? Is she pissed off?*

I spent the day at Flat White feeling nervous. Where I'd been euphoric about my prospects a few hours earlier, Clotilde's note had sparked an overwhelming sense of uneasiness in me that sent my anxiety spiraling. I threw myself into scrubbing dishes like it was the most important thing in the world and I soon lost count of how many times I'd replayed my sleepover at Gaston's in my head.

I was exhausted at the end of my shift and I bided my time waiting for Clotilde with a glass of white wine, staring at the people passing by and worrying what she might say.

Half an hour later, she arrived, shimmying into a seat, her arms laden with shopping bags. She looked bronzed and relaxed from her sojourn in Ibiza; the beachside lifestyle suited her well.

"What did you buy?" I exclaimed. "Or what *didn't* you buy?"

"Oh, just a few little things." She looked at the bags and laughed. I laughed too, more out of relief that she didn't seem angry with me. "Perhaps I got more than I should have. But I just got paid for a shoot and had some spare cash I felt like burning."

"Cool, who was the shoot for?" I asked. She was always shy about her modeling, brushing off my questions or saying it was "dull" whenever I asked, leaving me to wonder what was boring about being a model in Paris. This time, she countered my question with one of her own: "So, what happened while I was away? Tell me everything."

"Well, you somehow managed to get me a job at Food To Go Go," I said.

"Tim gave you the job?" she shrieked excitedly. "We're going to be colleagues!"

"Yes, it was quite out of the blue," I replied.

Clotilde looked sheepish. "I'm so sorry I forgot to mention it."

"No worries. I'm guessing you must have put in quite a good word for me. He wasn't even going to bother with an interview."

"Yeah, he's a little manic, our Tim, but he's a great boss. You'll love working with us . . ." She paused. "And now, any other dates you want to mention?"

I tried to stifle the grin that was spreading across my face. "I don't know what you're talking about."

"I wasn't sure if you wanted to date at the moment, but when Gaston called to ask if you were coming to Ibiza, I had a feeling he was planning something."

Oh dear, I wonder what else she knows!

"And you had fun?" she asked.

"Have you spoken with him?" I cut in.

"No, only before I went away. Why?"

Since my date with Gaston, I'd been desperate to dissect the night in detail like I would have done with my friends back home, and knowing that Clotilde hadn't already heard his version of events encouraged me.

I'd spoken to Chris about the date earlier in the day, telling him about how Gaston had been a little hot and cold with me over the two dinners; I'd blushed when he had me reenact the foot-up-the-dress moment and had agonized over Gaston brushing my hand away on the second night. And all I'd gotten in return was, "Welcome to Paris, newbie. Love ain't all shared bank accounts and brunches here," before he tried to convince me that I'd learn to love these feelings of uncertainty and excitement that came with dating the French. "Why do you think I persist?" he'd asked. I figured that it must be easier for guys to play the dating game here, especially laid-back ones like Chris.

Clotilde, on the other hand, was begging for details . . . I launched into a description of the restaurant and the food on the first date, but she cut me off.

"Yes, yes, yes. I've been there. The food was good but it's a bit pretentious, *non*? Can you just skip to what happened *après* dinner? Gaston will not tell me anything, but knowing my cousin like I do, I'm sure that something must have happened. Spill the beans, *ma belle*."

"What do you mean, 'knowing my cousin'?" I asked, feeling the blood rush to my cheeks.

"Oh, you know what I mean, Ella. Boys will be boys. So?"

"Well, he took me back to his place."

"Ooh," Clotilde said. "And?"

"And I don't kiss and tell," I told her with a grin, despite an

internal worry that perhaps the encounter hadn't been as special in Gaston's eyes.

Before I had the chance to ask Clotilde more about her cousin's playboy reputation, she said, "Let's go get some cheese.
After a week of eating seafood and fruit, I'm craving something
gooey."

I didn't need much convincing. A short time later we were
walking into Serge's.

"*Bonsoir, mesdames,*" he sang out as we walked through the
door. "Ella, it's been a while since I've seen you."

It'd only been a week since I'd last been in. And I had been
eating cheese, just not from his shop. I'd actually been a little
too busy, what with my jumping into bed with a hot Frenchman
and all, but I wasn't about to divulge that detail.

"I thought perhaps you didn't want any more cheese. But
maybe you're just finally ready for our dinner?" he added.

"Oh, I've been out of town. In Ibiza with Clotilde," I lied,
motioning to Clotilde, who raised an eyebrow.

Why did I just lie?

"Clotilde and I live together," I said by way of introduction.
"Clotilde, Serge is the owner of Paris's best cheese shop."

"*Enchanté,*" they both said in unison. If it weren't for the smell
of the cheese to remind me I was in France, their politeness
certainly would have done it.

Clotilde made quick work of ordering a log of Sainte-Maure,
the lightly barnyard-smelling goat cheese from the Loire that
I'd also come to love, especially coupled with fresh figs or
honey. The girl knew what she wanted.

"What else should we get?" she asked me, scanning the cabinet.

"Ella, there is something you must try," Serge interrupted. "I
know how much you love blue cheese." I nodded in agreement

but immediately felt apprehensive. Serge's blue recommendations were always quite intense.

"Well, you're in for a treat," he said. "This Bleu de Corse recently arrived. It's from La Corse, you know the island off the south of France? I'll wrap some up for you—on the house. You can tell me how much you enjoyed it next time you come in."

I couldn't help thinking that Serge's accent seemed to have gotten stronger—and slightly more adorable—over the past week. But I was getting distracted. I made a concerted effort to listen more closely to what he was saying.

"It tastes a lot like sheep's wool might, if you ate it. It's very delicious!"

"Are you sure?" I asked, unconvinced.

"*Mais oui,* especially with a glass of rosé."

He turned to Clotilde, asking her in French if she'd sampled it before.

"*Oui, oui, je l'adore,*" she almost sang in reply, playing up her Frenchness. She went on to say that it was super strong, shaking her fist and scrunching up her eyes in effort, looking more like a hiker reaching a mountain's summit than someone buying cheese.

"Your friend has good taste," Serge said. "Nearly as good as yours, Ella. At least when you're not posting pictures of cheese on the Internet."

"Oh, that reminds me, did I tell you I got a new job, Serge?" I interrupted. "I'm going to be writing the social media content for a start-up."

He looked at me, confused. "Tell me this doesn't mean more pictures of cheese," he said, sighing.

"It's a food delivery app, so not just pictures of cheese, but *all* food," I explained.

"And someone will pay you for this?" he asked quizzically.

"They sure will," I replied, still surprised myself at how lucky I was.

He looked at me sideways, probably trying to figure out how he could get me out of his shop, but instead he said, "Well, I hope you'll still find time to visit your old friend Serge."

"Don't worry, the new office isn't far away," I assured him.

———

"He likes you," Clotilde said as soon as we'd walked out.

"Who? Gaston?" I asked, picking up our conversation from before we'd entered the cheese shop. "Did he tell you that?" I heard desperation in my voice and it wasn't becoming.

"No . . . the cheese guy."

Serge? What would make her think that?

"He's just a friend. He recommends good cheese for me to buy. There's nothing more to it than that."

"He flirts with you," she said.

"He probably just wants to keep me coming back," I told her. "I must be one of his most profitable customers. And anyway, he's sort of giving me an education in *fromage.*"

"Ah, so it's just about the cheese. My bad." She held up her hands in mock surrender.

"Seriously, there's nothing going on between us. Serge isn't really my type."

"Well, yes, we all know your type: tall, dark, and with a hint of Gaston," she laughed.

I joined her, remembering that Billie had made a similar joke when she'd visited the *fromagerie.*

Luckily, I was sure Serge didn't think of me that way. If anything, I was just the annoying girl who wouldn't stop pestering him for recommendations.

FROMAGE À TROIS

I fell into step with Clotilde as we walked back towards home. She chattered on about her holiday, about the cocktails on the beach, clubbing until the early hours, and meeting up with friends she hadn't seen in years . . . but for whatever reason, I couldn't really concentrate on what she was saying.

⁓

By the time we arrived home, I'd given up on trying to find out about Gaston's dating history; Clotilde wouldn't say a word against him. Instead, I began divulging the details of my other current preoccupation: my mother's surprise engagement.

"And do you like the man she's marrying?" Clotilde asked, after I'd explained that Mum would be introducing me to her new fiancé when she visited at Christmas.

"I have no idea. I don't really know him," I admitted. "I only met him once when he was helping her in the garden. To be honest, I didn't even expect her to start dating again, let alone get married."

"Ella, can I ask what happened to your father?"

"It's a long story," I said, not really wanting to get into the details but not wanting to brush off Clotilde's question.

My father left me and Mum when I was little and I hardly remembered him. He was a young American artist working in some studio in Australia when they met. Shortly after, they got pregnant with me. They made it work for a few years, and were happy despite having no money and living in a sort of artist commune, but then he was offered a residency in the States and he disappeared. We never saw him again.

When I turned sixteen, I asked Mum to help me get in touch with him. After a few weeks, she told me she'd tried but to no avail. Mutual friends had said he was living off the grid in the mountains. I never knew if that was a lie or not, but a few months later, we received a letter telling us that he'd died unexpectedly of liver failure.

The news had put Mum into a bit of a spin, which had surprised me because she'd mostly seemed to dismiss him up until that point. Her reaction made it clear that her feelings for him had been greater than I'd suspected. Even though he'd been gone for most of my life, his death felt very final, for both of us.

I was almost certain that Ray was the first man she'd been with since my father. From the little I knew about him, he seemed like the epitome of an Australian bloke: friendly, reliable, and kind. He just didn't seem particularly interesting.

As I recounted all this to Clotilde, I realized just how fast I was speaking. The thoughts that had been buzzing around my head since my phone call with Mum came oozing out of me like a soft-centered cheese. It felt good to let them out.

"Oh wow, Ella, I had no idea," Clotilde said, tears in her eyes.

"It's fine. I've had years to come to terms with it."

I unwrapped the Bleu de Corse to think about something other than my father. The block looked wet, slimy, and unappealing; it was punctured by faint lines of mold rather than the deep pockets that were synonymous with other types of blue.

"Wow, this stuff really smells like a barn," I said, struggling not to scrunch up my face in horror. Clotilde bent over to sniff the cheese nonchalantly.

"I've smelled worse," she replied, grabbing a knife and chopping off a huge chunk. I cut a much more modest amount for myself, wary that this could be the first French cheese I might truly hate if the smell and texture were anything to go by.

The first bite was overpowering. Clotilde encouraged me to

take a second. It was creamy, despite the wet rind, and grainy, and had that unmistakably sheep milk cheese pungency; it tasted almost as though I were licking the animal itself. It didn't have quite the same sensation of salt bursting on the tongue as Roquefort did, but rather had an overall saltiness, which might have been moreish if I could get past the overwhelming smell that lingered in the air.

"You should always taste more when it comes to difficult cheeses," Clotilde said seriously. "Sometimes I hate the first bite, then on the second, it brings me around, and by the last, I'm hooked. Like a child trying vegetables for the first time."

"Clotilde, you sound like Serge!"

"Ah, so he's still on the brain then?" She ate some more of the cheese and sighed in delight. "Cheese can be very addictive, *n'est-ce pas?*"

I agreed with her in theory, but believed this Corsican blue might just prove to be the exception to the rule.

I begrudgingly cut another slice, this time even thinner than the last, and placed it in my mouth. I could tolerate it, but was sure I could never get to the point of being hooked.

"What's Ray like then?" Clotilde asked, serving herself more cheese.

"He's OK, from what little I know," I said, thinking about how he was the complete opposite to how I'd always pictured my father. "A little boring, perhaps. He's like the Cheddar of the cheese world. I don't think he's ever been overseas before."

"You must be excited to get to know him over Christmas then," Clotilde said.

I nodded unenthusiastically.

If I was being honest, I wasn't particularly looking forward to spending time with this strange Australian neighbor who was to become my stepfather and I certainly couldn't figure out what had endeared him to Mum. *And why now, after twenty years of being neighbors? Has she just settled for a safe option because she's lonely? Is it payback because I moved overseas?* The thoughts were still running. And I knew I was being a brat, jealous that Mum had moved on and kept me in the dark about her new relationship, but I couldn't help it. Her springing this news on me reinforced the fact that I wasn't part of her day-to-day anymore, and it made me feel horribly homesick.

That night, as I lay in bed thinking about Gaston, my parents, and blue cheese, I realized that somewhere along the way, my personal life in France had become nearly as complicated as the one I'd left behind in Australia. Where summer in Paris had been slow and at times lonely, autumn and winter were shaping up to be eventful. I posted a picture on Instagram of the Bleu de Corse and wrote in the caption that I had mixed feelings about the cheese. I received a few quick comments on the photo, both agreeing and disagreeing. The more time I spent in France, the more I understood that some types of cheese could be quite divisive. It made me thankful that there were so many varieties—it allowed you to swiftly move from one to the next if you didn't like the taste a particular kind left in your mouth. It was a valuable lesson that could also be applied to life.

My phone buzzed and Gaston's name appeared on my screen. My heart beat faster as I read his message saying he'd had a great time at dinner, and after dinner, and that he wanted us to do it all again soon. *All of it again? Yes, please!* I dozed off, hugging my phone.

Chapter
25

THE DAYS WERE FLYING BY and before I knew it, the cold December weather had arrived. Although I didn't feel ready to pull on boots and a warm jacket, adding a chunky knit sweater over my cheese belly was actually turning out to be a welcome convenience.

One particularly bitter-cold and gray Saturday morning, I decided to embrace the change in temperature by hanging out in bed with a bowl of coffee before heading to Flat White to start my shift.

I was updating my cheese journal, which I'd started in the notebook Billie had given me when she'd left Paris. I'd been writing in it frequently over the past couple of months and it was a pleasure going back over all the entries and remembering how I'd worked cheese into almost every aspect of my French life. Clotilde loved it, Serge adored it, and Gaston secretly enjoyed eating it, when coerced, although never in a restaurant.

My 365 Days of Cheese Challenge was mostly on track. I was slightly behind where I should have been, in terms of total varieties tasted, but that was nothing that couldn't be made up over an indulgent Christmas.

I chuckled as I came across one particular entry, which had

started as dinner with an old friend and had ended in a cheese hangover that had made me question if my 365 Days of Cheese could, would, and should continue.

My friend Henry had been visiting Paris from London. We'd met on our first day at university in an art house film class and had been friends before I'd started dating Paul. Henry knew the real me. Me before Paul. The adventurer.

We settled in for the night at a quaint little neighborhood wine bar. Once the drinks were flowing freely, Henry congratulated me on having left Paul.

"Ella, I was never a fan," he told me. "God, I can be honest now, he was bloody dull."

I appreciated the feeling of vindication.

I told Henry about work, Gaston, and Clotilde, but it was when I came to explain my cheese challenge that his face lit up with joy. He joked that he could do the same thing in the UK but with ales, and then ordered the bar's largest cheese plate in near-indecipherable Franglish.

When the glorious assortment arrived, I outlined the different varieties, impressing him—and myself a little—with my accumulated knowledge. We had a hoot tasting them all—Langres, Ossau-Iraty, and Saint Agur—and jovially imitated food critics, dramatically dissecting the flavor of each one, getting louder as we went.

As the night rolled on and the dinner crowd thinned out, we decided we hadn't had enough cheese and we moved on to some Munster.

As one of the more stinky French cheeses, Munster isn't for those with a delicate palate. It punches you, first in the nose and then in the mouth. I remember hating my first bite, and even the second and third, but as Clotilde had promised when we were eating the Bleu de Corse, I eventually came to appreciate it, relatively speaking. Henry, on the other hand, hadn't had the same lead time to get used to France's smellier cheeses and immediately despised it. He valiantly tried it a few times, but his opinion wouldn't budge, which is how I—heroically—ended up eating the entire generous serving we'd been given.

"I've missed you, Ella," Henry said as we stumbled home and I dropped him off outside his hotel. "I've missed the old you. It sounds clichéd, but I'm happy to have you back."

We hugged and said an emotional good-bye, laughing like drunken idiots before parting ways. I don't remember much of my walk home, other than feeling deliriously liberated wandering the quiet streets of Paris. I do, however, remember—in hideous detail—the indigestion that night, so violent I'd considered forfeiting the challenge.

At the time, I didn't think I could ever stomach *fromage* again; it was a sad prospect. But it did help me realize that I didn't need to finish every uneaten bite, particularly when it came to the more stinky varieties.

Serge would have probably agreed.

~

The next entry was one of my favorites, mostly because it involved Gaston, who now filled the majority of my non-cheese-related thoughts.

It was an unseasonably warm and sunny day in November, and I was in a wonderful mood because Tim had called and offered me an extra day per week at Food To Go Go. The start-up hadn't received the huge cash injection he'd been hoping for, he'd explained, outraged, but they'd still received a significant boost, which meant they could afford to pay me for three days a week. I was chuffed because it meant that I'd be getting some extra cash in addition to keeping my job at Flat White, which I wasn't quite ready to give up.

High on good vibes and keen to splurge on tasty fare, I headed to Serge's to get some picnic goods. I realized that since I'd started seeing Gaston, I hadn't been on one picnic—what with him whisking me around to Paris's newest restaurants— and I wanted him to realize that DIY alfresco dining could still be decadent and romantic.

Gaston arrived at our agreed spot by the Seine twenty minutes late, flustered and sweating in his chic gray suit, saying that he hadn't been able to get a cab or an Uber after his meeting with his editor. It didn't matter that he was late; I'd been happy to wait and soak up the pre-winter sunshine, but even so, it took him half an hour to calm down. He sat awkwardly on a folded newspaper—not wanting to crease his suit—and we dove into the cheese-heavy picnic I'd thrown together. We munched on Pont-l'Évêque and Neufchâtel—a romantically heart-shaped cow's milk cheese that seemed fitting for our date—and drank white wine from Jura that was grassy and fresh. I was feeling victorious.

Just as Gaston was starting to relax and enjoy himself, he startled, touching his hair in a panic.

"*Merde!* Ella, I think a bird went to the toilet on my head."

I laughed. The expression of disbelief on his face was priceless. "It's meant to be good luck."

"Good luck for whom? The bird?"

"No, for you," I gasped. "Now put your head down and show me the damage."

He complied, looking at the ground like a schoolboy who was being told off.

"There's hardly anything there," I told him, but he still wasn't happy.

"Let's go," he said.

"It's just some pigeon poo. Don't worry."

"*Just* pigeon poo? Have you seen the pigeons in Paris? They're filthy."

I know, you made me eat one once, I thought, but straightened my face because I could see Gaston didn't find the situation in the least funny. He started to pack up, even though we still had food and half a bottle of wine left.

"Come back to my place," he said. "I need to shower . . . and I want you to join me."

Gaston's offer was too good to refuse, so I wrapped up the cheese with regret and we cabbed back to his place. As I washed Gaston's hair for him, his smile returned. We ended up having the most amazing afternoon, opening the windows wide to capture the last of the sun streaming into his bedroom, keeping a safe distance away from any pigeons. We set up a rug on the floor and had the picnic inside, subbing the plastic cups for wine glasses.

Gaston obviously wasn't used to roughing it in the great outdoors but I had to admit that his version of casual dining wasn't all bad either.

~

Looking back on all my adventures, clumped together in my cheese journal like this, really reminded me that I was living a different life to the one I'd left behind with Paul. I couldn't believe how many types of cheese I'd gotten through during the past few months. While my day-to-day life here passed by gradually, the time since I'd arrived in France seemed to have flown by.

Serge had remained incredibly supportive of my cause, teaching me about new cheeses and steering me away from varieties he thought I wasn't ready for. Bizarrely, he was still baffled about me posting pictures on Instagram, saying that people obviously had nothing better to do with their time if they were interested in looking at my cheese eating. When I argued with him that France's dining culture was changing and that he would do well to keep up, he argued back that French traditions were more important than the latest Nordic culinary fad. What would start out as a light discussion always turned serious. But when it came to French food, Serge was a serious guy.

I flipped through the remaining pages of my cheese journal and imagined all the winter cheese dishes in France that I could fill the pages with: *fondue, raclette, tartiflette!* I knew that these dishes—too heavy to eat in summer—would help motivate me through the cold days when I needed encouragement. Everything I'd heard about winter in Europe had me worried. Melbourne never got seriously cold, and with my wardrobe mostly filled with dresses and T-shirts, I already felt underprepared. Just anticipating these dishes made me feel warm and cozy. Accompanied by this more positive train of thought, I was finally able to leave my bed and face getting ready for work at the café.

~

Not long after I'd arrived at Flat White and donned my apron, Gaston came in. I was carrying a stack of plates out to the front of the café and hastily put them down. I brushed my hands over my apron and waved.

"*Bonjour*, Ella," he said, waltzing over to me by the coffee machine and kissing me on both cheeks.

"*Salut*, Gaston," I said, slightly mortified that he'd caught me with a pile of dishes. He hadn't been to the café in weeks and I still hadn't corrected him when he kept referring to me as a barista.

"I was in the area and realized I've never tasted your coffee," he said.

Chris looked at me suspiciously. I gave him a pleading look and he said, "Ella, aren't you meant to go on your break now? Why don't I make you and Gaston a couple of coffees?" I mouthed "thank you."

With a little coffee courage under my belt, I figured it would be a good time to clarify what I actually did at Flat White. "Hey Gaston, you know I'm not a barista, right?" I said casually.

"*Non*, you told me you were."

"Well, I'm not exactly," I explained. "I actually help out in the kitchen."

"You cook?" he asked, sounding as surprised as I had when I'd thought Chris had been offering me kitchen work.

"Not really. I wash dishes."

I saw Gaston's expression change and we sat awkwardly in silence for a long moment.

"Do you enjoy washing dishes?" he asked nervously.

"Of course not. I'm just doing it for extra cash while I'm still part-time at Food To Go Go," I improvised. *Was it such a bad thing to enjoy washing dishes?* I thought, sensing that Gaston found it to be quite a lowly task.

He looked pensive, as if trying to decide if he could date a dishwasher.

"One summer, I worked selling ice cream on the beach in Saint-Tropez," he said, sounding relieved. "At least you've got the writing job. And I imagine you'll probably give up the dish-washing soon, *non?*"

"Sure will," I said, knowing full well that I probably wouldn't. What Gaston didn't realize was that the free coffee and good company gave me more than reason enough to stay.

Chapter
26

MUM AND RAY FLEW IN on the 23rd of December but I was struggling to get into the festive spirit. In Australia, I would have been enjoying the lead up to Christmas at the beach, but instead I was shopping for a small, overpriced tree in my scarf, coat, and gloves. The weather I'd found to be chilly in autumn was now beginning to look mild in comparison. It was safe to say I was still figuring out how to navigate the low temperatures of a European winter.

Paris had become increasingly lonely the week before Christmas, as people left the city heading to their family homes or on holidays to somewhere warmer. Clotilde had wisely gone to Thailand with her dad for a couple of weeks, and Gaston had gone to his friend's house in Nice. Work colleagues were dropping off the radar and I was left counting down the hours until Mum and Ray arrived.

On their first day, we walked all over Paris. We started locally, where I showed them my fruit-and-vegetable market and took them to Flat White for a coffee. Then we strolled past the Louvre, through Tuileries Garden, and down to the Champs-Élysées, which had been transformed into a village of little wooden chalets selling gingerbread, hot wine, and Christmas trinkets. As the hours whipped by, I watched Ray carefully, trying to get a better sense of the man my mum would soon marry.

When I'd met them at the airport, they'd walked out of the arrivals gate, hand-in-hand. For some incomprehensible reason, Ray was wearing a beret in addition to his standard flannel shirt. *Oh dear!* He'd stood awkwardly off to the side while Mum threw down her luggage to pull me into a massive hug. But after she had reintroduced us, he'd said, "Come here, lovie," and bundled me up in his arms. His strong Australian accent rang in my ears as I wriggled out of his embrace and shuffled them outside to the cab rank.

Ray bumbled about Paris like a child, full of wonder and amazement, looking at everyone and everything with fresh eyes. He marveled at the efficient metro system, stopped for Nutella crepes what felt like once an hour, and made Mum and me pose in front of every monument while he snapped pictures with a disposable camera. *This man is almost too much*, I thought to myself, wondering where he could have even purchased such a relic.

"So how are things going? You both seem happy," I told Mum later while Ray had gallantly set off to order us another round of mulled wine—a drink he'd started referring to as "bloody genius" since discovering it that afternoon.

"He's wonderful, isn't he?" she said.

"I really don't know him that well," I told her.

"But you will. He's so kind and generous. I'm so happy you'll get to spend some quality time with him."

"Me too," I told her, although I still couldn't help wishing I could have had Mum to myself this Christmas.

After a day of walking and sight-seeing, Mum and Ray were hit by a wave of jet lag. I started steering them towards home, conveniently planning a route that would take us via Serge's shop. I suggested we pick up some cheese for dinner.

"What a cracker of an idea," Ray said, as if we were the first tourists to ever think of it.

"This is my local cheese shop," I said, probably with more excitement than I had when introducing the Louvre.

It was funny watching Mum and Ray stand at Serge's window ogling the cheese on display, just as I had months earlier. I pushed them through the door and out of the cold.

"Mum, Ray, this is Serge. Owner of my favorite *fromagerie* in Paris."

"*Enchanté!*" Serge said, shaking both their hands over the counter.

I pointed out to Mum what I had planned to get for our Christmas dinner. Like many French families, we were going to feast on the 24th. I'd already ordered my traditional yule log for dessert and had paid through the teeth for some foie gras. I was also planning on roasting a turkey, but had a freezer full of Picard meals just in case.

The men made their way to the front of the store so Serge could show Ray the selection of truffle cheeses he'd gotten in for the festive season. I felt mortified as I overheard Ray asking whether it was safe to eat moldy cheese, but Serge, used to foreigners, took his time explaining the intricacies of French *fromage* in unrelenting detail. Surprisingly, their rapport was immediate; two old souls agreeing like bread and cheese.

Mum too seemed completely charmed by Serge's shop and kept adding to our already-large order.

"Mum, I think that's probably enough for the next couple of days. Don't forget there's only three of us."

"Darling, we're only in Paris for Christmas this once. Why not indulge?" she said, which felt out of character. She was getting swept up in the excitement of cheese shopping and I couldn't help but grin and wrap my arm around her.

But then Ray opened his mouth and suddenly things started moving in slow motion. "Serge, mate, why don't you come 'round for Chrissy dinner?" he asked hopefully. "You can give us a hand getting through all this cheese."

I froze.

"Oh, what a lovely idea," Mum chipped in.

"I'm sure Serge has plans already," I said hastily.

"Actually, I'm not heading to my friends' place in the Loire until Christmas morning, and I'll be working late on Christmas Eve," he said, looking at me quizzically, as if trying to read my reaction to the invitation. I gave him a guarded smile.

"I'd love an Australian-style dinner," he added, "as long as that's OK with you, Ella."

His response hung in the air for a few seconds before I was forced to say that he was more than welcome to join us.

"*Parfait!*" he said with a smile.

"Bloody parfay," Ray mimicked, and the two men shook hands jovially.

I wasn't sure how comfortable I felt about Serge joining us for such an intimate celebration, but I tried to go with the flow. I gave him my address and convinced him not to bring any more cheese.

"And how did you meet Serge?" Mum asked as we left the store.

"In the *fromagerie*."

"You didn't know him before? Outside of the cheese shop?"

"No, of course not. I didn't know anyone in Paris when I arrived."

"How much cheese are you actually eating these days, Ella?" She sounded concerned, but I wasn't having any of it.

"Actually, it's a funny story," I told her. "One I'll tell you tomorrow after a good night's sleep."

Similar to how I'd felt with Billie, I was reluctant to tell Mum about the cheese challenge, worrying she'd think it was futile, or that I was wasting my time in France on a gluttonous mission. Perhaps it would be easier to explain the stakes of the bet after dinner with Serge. The way both Mum and Ray spoke of him made it seem like he was the best thing they'd seen in Paris all day. Thankfully, after a quick bite, their exhaustion took over and they were in bed early, leaving me to continue planning our Christmas dinner. With Serge coming over, I felt an increased pressure to cook a wonderful meal. *The turkey would have to triumph!*

⁓

I spent Christmas Eve rushing between the supermarket and the apartment, doing dishes and frantically consulting recipes online. Mum kept offering to help, but every time she came into the kitchen, Ray would follow her and I'd end up shooing both of them out. I sent them on a long walk down to the river so I could concentrate.

Serge arrived right on time.

Out of his work apron, he looked dapper, dressed in a well-ironed white shirt and a sweet, floppy, green-and-red bow tie. *And was that a haircut I noticed?* He was bearing a bouquet of Christmas lilies, two bottles of champagne, and what I could only assume was a large wheel of cheese.

"Serge," I said when he handed it to me, "you were meant to help us eat the cheese, not bring more!" I ushered him in and busied myself putting the flowers in a vase, feeling a little embarrassed at his gifts. Luckily, Mum broke the tension and got straight to opening the champagne and handing out glasses. Ray joined us for a cheers, took one sip, and then cracked open a beer.

I took a few quick sips myself to help ease any awkwardness that could arise from putting Mum, my stepfather-to-be, and my cheesemonger together for Christmas dinner and went to check on the state of the turkey. Surprisingly, dinner was turning out to be the least of my concerns.

"So, tell us what you think of our Ella?" I overheard Ray ask Serge.

Merde, I thought. *Ray can't be left alone out there.*

I took a large gulp of champagne and sung out for Ray to come and help me in the kitchen.

Thankfully, dinner was mostly a success. Despite the turkey having dried out a little, it was masked by the plentiful gravy and I somehow managed to whip up the most delicious mashed potato accompaniment with the help of an unhealthy dose of French butter.

I assembled the cheese board in the kitchen, making sure Serge didn't see me snapping tens of photos of the decadent collection. It was by far the most cheese I'd had in a single sitting and it looked damn fine.

"So Ella, you were going to tell me why you eat so much cheese?" Mum asked as I returned with the board.

"Ah . . ." I stalled. I'd forgotten she didn't know about the cheese bet and now I was going to have to divulge the details in front of the man himself.

"Well, I'm trying to eat a different French cheese for every day of the year," I said quickly, avoiding going into too much detail.

Serge nodded along supportively.

"Why?" she asked, sounding surprised.

"Why not? It's cheese after all." I blushed and looked at Serge.

"Well, I'm glad you're having fun in France, but . . ."

Shit, here comes the but . . .

"But, has it all been worth giving up your stable life in Melbourne for?"

"What do you mean?" I asked, surprised at the sudden turn in the conversation.

"Well, your gap year is half over, Ella. It's time to start thinking about what comes next. You're not going to stay in France forever."

"No, perhaps not, but I'm here now so I may as well enjoy myself," I said heartily, trying to break the tension and get back to enjoying the rest of dinner.

But Mum hadn't finished. She went on to say she was *still* surprised I would give up my life in Melbourne to come to Paris and wash dishes in a café. She was also upset that I'd burned through my savings. She didn't even seem impressed by my cheese eating.

"Well, I hope you won't mind me saying 'I told you so' when you're back in Australia without a job, any money, or a boy-friend."

"I wouldn't expect anything less," I said. I knew she meant

well, but she'd been dismissive of my life in Paris ever since I'd moved here and I was tired of having to defend it.

Unexpectedly, Ray interrupted Mum's rant and told me that what I had achieved since arriving in France was admirable. "What an adventure," he said, squeezing Mum's hand.

"Thanks, Ray," I said. "I'm glad one of you gets it."

"You've got the rest of your life for hard yakka, Ella. May as well go on adventures while you're young," Ray added. "I'd never even left Australia until now. And look at everything I've missed out on."

Before I had a chance to feel sorry for him, Mum interrupted saying, "She's not that young anymore," motioning at me with her head.

"Hey! I'm sitting right here," I said, again trying to lighten the mood.

"At her age, I already had a two-year-old," Mum said.

"Yeah, but I reckon it's different for kids now. They're taking their time figuring life out," Ray said.

"Maybe. But Ella can't just up and run away from her life in Australia. Leave us all behind," Mum replied. Exhaustion and too much Christmas cheer had clearly caught up with her.

I shot an embarrassed look at Serge who was closely examining his hands.

We fell into an uncomfortable silence, looking at the cheese board in front of us.

But then Serge cleared his throat. "I agree with Ray. What Ella is doing in Paris is wonderful. It's not easy to find a job here with all the unemployment, and she has two jobs. And she is becoming nearly an expert in cheese. This is *très important* in France."

Mum looked surprised as Serge continued to justify my life here. "If you can understand France's love for cheese, you can actually understand a lot about the French psyche."

What I'd been unable to put into words, he was able to express succinctly, even in a foreign language. I gave him a relieved smile that I hoped conveyed how grateful I was. *He is full of surprises, this man!*

Mum huffed off to the bathroom and thankfully, when she came back, she'd calmed down a little. We finally dove into the cheese after Serge enthusiastically explained the different varieties. All seemed well again.

Miraculously, the rest of dinner passed without another scene, and Mum headed off to bed early, saying she was unable to keep her eyes open any longer.

I went to make Serge a coffee and Ray caught up with me in the kitchen.

"Don't you worry about your mum, love," he said, as he reached into the basin to wash the wine glasses and champagne flutes with his big, gardening-calloused hands.

"Oh, I'm not worried," I said defensively. "I just don't get why she's so judgmental of my life here."

Ray was silent for a moment, as if trying to figure out how to respond.

"I think sometimes she worries that you'll pull up stumps like your old man did. You know, leaving behind those you love when the opportunity for something more exciting comes along."

And then the penny dropped. It had never crossed my mind that Mum worried about me leaving her like my dad had. I was surprised Ray knew so much about it, knowing that Mum didn't open up about him easily.

"Oh. Of course," I said in reply.

"She thinks you're a good egg, you know," he said after a few moments.

"I know," I said.

"I do too," he added.

"Thanks, Ray," I said.

"Well, I'll leave you two young'uns to it," he said, making his way to say good-night to Serge and thank him for all the cheese.

———◠———

I took the coffee pot, two cups, and a bottle of brandy back to the living room. Thankfully, our festive consumption of wine during dinner made it feel completely normal to be having a nightcap with my cheesemonger in my apartment.

"Is everything OK, Ella?" he asked as I sat down next to him on the sofa.

"Oh sure, Christmas is a time for arguing with family, right?"

"It's been a while since I've been able to, but I remember it well."

"Oh, I'm sorry. I didn't mean to be insensitive," I said.

"No, it's OK. I'm an only child and my parents have both died. That's the problem with small families. But I'm lucky: I have good friends—although at the moment they're all having babies and leaving Paris for the countryside."

"Friends are the family we get to choose," I offered.

"What a wonderful thought," Serge said, as though I was the first person to ever put this idea into words.

"It sounds like your mother has really missed you in Australia," he added.

"And I miss her, but I'm only here for one year and I want to make the most of it. I don't need to be judged for the decisions I make."

"You're only here for one year?" Serge sounded surprised, sitting up straight.

"Yep, I'm on a one-year visa."

"Oh, that's a shame. Paris suits you," he said, and then leaned back into the sofa.

I took a large sip of brandy, basking in the thought of becoming a Parisienne.

"Perhaps you'll find a reason to stay a little longer," he added with a cheeky grin.

"Well, fingers crossed," I said, thinking briefly of Gaston before wondering what Serge thought that reason might be.

⁓

By the time Serge left, it was after midnight and I was beginning to feel jet-lagged *myself*. He wished me a happy Christmas and kissed me good-bye on both cheeks while gently holding my shoulders. His woolen coat was soft with wear, and under the glow of the Christmas lights in my apartment, I could have snuggled into it for hours. When we separated, he hovered a moment, as though he was about to say something.

Worrying what that might be, I quickly thanked him for coming and wished him an equally happy Christmas, telling him that I'd see him at the *fromagerie* soon.

Despite feeling exhausted, I couldn't sleep. I was spiraling into confusion over what Ray had said. I was shocked that Mum could even equate me leaving Australia to my dad abandoning us when he moved back to America. My intentions were nothing like my father's. I hadn't been trying to escape responsibility; rather I had an idiot of a boyfriend who left me to go and "find himself." If anything, I was the opposite of my dad. I'd tried to settle down and make a life with Paul, and he'd left me.

Although Ray had been careful when mentioning Dad, I wondered if Mum had told him everything. Knowing how private she was on the subject, I figured that Ray had probably had to piece together a lot of what had happened before he whippersnippered his way onto the scene. Perhaps he wasn't the simpleton I'd initially taken him for.

⁓

The next morning, things were a little awkward between Mum and me.

"You know I'll be home next year," I said, pouring everyone large bowls of coffee.

"Ella, I know you're enjoying yourself here and I'm happy for you. I just don't want you to think that running off overseas in the pursuit of pleasure is the responsible thing to do at your age. I mean, just look at your cheese thing. It all seems a little ridiculous," she said, not quite letting her disappointment in me go.

"Relax, Mum, my visa is only for a year. I'll be back in Melbourne and settled down before you know it. Unless, of course, I find a gorgeous Frenchman to marry . . ." I said, somewhat jokingly. An image of Gaston and me walking through a flurry of confetti flashed into my mind but I pushed it away; it was definitely too soon to start hoping for a proposal.

"Don't be ridiculous, Ella. You're not going to marry a Frenchman," Mum scolded.

"Well, moving to Paris has been one of the best things I could have done," I told her honestly.

"Just don't get too comfortable here. You can't run away from your problems forever. It's painful for those you leave behind."

I hugged her and reinforced, for what felt like the millionth time, that I'd be home before she knew it. "And don't worry, I'm not going to disappear into some artist commune here," I said hesitantly, worried to overstep my mark.

"I know, Ella darling. I know."

⁓

Mum and Ray flew out a few days after New Year's, arm-in-arm, content to be going home to sunshine and warmer weather. I waved them off at Charles de Gaulle airport, wishing them a safe journey and thinking to myself that I'd actually come to quite like Ray. He was reliable and sturdy and seemed to have found a place in my mother's heart. I felt confident they'd be happy together and quietly hoped that by having Ray to focus on, Mum wouldn't have time to hassle me about coming home.

On the metro back into Paris, I scrolled through my phone looking at old messages from Gaston. I'd texted him a few times over the Christmas period but hadn't heard much back, apart from him telling me he was looking forward to getting back to Paris and seeing me. I was so excited to see where things would go with him this coming year and I couldn't wait until he was home. I wanted to message him again but I also didn't want to appear desperate—although I couldn't have been more so—so I opened Instagram to distract myself with other people's happy holiday photos.

I looked at my own feed, showing the amazing cheese plate we'd put together for our Christmas Eve dinner. I thought about Serge and wondered if he was enjoying his break with his friends in the Loire. It was strange imagining him outside of Paris. He'd been so sweet and sincere when we were chatting after Mum and Ray had gone to bed, and I couldn't stop thinking about how he'd stood up for me in front of my mother.

I was really looking forward to spending more time with him in the *fromagerie*. Or maybe now that we'd transitioned to being friends who saw each other outside of the cheese shop, he'd be in my life even more. The thought cheered me greatly.

• PART •

Four

"The early bird gets the worm, but the second mouse gets the cheese."

—WILLIE NELSON

Chapter 27

THE WEEKS FOLLOWING CHRISTMAS AND New Year's Eve were a blizzard of activity. Thankfully, I had been mostly too caught up with work, eating cheese, and sleeping with Gaston to notice how seriously cold it had become in Paris. Even on the occasions I was aware of my nose and toes going numb I didn't mind, as I was preparing mentally and physically for my inaugural French ski trip.

Gaston had invited me to spend a few nights in a lodge that he co-owned with some friends—*because of course he owns a ski lodge*—and I'd leaped at the offer. I was beyond excited to see the imposing Alps, throw snowballs, and flounce around the chalets. The fact that I hadn't hit the slopes since a school camp when I was sixteen—and on the much smaller mountains of Australia—didn't cross my mind until Clotilde asked me if it even snowed Down Under.

Gaston and I arrived at the lodge late on a Friday night after taking the fast train to Lyon and driving a hired car through the evening fog. It'd been a long day's commute, and despite my best intentions to have rampant sex all night on a bearskin rug in the dappled light of a crackling fire, we had crumpled onto the couches, pumped the small foot heater, and fallen asleep following a quick glass of wine.

The next morning, after marveling at the wash of fresh snow from Gaston's balcony and picturing myself as a veritable ice-queen in my very own whitewashed tower, I was up the mountain with my winter gear on and my skis and poles scattered around me. The blissful feeling of the cozy lodge had gone and I was clearly out of my comfort zone.

We were halfway down a particularly long *piste* somewhere in Chamonix, surrounded by epic scenery, and I was too distraught to pay attention to anything but the terrifying path ahead.

When Gaston had asked me if I was a good skier, I'd boasted that *of course* I was. I didn't want to lose face in front of my new beau; and from memory, I'd been good enough at navigating the slopes when I was in my teens. But now, a few years on and maybe a few kilos heavier, my internal satnav seemed to be malfunctioning and I couldn't seem to coordinate standing up and turning my skis at the same time.

Seconds after tumbling out of the chairlift and landing rear-first in the snow, I was on the brink of my very first ski-holiday breakdown. By my tenth fall—after only managing to success-fully move about fifty meters beyond the chairlift—I was ready to pack it all in and retreat to the lodge where I could lick my wounds.

"I can't do it. I'm sorry, Gaston. I'm not cut out for this." I looked at him, tears welling in my eyes. I tried to hold them back, but that all-too-familiar ball of anxiety in my throat wasn't diminishing. I felt like a kid with a grazed knee in need of a hug. Instead, Gaston looked at me, rather bemused, as he tried to explain—*again*—how to snow plough and turn. While I understood in concept what he meant, aided by his wild hand movements and dramatic demonstrations, I couldn't seem to make it work.

"Just get me down the mountain. Maybe I can take a lesson tomorrow and then I'll find my ski legs."

"What do you mean, 'ski legs,' Ella?" he asked earnestly.

"It's a joke," I snapped.

"OK, OK. Let's get you down to the bar for a break," he said, scooping me upright and navigating me down the remainder of the run.

⌒

"Let me buy you a drink," I said, attempting a smile once we'd finally reached the bottom of the mountain. "For getting me down in one piece."

"Sure," he said, taking off his skis and helping me out of mine. "Then maybe we can try again on an easier *piste*."

"We'll see about that," I muttered under my breath.

I walked proudly through the ski chalet and into the bar with Gaston, who was by far the most handsome of all the stunningly-dressed skiers lounging around.

"What do you want to drink, Ella?"

"I'll have a *vin chaud*, please," I said, warming up both physically and spiritually to my new habitat.

Comfortably ensconced in the chalet, I recognized that I'd confused my desire for ski legs with a more real desire for chalet legs. Drinking mulled wine while overlooking the mountain was what my heart truly wanted. I was a snow bunny on the most fundamental level.

One glass of *vin chaud* down and I felt like I was slowly

beginning to recover from the morning's trauma. That was, until I heard a woman call out from behind me.

"*Gaston!*" The voice was familiar, but I couldn't think where I'd heard it before. I turned around to see who was behind it and—*dammit!*—there was Camille. My mind flashed back to the "bistro" where I'd had the displeasure of meeting the skinny model-slash-waitress-slash-whatever for the first time.

What the hell is she doing here?

I scanned around, hoping to find a suave model-slash-boyfriend accompanying her, but no such luck.

We exchanged pleasantries and Gaston asked her to join us for a drink. As they nattered away in too-fast French, I grasped that she'd come to the snow with her dad. *Of course, little rich girl with her papa at the resort . . .* Still in French, I managed to translate that she'd just broken up with someone named Antoine and had come to the slopes to clear her head. Of course, my excitement at understanding some of the conversation was trumped by the reality of what she'd said. And I couldn't help but wonder why she was telling something so personal to Gaston, who claimed they were only acquaintances.

They continued chatting and laughing until Camille apologized for being rude and switched to English. *Ha! The joke's on you, Camille.* She was clearly unaware that I'd understood most of what they'd said: mostly industry stuff, mostly boring, and all seemingly overlaid with innuendos and flirtation.

As I watched a young boy outside eyeballing me and pelting snowballs at the window, I couldn't help thinking that this ski weekend wasn't working out quite as I'd planned.

Polishing off her espresso, Camille suggested we all head out for a few runs and Gaston asked me if I was ready to try again.

Seriously? I thought. *I'm not about to go subject myself to that kind of embarrassment, especially in front of Camille.*

I mumbled something about having a sore knee from an old injury I'd suffered playing netball at the Commonwealth Championships. I justified the exaggeration, reminding myself that I had easily been the best goal shooter in my Tuesday night league.

"Do you mind if I go out with Camille?" he asked, clearly not realizing the double meaning of what he was saying.

Of course I do. You should stay here and keep me company, I wanted to say, but didn't. Instead, I settled on, "No, of course I don't mind. Go for it and have fun."

Images of Gaston and Camille making out on the chairlift and then gliding effortlessly hand-in-hand down the mountain surged into my mind, but it seemed like a choice between letting them go alone and having to go with them myself. Self-preservation won out on this occasion.

As they left, I overheard Camille asking Gaston what netball was, to which he shrugged his shoulders.

I watched them saunter out of the bar and towards the chairlift and saw them giggling as they got pushed together into the seat. I continued to spy until their beanies diminished to specks on the horizon before slipping over the mountain. My gut told me I shouldn't have let them go off together, but I tried to reason with myself. After all, Camille was just an unhappy surprise guest. Gaston had chosen to take *me* to his ski lodge.

"Waiter, I think I'll need another drink," I sung out in panicked French. "Make it a double."

I sat in the same seat for the next hour, my muscles already tense from my short but physically-demanding burst of skiing. At first, I reveled in the snow-bunny life, checking out the crowd, scrolling through Instagram, and reading magazines. But then as the minutes ticked by, I ran out of things to do to entertain myself. I tried calling Gaston's phone to get directions back to the lodge, but it went straight to voicemail—out of coverage, I supposed.

I started to feel a little helpless. Memories of being in primary school and waiting in the rain at the gate for Mum to pick me up came flooding back. Even the waiters gave me apologetic little shrugs, as if to say, *Don't worry, love, I'm sure you haven't been forgotten.*

Well into my second hour of flying solo, I was considering the potentially lethal prospect of going back up the ski lift to look for Gaston. I started to fret. I felt deserted in the ski chalet; left to wither away from boredom or alcohol poisoning, whichever came first. I was sure Gaston and Camille were probably shacking up in some ice cave that he'd made with his bare hands, having forgotten all about me.

"Who cares about Ella?" I muttered to myself bitterly. "She can't even ski."

I flicked through a menu, wishing I were back in Paris where I could console myself with cheese, which made me think of Serge. I wondered if he too could ski . . . I was sure *he* would never abandon me to go up the mountain with some floozy.

But back to my present concerns. *Where the hell is my boyfriend?* I mentally rehearsed a speech in case Gaston ever emerged from his snow cave with his new and improved—i.e. able to ski with grace and decorum—ice queen. A flood of tears was threatening as I internally accused him of desertion, only to be interrupted by the man in question tapping me on my shoulder, his cheeks glowing adorably from the cool snow air.

"You're back," I squealed, forgetting my monologue and throwing my arms around him.

"Are you OK?" he asked, squirming out of my embrace and fixing his hair.

"Where's Camille?" I asked.

"Oh, she went to meet her father's friend. He's the head of some big modeling agency back in Paris."

"Did you have fun?" I asked, searching his face for clues that their jaunt may not have been so innocent.

"Sure. It was good. You would have hated it, though. Lots of black runs and back-country exploring. Even *I* had trouble keeping up with Camille."

"I thought you'd forgotten about me," I told him, still trying to hold back the tears. All of a sudden, I didn't want him to know how angry I'd felt while he'd been away.

He looked at me and said, "Why would I do a thing like that, Ella? *Je t'aime bien.*"

Holy shit! Did he just say he loved me?

I paused, idolizing him.

"Wow, Gaston," I said. "*Je t'aime, aussi.*"

He stood back a minute, looked like he was about to say something and then stopped himself.

"Everything OK?" I asked.

"Sure. Let's go have a spa. I'm freezing! And then tonight, I've booked a table at a restaurant in town. It's very cozy, right up your alley. There will be plenty of cheese."

He grabbed my hand and we headed back to his lodge.

Our afternoon lazing in the hot tub helped to ease any remaining tension from my earlier freak-out. I'd been feeling rejected due to my lack of ski skills, that was all. Of course Gaston would never do anything with Camille, however beautiful she may be. By the time we were ready to leave for dinner, I was back to being smitten with him.

~

Walking into the restaurant, I was immediately charmed. Wooden chairs and tables lined the dining room and a raging fire burned brightly in the corner. Most of the seats were filled with either families or lovers, hunched over a flaming pot. Faces were rosy, made brighter with smiles, and there was an indescribable sense of joy filling the room.

Gaston told me that it was a fondue restaurant. He indulged my love of cheese details, adding that it specialized in Savoyard cheese fondues, using a mix of Comté, Emmental, and Beaufort. My mouth started to water as he explained the tradition of fondue and I gazed on adoringly. Originating in the mountains, the melted cheese is served in a big, communal pot, with each diner dipping hunks of bread into the mix with long forks. It reminded me of how my mother used to serve a chocolate fondue at dinner parties when I was a child, although this savory iteration now seemed so much more appealing.

Gaston's choice of restaurant made up for ditching me to go on black runs earlier that day. He certainly knew the way to my heart.

By the time the pot arrived at our table, I was drooling with anticipation. In my excitement to dunk some bread into the cheese and try it, I immediately burnt my tongue. I took a huge swig of wine to try and limit the damage. Gaston laughed and called me a novice but I didn't mind. I'd never been very patient when it came to trying food.

The fondue, which Gaston brushed off as the ultimate "cheesy" French mountain cliché, represented to me all that was good in the world. I dipped chunk after chunk of bread into the dangerously bubbling pot, occasionally getting distracted by the accompanying charcuterie and cornichons. Once I gave the cheese a moment to cool, I tasted hints of garlic and white wine, with a distinct farmyard feel. I found it incredible how food could be so soothing and warming, especially after a long day on the slopes—or a long day in the bar, in my case.

"So is fondue the *real* reason why people come to the snow?" I joked.

Gaston leaned over and pinched my cheek. "That and, you know, the skiing," he laughed.

"So you don't mind that I'm a disaster on the slopes?" I asked.

"Of course not, you're Australian!" he said. "You're probably more at home on a surfboard, right?"

Of course I was, I boasted, making a mental note never to agree to a beach holiday with Gaston.

Looking at the gorgeous specimen in front of me, I felt like an idiot for having worked myself into a state earlier. I thanked God that I hadn't voiced my concerns about Camille; if I had, Gaston mightn't have said that he loved me.

I was high on cheese, wine, and newly declared *amour,* and I soon settled into a sort of fondue stupor; the experience was almost orgasmic. And thankfully so, because after dinner, both Gaston and I were too full to move, let alone get naked. When we got back to the lodge, he suggested we watch a movie and fell asleep promptly after the opening credits. When I heard him snoring softly, I turned down the sound so as not to disturb him and reminisced over what a magical evening it had been. Sore calves and wounded ego aside, I couldn't help thinking that I was probably the luckiest Australian to have ever moved to France.

Chapter
28

LEAVING THE ALPS A FEW days later felt bittersweet. Sweet because Gaston had said he loved me—and because I knew that I'd never have to go skiing again—but bitter because it meant that my romantic getaway was over and I had to go back to the real world.

Gaston seemed a little aloof and gruff on the train ride back and I hoped it wasn't because of my terrible attempt at skiing. I tried to cheer him up with the suggestion of joining the meter-high club in the bathroom, but he did not join me in my enthusiasm and opted to fall asleep for the majority of the journey instead. When he woke, he wrapped his arms around me and kissed my neck. Our romantic mini-break had obviously worn him out. I invited him over for dinner, but he told me he had a deadline the next morning so we went our separate ways, him in a cab and me on the metro, to which he gave a laugh and a shake of the head. He never understood why I insisted on taking public transport, saying it was full of "beggars, buskers, and people huffing and pushing to find space." But I enjoyed it: The crowd was so diverse—therefore one of the best people-watching spots in Paris—and I loved it when a singer or piano accordion player serenaded my journey. It also meant that I didn't have to try and hail one of the very elusive—and expensive—cabs in the city, or navigate a pickup location in French to an impatient Uber driver.

~

Coming out of the metro, I started to think about dinner. Hyped up on love and hungry from all the fresh mountain air, I was in the mood to sample a cheese that was decadent and warming—something that would continue to make winter more bearable. I also wanted to get a little something to put in the fridge to celebrate Clotilde's return from her trip to Thailand with Papa Jean, which they'd ended up extending beyond the original two weeks because apparently sitting on the beach in Southeast Asia was nicer than spending winter in Paris. They were due back late that evening and I knew she would have missed her French cheese.

I headed directly to Serge for a recommendation and to say a belated thank-you for the Christmas cheese; I was also excited to tell him about my fondue discovery. It'd been an eventful few weeks and, feeling like we'd left our friendship in a really good place after our Christmas Eve dinner, I was looking forward to seeing him.

"Happy New Year," I said, grinning as I opened the door. "How was your holiday?"

He told me it was great—in French—testing whether my comprehension had gotten better over the break.

"Wonderful," I replied in English.

"Tell me, did you manage to finish the leftover cheese from Christmas dinner?"

"Don't get me started, Serge. I ate too much."

He made a face of mock horror and said, "There is no such thing as too much holiday cheese."

Ah ha, I thought excitedly. It seemed that overindulging in food was acceptable in France so long as it was attached to an event or holiday. *Good to know!*

"I feel like something delicious tonight," I told him. "Something luscious and creamy. What would you suggest?"

"Let me see," he said, running his hand over the counter. "Have you tried Mont d'Or before?"

"No, I haven't even heard of it," I admitted.

"*Oh là là,*" he exclaimed before telling me that this "very special" cheese was only available in autumn and winter. He gave me a mouthwatering description of how it can be baked in the oven with a little garlic, salt, and a splash of dry *vin blanc.* It sounded heavenly.

"Mmm." I made a murmur of approval as I looked at the white, pillowy cheese encased in a round, wooden box. "Better wrap one up then."

"You know, it's a terrible shame to eat cheese like this alone," he said wistfully.

"Really? Why?" I asked. Not that I would be alone after Clotilde got back anyway.

"Well, it's the kind of cheese that is best shared . . ." He paused and I nervously waited for him to continue.

"If you don't have plans tonight, why don't you come to my apartment for dinner? I'll bring the cheese."

"Like a date?" I asked fearfully. I hoped he hadn't somehow gotten the wrong idea about us after our Christmas dinner.

"I would like to repay your hospitality," he responded, skirting the question.

I was about to tell him that I was too exhausted from my trip to the snow, but then I thought about how fun it would be to eat cheese at Mr. Cheeseman's house.

"OK. Why not?"

At that moment, an impeccably-dressed woman around eighty entered the store, leaving me with only a few more seconds to agonize over whether or not Serge had just asked me out. *Maybe he doesn't understand the nuance of the word "date." Besides, I'm sure I've told him about Gaston . . .*

"Come over around eight," he said, giving me his address.

I rushed out of the shop, relieved to get outside and replay the conversation in my mind. *Did I just agree to go on a date with Serge? Merde! Perhaps I'm simply overthinking things; it wouldn't be the first time . . .* I was probably just getting carried away thinking that all French men loved me in light of Gaston's recent declaration.

Whatever tonight was, I planned to drop Gaston's name into the conversation nice and early, and if it was supposed to be a date, hopefully the reminder that I already had a boyfriend wouldn't offend Serge and he'd take it in his stride.

⁓

Trying to find something in my closet to wear to this non-date dinner was harder than it should have been. I wanted to look casual—and not at all sexy—but I also didn't want to offend my host by turning up dressed sloppily. *Did high heels give off a "date me" vibe? Would faded jeans be too informal?* I glanced at the clock and realized I'd be late if I didn't make a decision quickly. I considered messaging Clotilde for advice but she was probably still in the air. Plus, I didn't want to tell her about dinner with Serge in case Gaston found out. Better to mention it when I was sure there weren't any romantic intentions. Things suddenly felt complicated.

After inspecting all the potential outfits currently on the floor, I threw on black jeans, a fitted black T-shirt, and a pair of ballet flats. I scooped up my hair into a rather chic chignon, grabbed my bag and coat, splashed on some lipstick, and rushed out the door.

I hadn't really thought too much about where Serge might live, but I was surprised at the splendor of his apartment's exterior as I walked through the pot plant–clad courtyard. He buzzed me in and told me fourth floor, apartment A.

Serge opened the door in an apron, holding a wooden spoon, and ushered me in. "*Vite, vite, vite*. Quick, quick, quick," he said, hurrying me along the short hallway. "We don't want anything to burn."

Looking around, I was surprised by two things. The first was how charming Serge's home was, especially for a bachelor. The second was the candle on the table and the dinner setting for two. *Merde!* It definitely appeared to be a date.

This might get awkward.

"Serge, this place is magnificent," I said as he handed me a glass of sparkling wine, a Crémant de Bourgogne. Exposed wooden beams the color of espresso lined the high ceiling, offset by creamy white walls and over-stacked bookcases. Two leather couches, soft like butter after years of wear, sat cozily by the windows. It was a small apartment but it gave off an impression of space.

"I never knew you were into interior design," I continued.

"Ella. There are many things you don't know about me," he said, winking while ushering me into the kitchen and stirring a pot bubbling away on the stove. My stomach fluttered and I was suddenly reminded of my first day in Paris when I'd met Serge in his cheese shop, full of aspiration and hopped up on the excitement of being in France.

"You're probably right. And I'm sure there are many things you don't know about me," I said, trying to find a way to bring up Gaston but instead sounding oddly mysterious. "Anyway," I continued, changing tones, "what are you cooking?"

"Homemade pappardelle," Serge said, telling me how he'd done a pasta-making course in Italy when he'd been there on holidays last summer. I kept asking him questions and tried to act casual, but found myself unintentionally interrogating him, all the while seemingly incapable of mentioning that I had a boyfriend.

I finished my glass far too quickly—Serge had only taken a couple of sips of his—and I was feeling a little flushed. I excused myself to go to the bathroom for a quick breather; I had to try and form a plan for the evening that didn't involve me chugging my drink and babbling like an idiot.

I sat on the loo and reprimanded myself for getting into this messy situation, thoughts flying around my head. Were Gaston and I even exclusive? We certainly hadn't had the talk, but he *had* said he loved me. *Am I cheating on him by being on a date? Is this a date? Is it too late to get out of it? Should I fake an illness? Maybe I can sneak out the window. But then I'd lose my cheeseman . . . Oh God.*

I washed my hands and headed back out.

"Is everything all right?" Serge asked, gallantly pulling a chair out for me at the dining table.

"I'm fine. Sorry. I must have had a little too much coffee this afternoon," I said, noticing two plates of delicious-looking pasta ready and waiting. I also couldn't help but notice that he'd refilled my glass. *Great . . .*

"*Alors*, first on the menu tonight we have pasta with truffles and Gruyère. Something simple and light so we can move swiftly on to the cheese course."

I laughed at his idea of simple and light, swirling the creamy pappardelle into a large ball and stuffing it ungracefully but satisfyingly into my mouth. *Perhaps he'll find my eating habits a turnoff* . . .

After the pasta, Serge didn't waste any time moving on to the baked Mont d'Or, serving it unadorned in its box with a couple of spoons. He studied me carefully as I heaped some of the warm, oozing cheese onto a hunk of crusty bread. Remembering how I'd burned my tongue on the fondue in the mountains, I waited a moment before slipping the warm cheese into my mouth.

"Serge, what have you done to me?" I asked, mid-chew.

"What's the matter? You don't like it?" He sounded surprised.

"I just don't understand how you could have hidden it from me until now," I said in mock anger.

"Ella," he said slowly. "You can't eat this cheese too often. First, it's only available for a few months every year. Second, it's very, very *riche*!"

"Well, I think my cheese challenge is over. This is, and always will be, the only variety for me. It's what I didn't even realize I was looking for. Can I marry this cheese?" I joked.

Serge laughed and told me to go ahead and forfeit our bet, he'd already gotten me to agree to dinner. It would have been the perfect moment for me to bring up Gaston, but it still didn't feel right. Instead, I changed the subject, asking Serge how he came to love cheese.

"It's a long story," he told me. "One for another time. And you?"

"Also a long story," I admitted, thinking about my picnic in Paris with Paul.

We ate in a comfortable silence for a few moments, both lost in our own thoughts, before Serge questioned me on some of my recent cheese discoveries, our usual fallback topic of conversation.

⁓

After finishing the meal, I stood to help clear the plates but found myself feeling a little light-headed after one too many glasses of wine.

Serge grabbed my arm to steady me. His hand lingered, almost like we were frozen in time, lulled into slow motion from the pasta and the cheese. I should have moved away but found my legs wouldn't cooperate.

Before I realized what was about to happen, Serge leaned towards me and placed his large, warm hands lightly on my cheeks. And then he kissed me so tenderly that I melted like a Saint-Marcellin on a warm day.

I knew I should pull away but his lips felt so right. Serge felt so right. The minutes passed as we stood entwined together.

And then I suddenly remembered Gaston and went rigid. I leaned back and blurted out, "Serge, I can't do this. I have a boyfriend."

"What? Why didn't you tell me?" He took a step backwards, bumping into the chair behind him, a horrified look falling over his face.

"I'm so sorry; I thought I already did tell you. But then there was the dinner, and the cheese . . ." I couldn't get my thoughts in order. All I could think about was kissing him again. I regretted having said anything and would have happily leaped back into his arms, but his face warned me forcefully against doing so.

"I'm so sorry, Serge."

He said nothing.

"Maybe I should go," I said. "Thank you for dinner." I picked up my bag and coat and hurried out the door.

Outside in the cold winter night, I wondered what had gotten into me. The combination of the delicious food, the wine, and of course the cheese, all must have wooed me into believing I had feelings for Serge. Clearly, he wasn't my type of guy. He was old-fashioned and traditional. His hair was already graying and he made terrible jokes. But there was something about him that was sort of charming—not charming in the same way as Gaston, but there was still something there. And then I remembered the kiss and wanted to melt all over again. *Damn!*

I opened my apartment door, still lost in thought, and was surprised to see Clotilde sitting in the dark, looking out the window.

"Clotilde, you're back! How are you? I feel like you've been gone for ages. How was Thailand?" I asked.

She turned to face me and I saw that her eyes were wet and red and that she had been, and was still, crying.

"Hey, what's the matter?" I said, rushing over to her. "Did something happen?"

"Oh God, Ella. It's a mess. It's too complicated to even explain. I wouldn't know where to start."

I thought about the evening I'd spent with Serge and empathized.

"It can't be that bad," I said. "Whatever it is, I'm sure we can figure it out."

She leaned around to grab her handbag, hauling it onto the table and passing me a leather folio. I opened it nervously.

What the hell am I looking at? I thought as I flipped through. The pages featured very suggestive photos, mostly of feet, but sometimes including a "prop" or two. At one point I was on the verge of laughing, but on seeing Clotilde's distressed face, I held it in.

"Clotilde, what's going on? What are these?"

"Ella, I'm so embarrassed," she cried. She burst into another round of desperate wailing. I'd never seen her like this. Between sobs, the truth came pouring out. Clotilde had been posing as a foot model. At first, it was all above board, mostly shoots for designer footwear labels—she did have exquisite feet—but then she'd fallen in with a stylist who was paying her increasingly large sums to take some of the more bizarre shots I'd seen in her folder.

She'd guessed that he was a fetishist, but the money was great, and she'd thought it was all rather amusing. That was, until Papa Jean had found her folio over Christmas.

"Ella, he's furious . . . he said it wasn't proper to fuel people's perverted fantasies."

My heart sank for my friend.

"I tried to tell him that people could enjoy whatever they wanted and that as long as the photos didn't have my face on them, it didn't matter. But he's so old-school and proper. He kept yelling at me and saying, 'Imagine if your mother was still around.' He told me she would be so disappointed in me and what I've become." She started crying again, her body shaking as she gasped for breath.

"Don't worry," I said, rubbing her arm. "I'm sure he'll forgive you. Can you just tell him that you won't take any more pictures?"

"It doesn't matter anymore; he wants to cut me off. Take back the apartment. Ella, what are we going to do?"

"He wants you to move out?" I asked, realizing this now affected me too.

I did my best to console Clotilde but I was struggling to keep up with what was so bad about what she had done. As far as I could tell, the photos seemed fairly inoffensive; sure, their purpose might have been a little less than innocent, but things would have been a lot worse if her face had been in the frame. I now realized why she'd been so secretive about her modeling, elusively rushing off to meetings and always keeping her folio hidden away in her giant bag.

"So, why have you been posing for these pictures?" I asked her. "Do you enjoy it?"

"Well, at first it was just for my friend, but then I started getting quite a few offers. Apparently people with foot fetishes can recognize specific feet. My toes became popular in certain circles . . ."

At that comment, a little bubble of laughter escaped me. Even Clotilde managed a meek smile, almost acknowledging the absurdity of the situation.

"Clotilde, I wouldn't worry if I were you. Your father adores you. Maybe wait until he cools off and then try apologizing again."

"I'm not sure it'll work this time, Ella. I've never seen him so mad. He said I need to learn the value of hard work and money; he said he wouldn't always be around to support me."

"Maybe you should consider modeling for real, then—all of you rather than just your feet?" I suggested.

"I couldn't," she replied. "Who would ever hire me?"

"Who wouldn't?" I argued. "Even your mascara-stained face is gorgeous."

⁓

After Clotilde had cried herself out of tears, I sent her to bed for a good rest and told her we would come up with a plan for how to deal with her father in the morning. I knew that we could find another flat if we needed, so that wasn't the primary concern—most of all, I wanted to help her make amends with her dad. I loved their close relationship and I couldn't stand the thought of Papa Jean angry with her over some silly feet photos. I considered calling him to discuss what had happened but decided it wasn't my place to interfere.

Going to see Serge, on the other hand, and apologizing for not having told him about Gaston, was probably the right thing to do. I resolved to visit his store first thing in the morning.

But when dawn rolled around, after only a few hours of fitful sleep, I was more confused than ever. I'd dreamed of Serge, of being in his arms, of him caressing my hair and laughing softly in my ear. The dream had seemed so real and so wonderful that I woke up and felt like he was actually in bed with me. I had to turn on my lamp just to check that he wasn't.

I decided to avoid Serge and his *fromagerie* for a few weeks until the memory of the accidental-date-gone-wrong had faded. I was so lucky to be with Gaston and I didn't want to jeopardize things with him.

Fortunately for me, there were plenty of other cheese shops in Paris where I could continue to get my fix.

Chapter

29

A FEW DAYS AFTER THE mortifying "non-date" with Serge, Gaston called me late at night and asked if he could come over. I was still awake writing some copy for work the next day and let him know that he'd be a very welcome distraction.

Just as I was beginning to think he might have gotten lost on the way, I heard a pounding on the front door. Worried he'd wake Clotilde and the rest of my apartment block, I rushed to let him in. He stumbled past me, mumbling something about having been at a dinner, and giggled as he whipped off his jacket and spun it around his head, humming a striptease ditty. I laughed as I looked at him; I couldn't remember ever having seen him this drunk before. I whisked him into my room so he could continue the show.

Flinging my door shut, Gaston grabbed me from behind and pulled me roughly towards him, nearly falling over in the process. I tried to get him to slow down but he was absolutely sloshed, pushing me to arm's length and then pulling me closer, as if we were doing a strange dance. His drunken gaze was intense, as if he were assessing me. I turned off the lights and guided him to bed.

Pulling off his shirt and running my hands over his torso

seemed to settle him down a little. He ripped at my underwear and succeeded in getting off my bra. I helped him with the rest while he kissed me desperately. The sex was over nearly as abruptly as it began, and shortly after, Gaston was asleep, snoring a wine-drunk snore.

I groped around in the dark for my pajamas and slid them on, spending the next hour or so wondering what the hell had just happened. Gaston had somewhat crudely grabbed my arse seconds before finishing—and not an affectionate grab either, rather a rough, jolting grab more intended for his pleasure than my own. *Is this what it's like after settling into a relationship with a Frenchman?*

I felt insecure and I was sure it wasn't *all* in my head. Perhaps I'd just never feel like I could live up to the Parisian girls Gaston hung out with. *Did I even want to?* With Paul, I'd never fit into his social life and look how well that turned out.

I tried to visualize things long-term between Gaston and me. Getting married in a glamorous French chateau, having adorable *bébés* that called me *Maman* and spoke better French than I did. I imagined a country house filled with flowers and big wheels of cheese to be shared with our large family. Despite my vision of this idyllic French future, I couldn't really see Gaston in that kind of life. I couldn't see him leaving Paris and its restaurants behind. For the first time since I'd met him in Flat White, I wondered if we were well suited. Or was that just the 3 a.m. anxiety talking?

I woke early to the sound of pigeons outside my window. I'd been in such a hurry to turn off the lights the night before that I'd forgotten to close the shutters. Listening to the birds, I imagined that I'd unintentionally eaten their brother on my first date with Gaston, and now they were here for retribution. I slid out of bed, taking care not to disturb the sleeping man beside me, and decided to nip down to the bakery and pick up some breakfast.

Stepping outside into the crisp morning air felt invigorating. I tried to bask in the little bursts of sunlight streaming through the gaps between buildings, but kept getting distracted by thoughts of Gaston's booty call. Sex with him had never been so awful, or short-lived; I wanted to put it down to a drunken one-off.

I walked into the bakery and noticed the lady behind the counter placing little walnut bread rolls into the cabinet from the baker's tray.

"*C'est chaud?*" I asked, pointing at them.

"Yes, they're warm," she replied.

I still couldn't understand why every Parisian had to reply to me in English when I spoke to them in French.

I pointedly replied in French, asking for three.

The lady wrapped up the walnut rolls and wished me a nice day. As I walked back to the apartment, I passed a cheese shop that I'd been meaning to try and saw some delightful-looking rounds of raisin-covered goat cheese in the window. *They'll be delicious with this bread,* I thought, ducking into the store for a few small balls.

~⌒~

Back at the apartment, I noticed Clotilde's door was ajar and went to check if she was in her room. She wasn't, but had left a note on the kitchen bench that said:

Gone to the gym. Let me know if you have time to grab coffee before work. C xx

Gaston came slowly out of my room wearing my pink dressing gown.

"Is Clotilde home?" he groaned from the doorway.

"No, she's gone out. Feel like breakfast? I got some fabulous-looking goat cheese from that little store next to the bakery down the street. Have you seen those little rounds before? The ones covered in—"

"*Oh non*, Ella, not more cheese! After all the fondue we ate at the snow?" He slid up behind me and grabbed my arse again.

I shrugged off my disappointment at his lack of enthusiasm and spun around, all smiles, telling him that we didn't have to eat it right away. But as I sat buttering the warm walnut bread, I envisaged how great the cheese would taste and looked forward to the moment I'd be able to sneak a bite. Gaston's comment about my cheese consumption, accompanied by the incessant arse grabs, hadn't gone unnoticed. *Is he saying I'm fat?* I shook my head to escape this pointless train of thought.

"How'd you sleep?" I asked. "It seemed like you had a big night, did you have an event on?"

"No," he replied. "I was out catching up with some friends."

"Anyone I know?" My voice trembled as thoughts of him "catching up" with Camille flashed through my mind.

"Oh, no one you've met," he said.

I breathed a sigh of relief.

A few seconds later, Gaston flipped on the TV and settled onto the couch. I went to the bathroom to start getting ready for work and took the opportunity to examine my arse in the mirror. It wasn't an angle I often checked out, but I thought it was probably best to know if things had suddenly gotten wildly out of proportion back there.

After a thorough inspection, I confirmed that all was well; yes, there was a little additional padding but it certainly hadn't morphed into a Mont Blanc—sized issue. I reprimanded myself for letting the old, insecure Ella creep back into my brain and focused on changing my thinking to reflect the confident and self-assured Parisian that I'd been working hard to become. I knew I couldn't eat cheese every day and have a supermodel's arse—I didn't need a dietician to tell me that—but I had my priorities. I jumped in the shower and scrubbed away any remaining negativity in a cloud of steam and almond-milk body wash, leaving the bathroom in a much stronger frame of mind.

Checking my phone, I realized I still had time to meet Clotilde for coffee before work, so I pushed Gaston—who had at least managed to get dressed—begrudgingly out the door so I could finish getting ready. He didn't kiss me good-bye, but muttered something about dinner soon. I decided to give him a few days to get over his hangover before contacting him again. *Hopefully, absence will make the heart grow fonder.*

As I was hunting for my keys on the kitchen counter, I noticed an unread email notification staring at me from my laptop. It stopped me in my stride. It was from Paul. I gasped. The subject line read: "I'm so sorry, Ella, you have to forgive me."

Oh shit. I slammed my laptop shut as if it were on fire.

I stood immobile, wondering what Paul could possibly have to say after so many months of zero contact. Despite believing I was over him, seeing his name on my computer screen made that unwelcome Paul lump return to my throat. I took another few moments, trying to convince myself that I should simply delete the email, before giving up and lifting the screen. I couldn't resist reading it, my curiosity greater than my pride.

Ella,

I'm so sorry for how things ended between us. I never imagined you would move to Paris so quickly after that night we had the chat.

I wish you had stayed in Melbourne. If you had, I could talk to you about this in person right now, rather than sending an email, which has already taken me an hour to write.

I want to be honest with you. After the retreat I started dating Jessyka. You remember her from Cross-Fit? Anyway, things didn't really work out between us. If anything, dating her just made me realize that my life is with you.

Please come back. I'm ready to start thinking about marriage now. I promise.

I miss you, babe.

Paul

I slammed my computer shut again. *What the hell is he thinking?* A few seconds passed and I carefully reopened my computer, surprised it hadn't broken by now, and drafted a reply.

Paul, you dickhead!

I stared at the words on the screen and felt a rush of endorphins. Yes, I could do this.

How dare you send me an email, let alone an email in which you ask me to take you back.

First, I want to tell you that I'm thrilled things didn't work out with you and Jessyka. I think some time alone will do you the world of good. Didn't they teach you that at the retreat?

Second, leaving Melbourne was the best thing that could have ever happened to me. Paris may have been where I thought I'd fallen in love with you, but now I realize how blind I'd been. You and I were never meant to be. The only thing I regret is not realizing that long before you left me to go and "find yourself" (yes, that's the reason I left Melbourne in the first place, remember?).

Third, you say that you're "ready to START thinking about marriage." Well, how very gallant of you, but I'm no longer interested. I'd even go so far as to say I'd marry a wheel of cheese before I'd contemplate spending my life with you.

Finally, don't ever call me "babe" again. You lost that privilege a long time ago, and to be honest, it always pissed me off anyway.

Please never email me again.

Ella

I hovered my cursor over the send button, amazed at how eloquent I'd managed to be despite my rage. Then I paused, remembering a piece of advice I'd once received from my old boss: Never send an email when you're angry.

Fuck it! I thought.

I hit "send."

Chapter

30

I MET CLOTILDE AT A cute little French café near work. I was surprised to find her in good spirits considering her father had threatened to cut her off, and it was a relief to see her smiling, especially after the weird morning I'd had.

"So, it seems that one of us had a late-night caller," she said, kissing both my cheeks, which immediately reddened with her words.

"Oh, you heard him come in. I'm so sorry. I tried to keep him quiet."

"Ha, never mind. I know how he gets. Was he at a work dinner?"

"No, out with friends apparently."

"Which ones?" she asked, to which I replied that I had no idea.

I was about to launch into a monologue about how I was worried Gaston had changed since we'd first met but Clotilde jumped in before I could get my thoughts in order. "So I've got some news," she said. "I've got a meeting with an agency tomorrow morning about some real modeling work."

"That's great!"

"The photographer who took my feet photos helped set it up. It's totally legit."

"And you want to do it?" I asked.

"It's weird, I never even considered modeling for real, but this guy tells me he thinks I'd be perfect. Anyway, I'll keep working at Food To Go Go with you for now and see how things go. I don't know if it's a long-term thing but I can't help thinking why not give it a try? Maybe it'll help me figure out what to do next."

"So will you do runway shows?" I asked, totally oblivious to how the modeling world worked.

"No, campaigns only. And just for brands that I'll be able to get past Papa."

"Have you already spoken to him about it?" I asked.

"I'm meeting him tomorrow for lunch. I told him I wanted to apologize for everything by buying him a nice meal. If the meeting with the agency goes well and Papa seems open to my apology, I'll ask for his opinion. But if he's still pouting about everything, then perhaps I'll wait a few more weeks before mentioning it. When I spoke to him on the phone he seemed to have softened a little. I think he's missing me."

"I'm happy it's working out," I said.

"Ella, I couldn't have done it without you. I would have been a miserable mess for weeks. You were the one who encouraged me to pursue modeling seriously."

"It was an obvious solution," I said nonchalantly, but it felt wonderful to have been able to help Clotilde for once.

"Now tell me all about you," she continued. "How are things with Gaston?" I was relieved she'd brought him up; I really wanted her input. I still couldn't help thinking something wasn't quite right between us recently, although I wasn't sure what that was, or how to explain it. Part of me wondered if I was imagining things. Perhaps my suspicions had been blown out of proportion following my kiss with Serge. And then there was the email from Paul . . . *What a mess!*

"Things are OK. I mean, it's been pretty hectic since we came back from the Alps."

"Mmm. I heard about your skiing," she said, stifling a giggle.

"Oh God, did Gaston tell you I was terrible?"

"He may have mentioned something along those lines."

"Well, apart from the ski trip, I haven't seen him that much. He's really busy with deadlines at the moment."

Clotilde stopped stirring the sugar into her espresso and looked up at me suddenly. "Really?" she asked.

"Yes, he's out a lot during the day and most evenings. That's why he came by so late last night."

"That's weird," she said. "Normally, he's quiet with work this time of year. Oh well, I'm sure something must have changed. Maybe he has a new editor or something."

I blushed and pushed away the doubts that seemed to be accumulating in my mind. Perhaps I needed some more time to analyze the situation before discussing things further. It was my turn to change the conversation: "You'll never guess who emailed me."

"Who?" she asked, excited.

"Paul."

"No! What did he want?"

Ever since I'd first divulged all the details of Paul and my breakup, Clotilde had been incredibly supportive of me having ditched him. She kept trying to convince me to contact him and rub my happy Paris life in his face.

"He wants to get back together." Even saying it aloud felt strange.

"And?"

"Well, there's just no way. I would never give up what I've

got here for our comfortable old life in Melbourne. Sure, his apartment is gorgeous, but I couldn't do it."

"Is it because you're too Parisian now?"

"Exactly," I laughed. "And there's too much going on with work and you and Gaston. And I couldn't give up on French cheese. I love my life here."

"So, did you reply?"

"Yep."

No matter how many photos of food I tried to distract myself with at Food To Go Go, I couldn't stop thinking about Gaston and Paul. It seemed odd that Paul would email me at the same moment that Gaston and I were having troubles, but I knew it was just a coincidence.

What was eating away at me more was the realization that my budding French romance, which had been mostly dreamlike up until last night, might not be as perfect as I'd imagined.

On my way home, all I wanted to do was buy some kind of new, wonderful cheese that I could write up in my cheese journal. I didn't feel like I could go to Serge—I was still too embarrassed about the disastrous, but also perfect, kiss—so I tried a different shop.

I greeted the lady behind the counter with a big smile and a *bonjour*. She didn't reciprocate my friendliness and asked me grumpily what I wanted. I panicked, got flustered, and ended up requesting a slice of Comté. Without Serge to help guide me, I was overwhelmed when faced with so many glorious mounds of cheese.

Oh well, I thought, walking out of the shop disheartened. *I guess I could do a lot worse than good old reliable Comté.*

Chapter

31

I WOKE WITH A START the next morning, feeling anxious and agitated. I hadn't slept well since hearing Clotilde get home at midnight and then thinking about Gaston until I saw the clock tick over to 2:00 a.m. I somehow stumbled through the morning at work, and after a few espressos and a buttery croissant that I slathered with even more butter, I finally started to feel normal again.

During my lunch break, I sat in a café and mulled things over.

Paul's email had reminded me how great Gaston was, and what fun we'd had since we'd gotten together. As I made my way through a *croque-monsieur*, I felt certain that I'd been overthinking things—the snow, Camille, and our recent late-night encounter—and that I needed to get out of my head and back into my heart.

I decided that I had to do something special to bring things with Gaston back to perfection. I suddenly had a vision of us getting naked and drinking champagne in bed. *It would be the perfect rekindling*, I thought excitedly. *After all, what's sexier than a champagne-fueled afternoon frolic with a Frenchman?*

I knew Gaston worked from home on Thursdays so I hatched

a plan to sneak in and surprise him; thankfully, I still had his spare keys from when he'd left me to lock up the week before. *It was meant to be!*

I got approval from Tim to finish work early and left the office, the spring returned to my step. I stopped by the wine store to buy their cheapest bottle of champagne, feeling empowered that I was taking our relationship's future into my own hands.

In the past, I'd always waited for Paul to make the first move, but I wanted to show Gaston how much he meant to me. In Melbourne, I'd often felt boring and tepid, but in Paris, I could be spontaneous and sexy. The new Ella adored surprising her lover and drinking champagne in bed mid-week. I smiled at how much I'd changed.

After puffing my way up Gaston's stairs because the lift was too slow to match my level of excitement, I knocked loudly, singing out while turning my key. Seconds later, he came rushing out of his room.

"Ella, what are you doing here?" he said, shutting the bedroom door behind him and pulling on a shirt.

"Hi," I said, holding up the champagne bottle and grinning. "Were you asleep? I'm sorry I woke you. But anyway, turn around, I want you back in bed," I said, giving him a little nudge.

"Ella, look. Now is not a good time . . ."

I heard a voice coming from the kitchen and was surprised to see another shirtless man walk into the hallway.

What the hell is going on? I thought, feeling panicked.

"Oh, hi," I said awkwardly. "Sorry, I didn't realize Gaston had . . . err . . . company?"

"Ella, this is Camille's boyfriend, Antoine," Gaston said. "He's staying here while his apartment is . . ."

"Getting painted," Antoine pitched in.

OK, that makes sense, I thought, feeling relieved that Camille had gotten back with her boyfriend.

I gave Antoine a smile and shook his hand, still on the alert for weird vibes.

Gaston suddenly asked me why I wasn't at work and I explained that I'd taken the afternoon off. I apologized again for interrupting and asked them what they'd been up to.

"Well . . ." started Antoine before Gaston cut him off.

"Just hanging out, watching TV," he said. "The football."

I was surprised to hear Gaston admitting to watching sports. Perhaps it was Antoine's influence.

"Is everything OK?" I asked him.

As soon as the words had come out of my mouth, I spotted something in the hallway that made my heart drop. It was a pair of Chanel ballet flats. My mind raced, trying to place where I'd seen them before.

"Gaston? What's going on?" I asked, looking around the room for more potential clues, feeling increasingly uneasy.

"Nothing's going on. Look, we're a little busy now. Are you free to meet up later instead?" he asked.

I heard a rustle from the bedroom.

"Oh, God. Is there someone else here?" I asked.

"Ella . . ." Gaston started.

The appearance of a gorgeous woman walking out of the bedroom in her underwear interrupted him. It took me a minute to realize it was a near-naked Camille.

"Are you the house cleaner?" she asked in French.

I half screamed.

"Oh, sorry, Ella. It's just you. Did you change your hair?"

Was this really happening?

"Anyway, Antoine, we should probably go," she continued.

I stared at her as she unapologetically flung her luxurious mane of hair across her bare shoulders and searched around the room for her dress. She strutted across the hallway dramatically and I stood frozen, watching her beautifully-manicured feet move across the parquetry floor.

Gaston touched my arm. "Ella, relax. We were just fooling around. You know, like a *ménage à trois?*"

He paused, looking at Camille and Antoine, before continuing, "We can make it a *ménage à quatre*, if you prefer."

Hardly the most romantic proposition I'd ever received.

"Seriously?" I asked, looking around to see Camille and her boyfriend shrug as if to say, "Why not?"

What. The. Actual. Fuck?

"I think I'll just go. Leave you three to it."

"Ella, don't be so dramatic," Gaston said laughing.

With my mouth still agape, I slammed the door and got the hell away from them.

A few minutes down the road, tears working their way onto the pavement, I felt my phone vibrating somewhere in my bag. It was Gaston. I juggled the bottle of champagne that I was stupidly still holding and answered.

"What in the world could you want?" I said.

"Ella, look. Come back and talk to me. I'm sorry. I honestly didn't think you'd find out."

"Gaston! That's even worse."

"You know, what I was doing with Camille and Antoine, it was just a *cinq-à-sept*. Obviously, it doesn't mean anything to me," he said.

"Are you being serious right now?" I asked.

"Don't be angry, Ella. We're in France . . ."

What the hell is wrong with these people?

"Gaston, you're an arsehole. I can't believe you told me you loved me."

"What? When did I say that?"

"At the snow, after you'd been skiing with Camille all day."

"*Oh là là*, Ella. I never said *je t'aime*."

I paused, flabbergasted, wondering if I'd misheard him. *I couldn't have invented such an important memory, could I?*

"Please come back and see me. I told Camille and Antoine to leave. They're gone now," he said. "We can enjoy that bottle of champagne together."

"What? Do you really think I'd want to sleep with you after your little *ménage à trois?*"

"Look, Ella. It just sort of happened. We were all hanging out together, drinking rosé, and then we were naked. It was actually very innocent."

"Threesomes aren't 'very innocent,' Gaston . . . God, how is it possible I ended up falling for someone *worse* than Paul?"

"Who is Paul? What are you talking about?" he asked.

I hung up.

~

Struggling to coordinate walking, carrying the champagne, and crying, I sat down on a nearby park bench. It was freezing outside and the cold wind whipped up off the pavement and slapped me like an icy snowball directly in the face. I sat, oblivious to any oncoming frostbite, while simultaneously overheating from rage. I popped open the champagne and glugged it directly from the bottle. It was cool and crisp, offering a small consolation after busting Gaston having an affair, and, perhaps more importantly, dulling the realization that I'd been deceived by somebody I thought I loved. Again.

I dialed Clotilde's phone, relieved when she picked up immediately.

"Gaston is cheating on me," I blurted out.

"*Merde*," she said. "I was worried this might happen."

"What? Why? Has it happened before?"

"Yes, but Ella, I didn't want to tell you because I was hoping he'd changed. He told me that he was really into you. He said that with you, things were different."

"I feel so embarrassed," I told her. "He said it was a '*cinq-à-sept*.' What does that even mean?"

"Eugh. Men can be such pigs. *Cinq-à-sept* is like an after-work fling. Something to do between five and seven . . ."

"What the hell?" I said, disgusted. "Is this a common pastime for French men?"

"Not just for men, but for women too. It's not so common anymore, but you know, some people are just more sexual than others," Clotilde said, explaining the intricacies of French relationships to me like I was the world's biggest prude.

"But he said he loved me," I told her.

"Really? Gaston did?"

"In the mountains," I told her. "Why do you sound so surprised?"

"It's just that he's had commitment issues in the past. What did he say exactly? Was it in French or English?"

"What does it matter?" I asked.

"It matters a lot," she said seriously.

"He said, "*Je t'aime bien*'."

"Oh Ella, that can mean that he *likes* you a lot."

Oh, I thought, my heart almost dropping out of my chest. *Was my French really so terrible?*

She continued. "*Aimer* is a complicated verb because it can mean both like and love. Like '*Je t'aime beaucoup*' means 'I like you a lot,' but '*Je t'aime*' on its own means 'I love you.' Do you understand the difference?"

"Yes," I said, despairing.

"Where are you now?" she asked.

"I'm in the park behind Gaston's apartment. I'm drinking champagne," I said through tears.

"You're what? Oh Ella, come home and we'll get drunk together. It'll help you forget about men."

With the bottle still perched on my lips, an old man strolled past with his poodle and asked if I was OK.

"*Ça va, mademoiselle?*"

"*Ça va, merci*," I replied.

He asked me why I was so sad and I told him that life wasn't easy. He assuredly told me that everything would be OK and wished me luck. I couldn't help but laugh at our exchange. His attitude initially struck me as cold but he was right. Life could be hard but of course things would be OK.

So what if I'd just walked in on a guy who I thought was my boyfriend—who I thought loved me—only to discover that he was sleeping with someone else . . . and another someone else? I'd misunderstood the nuance of the verb *aimer* in French—a simple mistake—and then misinterpreted Gaston's and my relationship status. Embarrassing, yes; world ending, no.

Thankfully, I had a loving housemate who was ready and willing to help me ease the pain with more champagne. I started walking home.

A couple of blocks away from the safety of our apartment, I did a double take as a billboard caught my eye. It featured a gorgeous, scantily-clad model who was unmistakably Camille . . .

In the larger-than-life advert, she was wearing a bra—very similar to the one I'd just seen her in—under a chic jacket and paired with a short leather skirt. She looked ridiculously glamorous, strutting down a cobbled laneway, suggestively touching her inner thigh with her bedroom eyes staring down the barrel of the camera lens. I noticed a tiny smirk on the right side of her lips, as though she was saying: *I get everything I want, Ella. I'll have my Gaston and eat him too!* Her face made me both furious and sad.

"You beautiful arseholes deserve each other!" I screamed at the billboard.

"What did you say, Ella?" I turned around at the sound of a familiar voice.

Oh my God, what is happening?

"Jean-Pierre, what the hell are you doing here?"

"I was just passing by, then I saw you screaming like a crazy person," he said. It seemed as though he hadn't made much progress in the charm stakes. I wondered if he'd found a girl yet . . .

"Not now, Jean-Pierre. Get out of the way." I pushed past him and rushed home. *What on earth is the world trying to tell me?*

"I spoke with Gaston," Clotilde said, motioning to her phone as soon as I stepped through the door. "He's really sorry."

She grabbed two glasses and the partially-consumed bottle of champagne I was still carrying and motioned to the couch.

"What did he tell you?" I asked, wondering if he'd been honest.

"That you walked in on him having a threesome. He said you were very mad. He was looking for my sympathy but instead, I yelled at him. I've never done that before with Gaston. I think he was shocked."

"Did he tell you who he was sleeping with?"

"No, and I didn't even think to ask. Why, who was it?"

"Camille . . . and her boyfriend, Antoine."

"What! That skinny waitress-slash-model-slash-trust-fund girl and her airhead model boyfriend? I've met them both a few times out clubbing, smug as anything," Clotilde said. "She's a menace."

"That sounds like the same Camille," I said, feeling tears working their way down my cheeks. "What's worse is that I saw her on a billboard right after I'd busted her with Gaston."

"Who for?"

"Balenciaga. And she looked gorgeous, of course."

"Don't worry, Ella. I'm sure Gaston will regret this. Camille probably will too."

⤙⤚

That evening, I drowned my sorrows under Clotilde's watchful eye. When I was finally ready to drag myself to bed, she grabbed my phone, turned it off, and put it on the kitchen table.

"You should leave that here tonight. Just in case you fancy making any late-night calls," she said.

I may have had a few more glasses than usual, but I hadn't lost all my common sense, I told her. I gave her an unbalanced hug and stumbled off to my room.

Around half an hour later, when I was unable to sleep because the ceiling was spinning, I snuck out into the kitchen and grabbed my phone. I turned it on and pulled the bedcovers over my head.

I dialed.

"Hello," a voice on the other end said.

"Billie, are you there?" I whispered into the receiver.

"Ella? What's going on? Why are you whispering?"

"I'm fine," I said. "I just wanted to talk to you."

"Are you drunk?" she asked.

"No. I mean, yes. Maybe. But that's not why I'm calling."

"Is everything OK?" she asked.

"Not really," I said, starting to cry. "Turns out that French people are crazy."

"What do you mean?"

"Everyone is sleeping with each other! Gaston included. I'm pretty sure we just broke up."

"Oh dear," she said with a sigh.

"I know. It turns out he wasn't the complete package after all. Turns out he was an arsehole, actually. I busted him having a *ménage à trois*."

"I take it you weren't one of the three, then?" she asked.

"Not even," I said, sniffling. "They invited me to join but they were clearly only being polite."

"Ella, I'm so sorry. Are you at home? Why don't you make a cup of tea and you can tell me what happened."

"I can't leave my room," I said. "I stole my phone from Clotilde."

"Right . . ." she said pausing. "Maybe just go over all the details slowly then."

Over the next half hour, I told Billie what had happened that afternoon. I went into detail about how excited I'd felt leaving work early to sneak into Gaston's apartment, ready for an afternoon romp. Then I recounted how surprised I'd been when Camille's boyfriend had walked out of the kitchen—and my immediate relief that Gaston wasn't cheating on me with

Camille like I'd half been expecting. Finally, I told her how devastated I'd felt as soon as Camille herself had made her grand entrance from the bedroom, half-naked, asking if I was the cleaning lady.

When I'd finished, having stopped occasionally to sob or blow my nose, I was relieved to find Billie was still listening quietly on the other end of the phone line. She asked gently if I was done and then took a deep breath.

"Ella, seriously. You know I love you, but this situation you've gotten yourself into is ridiculous. I've seen you make all these mistakes before."

"What do you mean? Paul wasn't cheating on me," I said, hiccuping. "Was he?"

"Forget about Paul. Look, I'm going to be completely honest with you: The men you choose to date are arseholes."

Good cop Billie was clearly over; it was time for bad cop. I braced myself and she continued, "You date people you're not compatible with. And yes, they might appear glamorous, or exciting, or wealthy, but have you ever stopped to wonder why they treat you like you're not important?"

"No," I said, sobering up slightly as she unleashed a world of truths upon me.

"Because you let them. They never understand or care about what you want in life because you don't assert yourself in front of them."

"Yes, I do," I protested, unconvincingly.

"Paul was an idiot, and while yes, he could be sweet at times, he was never going to give you the life you wanted because he always put his own plans first. And this Gaston, from what you've told me, sounds appalling. Just like Paul, he kept you around while it was convenient for him, but the minute things started to appear serious between the two of you, he let you know he was still in charge. Trust me, he'll be better off with that model and her boyfriend, and you'll be better off without him."

"But I loved him." I realized how desperate I sounded, but the mix of heartbreak and wine was too strong to bear.

"Don't kid yourself, Ella. You loved the *thought* of him."

"So it's all my fault?" I interjected, feeling wounded.

"Of course it's not your fault, but choosing to date idiots is something you can stop. Immediately. You should never date another Paul or Gaston in your life. And yes, breakups will still happen, but it's better if it's because you're incompatible and not because he's got his sights set on another girl, or boy and girl. You need to value yourself more and make it damn clear to anyone you're seeing that you do."

"I'll never find love," I sobbed.

"Of course you will." She switched back to good cop. "You just need to look for a man with more substance than style."

"But I thought Gaston was that man."

"Why?"

"Because he was so handsome and French," I said, wailing.

"Ella . . ." Billie said, sounding worn out. "What about that guy from the cheese shop, Serge? He seemed nice."

"We kissed," I squealed. I couldn't believe I'd forgotten to tell her about the disastrous dinner with Serge. Too much else had happened.

"There we go," she said, sounding encouraged.

"But he's still not my type," I added quickly.

"Why not? Because you think he's not sophisticated enough? Because you think of him as a friend since he's kind and he cares about what's important to you? Do you see what I'm saying?"

"Kind of, but I think I'm going to be sick," I said, and rushed to the bathroom, leaving Billie on the line to hang up. After throwing up a bottle or two of wine and looking at my miserable face in the mirror, I went back to bed.

⌒

The next morning, fragments of my drunken conversation with Billie came flooding back to me when I saw a text message from her. I read it nervously.

"El, I hope you're OK. I'm sorry if I was harsh and I'm sorry you're upset. I really didn't think you'd fall for another Paul type after moving to Paris. When I saw you recently, you seemed really confident and happy. I'm so sorry it ended up like this. Call me any time if you need to chat."

I pieced together what I remembered Billie telling me. Something about always dating the wrong guys, something about Serge.

Although it was hard to admit, especially with a hangover, she did have a point. I did tend to date jerks. And I'd certainly gotten swept up in the idea of being with Gaston and with the magic of starting a French romance. I'd assumed I'd found the perfect boyfriend and had ignored the warning signs of him flirting with other girls and being aloof. I sent Billie a reply, apologizing for my drunkenness and letting her know that I appreciated her advice.

⌒

I spent most of the following week walking the streets of Paris. I didn't care that it was bitterly cold or that my nose was permanently numb; walking was the only thing that made me feel better. When I wasn't at work, I walked the length of the Seine from Bercy to the Eiffel Tower, trying to figure out when everything had gotten so complicated.

I did laps of the Jardin des Plantes, musing over how my year in Paris discovering *joie de vivre* had turned into me gate-crashing a threesome and avoiding my favorite *fromagerie*. I fought back tears thinking about how complicated my relationships with Gaston and Serge had become.

A few weeks earlier, I'd been ecstatic, in love with my life here, and now my mind was full of men. *This is exactly what I came to France to avoid*, I admonished myself as I continued to trudge around the city, breathing fog into the freezing winter air.

One day, as I was walking through the Square du Temple, I spotted a familiar silhouette. It was Serge.

He was standing alone looking out over the little pond and I could see him tearing up a baguette into small pieces and feeding it to the ducks. I knew I should go say hello and apologize for rushing out on him that night after he'd cooked us dinner. I desperately missed going into his store to buy cheese. I missed chatting with him.

Before I could muster up the courage, he walked briskly back towards his store. I could have gone in to see him, settled our differences on familiar turf, but I instead found myself lulled into Le Progrès, where I ordered a bottle of red wine.

"*Avec un seul verre?*" the waiter asked, looking at me with pity.

"*Oui*," I said, tears welling in my eyes, "only one glass."

In the warmth of the café, the sensation slowly came back into my fingers and nose. With each sip I tried to decide what I should do next. The bottle went down quickly as I sorted through the pros and cons of staying in Paris. The pros: Clotilde, enjoyable work, amazing cheese, the wine! The cons: homesickness, the cold, Gaston, Serge, and French men in general.

I decided that while I'd loved Paris up until very recently, maybe it was time to go back to Australia. I'd had some great experiences and had learned a lot about myself—most of all that I had terrible taste in men—but right now, I thought I'd benefit from being surrounded by my family, friends, and English speakers. It was also summer back home, and watching the darkness and fog descend over Paris, I felt like this was almost reason enough to call it a day.

I polished off the bottle and made my way home, determined to look at flights out of Paris. I made a cup of tea and hopped in bed with my laptop. I was asleep before I'd even entered my password.

⌒

The next morning, with a smashing headache, I went to make coffee and ruminate on my red wine–induced decision to move back to Australia.

As much as I tried to convince myself that it was for the best, I still couldn't shake a nagging feeling I had in my stomach. It was hard to justify, and I felt silly for even thinking it, but I really wasn't ready to give up on the cheese challenge. A dinner bet with Serge, who I was currently avoiding, hardly seemed like reason enough to stay in Paris, but then I couldn't leave without paying my debt for not finishing. And what about my Instagram account? My followers had been growing steadily over the last six months and I didn't want to lose the community I'd been fostering.

Cheese had been the impetus for my move to Paris, but was it important enough to make me stay? And why did I care so much about one specific food anyway?

Spying an empty bottle of Crémant de Bourgogne on the kitchen bench, I was reminded of the truffle pasta Serge cooked for us the night he kissed me. I paused as my dehydrated brain tried to piece together something my subconscious had already figured out. Suddenly, I knew I had to make things right with Serge.

I swallowed a few painkillers, checked my watch, and rushed outside.

Chapter

32

"**WHERE IS SERGE?**" **I YELLED** in French as I pushed open the door of his cheese shop. I had arrived during the pre-lunch rush and all the customers turned to stare at me.

"Who are you?" Fanny asked.

"I'm Ella," I said. "I once bought cheese from you. Remember?"

"*Qui?*" she repeated, looking at me blankly.

"It doesn't matter. Can you please tell me where Serge is?"

"He's out visiting suppliers *dans la Loire*," she said, adding curtly, "Now please, I have customers. Unless you plan to buy something . . ."

"When will he be back?" I asked, desperately.

"Maybe he will come back next Monday. He hasn't confirmed."

"Can you at least tell me which supplier he has gone to visit?"

"*Non, je ne sais pas.* He's gone to get more goat cheese. You should call him."

And with that, she turned away from me and started serving a customer. I heard her say in French that all American girls were crazy, which made them both snigger.

"I am NOT American," I said loudly as I left the store feeling deflated.

⁓

I didn't have Serge's phone number and I wasn't sure how to get ahold of him. I considered waiting outside his apartment until he came back, but what if that wasn't until Monday as Fanny had implied? It was freezing outside. I was at a loss for what to do.

Thankfully, Clotilde was out for lunch when I got home and I could skulk back to bed, hungover and heartbroken.

I couldn't stop thinking about Serge.

I was desperate to apologize for not telling him I was in a relationship and for running out on him rather than explaining the situation. I fell asleep full of regret.

I woke like a shot an hour into my nap, my eyes flinging open in a mix of panic and excitement.

A few hours later, I was on the train to Tours.

I'd dreamed that I'd run into Serge and his glamorous new girlfriend who were visiting a Sainte-Maure supplier. I got the strongest feeling that was where he'd be.

A quick online search had revealed the name of Serge's friend's B&B that he'd mentioned at Christmas dinner. I called the phone number but nobody answered so I ripped a page out of my cheese journal and jotted down the address. It was a long shot, but I figured I was due a little luck. And even if he wasn't there, I was sure his friends could help me find him.

I left a note for Clotilde and went to the station, making the train with only minutes to spare.

Zipping through the outskirts of Paris, I had time to catch my breath.

What the hell am I doing gallivanting off to the country to find a man who might hate me? I thought once the adrenaline had worn off.

I'd been so blind to believe the cheese challenge was more important to me than the man behind it. The more I thought about it, the more I saw that, even from the beginning, it had always been about Serge. Billie had been right; he was a good guy, so why couldn't he be *my* guy? *Is it worth a shot?*

With the final jolt of the train's brakes, I grabbed my bag and rushed out of the station and into a cab. After a few wasted minutes trying to get the driver to understand my accent, he told me that the town was really far away. I sat back, got out my purse, and told him to drive on.

~~

After almost half an hour of navigating winding country roads, the cab rolled through the quiet town of Sainte-Maure de Touraine. My hands shook with nerves.

"Is this it?" the driver asked, pointing at a small sign as he pulled into a long driveway.

"*Oui,*" I croaked, checking the address I'd scribbled down before leaving Paris.

Approaching the stone cottage with its lush green garden, I saw two men standing beside a pile of wood. One had an axe in hand. The other was Serge.

Relief flooded my body.

Serge was chatting to the owner of the bed and breakfast, Jacques; I recognized him from his photo on the website. I thanked God that I'd been paying attention when Serge had told me all about Sainte-Maure de Touraine. His lessons had led me directly to him.

Both men turned to look at the approaching cab, squinting in the winter sun to see who was in the back seat. The look of recognition, and then of shock, on Serge's face worried me, and I began to regret having traveled so far to essentially ambush him.

He left Jacques by the woodpile and started walking quickly towards the cab. I shoved a handful of euros into the driver's hand and asked him to wait a few minutes before driving off; I had to make sure Serge wasn't going to tell me to leave. I stepped out and the driver sped off, obviously not empathizing with the precarious nature of the situation and taking the extra money as a generous tip.

I didn't know what to say. *Why didn't I rehearse something on the train?* I thought. I had no idea how to tell Serge that I was sorry, that I really wanted us to start over, that I couldn't wait for him to kiss me again.

"Serge, hi," I said. *Killer opening, Ella!*

"Ella, what are you doing here?" he asked, sounding confused. "Are you holidaying?"

"Serge, I really like you," I blurted out.

"What do you mean?" he replied. "I thought you had a boyfriend."

"He is a massive pile of *merde*. We broke up."

Serge looked at me intensely with his deep blue eyes and didn't say anything. My heart sank. It was too late.

"I hope it's not too late," I said.

"Too late for what?"

"For this," I said, leaning in to kiss him deeply on the lips.

At first, he stood there frozen, and then his soft lips encased mine, the warmth of the embrace spreading through my body like I'd just slid into a hot bath.

The memory of our first kiss flooded back to me. The joy, the release, the abandonment, it was all there. This time I wouldn't be stupid enough to pull away. I brought him even closer and he happily complied.

After a minute or so locked together, I heard Jacques shout out "*Oh là là*," which made us break apart, breathless and laughing. I'd completely forgotten he was standing there and was relieved to see that Serge was blushing too.

I waved, calling out "*bonjour*," and we walked over to him. The two men chatted briefly in French and I stood there smiling like an idiot, lost in the moment.

After Serge shook Jacques's hand and said good-bye, he led me over to his little blue Citroën parked in the driveway. The car looked so quintessentially French against a background of farmland and a cloudless blue sky that I felt like we were the stars in a French film. He opened my door before getting in himself.

"Ella, Ella, Ella." He said my name slowly, almost like he was savoring each syllable. "This is such a surprise."

"I hope it's a good one," I said.

"How did you even find me here?" he asked.

"It's a long story."

"Have you eaten?"

"No, and I'm starving," I said, relieved. It felt almost too good to be true.

We drove the remainder of the driveway in silence, my heart pounding with anticipation.

Before turning onto the main road, he leaned over and kissed me again. It was tender but passionate, desperate but sweet, almost like we were making up for lost time. His touch felt electric.

When we finally broke apart, Serge looked into my eyes and said, "Ella, *je t'aime*." I paused, waiting for the '*bien*,' or the '*beaucoup*,' as I'd been taught by Clotilde, but none came. Instead he continued, "I know it's early and perhaps you don't know me that well, but from the moment I saw you, struggling with the door of my cheese shop that beautiful summer morning, I knew you were my girl."

Nobody had ever called me "their girl" before and it felt so perfect.

"It was, as we say in French, a *coup de foudre*," he continued.

"Love at first sight?" I asked, shocked he'd managed to even see past my clumsiness that day.

"That sounds about right."

I almost burst with excitement. I may have been the last to see it, but Serge was open and honest, kind and gentle. Now there was just one thing left to clarify.

"Serge, what do you mean by '*Je t'aime*'?"

He laughed. "Ella, I love you," he repeated in English, and wrapped his arms around me.

"I love you too," I said, surprising myself. "And I'm sorry it took me so long to realize it. I've been such an idiot."

I felt like I was apologizing both to Serge and to myself for every mistake I'd ever made that had postponed me from being there, with him, in that very moment.

Chapter
33

HAVING DECLARED OUR LOVE TO each other, Serge and I sat down that night to our first real date. Over a three-course dinner with cheese and a bottle of Chinon, we spoke joyfully, switching between French and English, furiously catching each other up on what had happened since Serge had cooked me dinner. He apologized for having kissed me prematurely that night at his apartment, and I told him the only thing that I regretted about that kiss was having pulled away.

"I was worried I'd never see you again," he said. "I've missed you coming to the store."

"I've wanted to come, to apologize, but I wasn't sure you'd want to see me."

"It might have been easier than coming all the way out here."

"Not nearly as romantic, though, right?" I said sheepishly.

As we got further into the bottle of wine, I explained what had happened with Gaston, how he'd tried to blame his infidelity on being French, how I'd been stupid to even date him. Serge rolled his eyes then told me very seriously that people like Gaston didn't represent all French men.

Finally, I confessed that Gaston's mistress had confused me with the house cleaner, at which Serge laughed so loudly and warmly that guests seated at surrounding tables couldn't help smiling. It was a relief to find humor in what had been, after all, a ridiculous situation.

When the waiter arrived with a huge cheese trolley, Serge recommended I try the Chabichou du Poitou and the Selles-sur-Cher.

As I bit into the first cheese, which was fluffy and sweet, he asked, "So how is the cheese challenge going? Or did you quit because you were avoiding me?"

"Ha! Don't flatter yourself," I said. "I'm still going and I'm not embarrassed to tell you that I'm up to 231 types of French cheese, 233 if you count these two," I said, motioning at my plate.

"I'm impressed," he said. "And now that we're talking again, I can help you get to 365. What's missing from your list?"

I looked at him, brimming with love.

"This is a Pouligny-Saint-Pierre," he said, offering me a slice. "The form is a topless pyramid. It resembles a Valençay but it's whiter. It's a personal favorite of mine."

"Another favorite?" I asked. "Why have you never mentioned it before?"

"Well, I don't eat it that often. For me it's more of a special occasion cheese. I like to save it for when something good happens," he said.

I blushed.

"I don't normally like telling people this, but seeing as you told me about your ex-boyfriend's mistress mistaking you for the cleaner, I feel I can be honest with you."

I laughed, "Go on then."

"Well," he began awkwardly. "This is the cheese that made me want to open a cheese shop."

"It sounds like a happy story, then," I said.

"Not quite. Right after I split up with my wife, I was sitting alone in my apartment, feeling miserable and eating this cheese, when I had the idea to change my life. In the weeks that followed, I sold my home, quit my job, and moved to Paris to open my *fromagerie*."

Serge's route to Paris sounded unnervingly familiar.

"I didn't know you were married," I said, adding, "or divorced."

"Don't worry. It's a good thing. My ex-wife and I got married when we were too young, and from the day after our wedding, we slowly realized that we were incompatible. Everything I liked, she hated, and it was the same for her." He took a deep breath before continuing, "She didn't even like cheese . . ."

"Wow," I said. "What a waste."

"It's OK. Our relationship ended in quite a friendly and mutual way. But I still couldn't help feeling miserable that I'd failed to have a successful marriage. It took the divorce for me to realize how unhappy I'd been all those years, and not only with my wife, but with my whole life. I hated my job as an accountant and I hated living in the suburbs of Paris. I was scared because I didn't remember how to be alone but I knew I couldn't continue the same life as before. It was then that I decided to open a cheese store in Paris. My father used to make cheese here in the Loire before he retired and he helped set me up the shop."

I nodded, relating more than Serge could have realized. Who could better understand the desire to completely change your life after a breakup? I decided to wait a few more days to tell him about Paul. *One bad ex-boyfriend story at a time*, I figured.

"Well, I'm glad cheese led you to Paris," I said.

FROMAGE À TROIS

Biting into an apple tart topped with a decadent ball of oozing vanilla ice cream, I was almost delirious with joy. Whenever I'd eaten out with Gaston, I'd never been fully comfortable. I always got the impression I was being judged for either liking something too much or not enough.

With Serge I felt at ease; his desire to make me happy was almost palpable. Admittedly, it was a little odd opening up to each other about our past loves, but my gut—now full of a hearty country meal—told me this relationship was worth taking a chance on. Serge felt like an old friend who I was conveniently looking forward to kissing again.

We ended up parking Serge's little Citroën at a hotel for the evening because the thought of staying clothed during the entire drive back to Paris was too much for both of us.

The next morning, after a breakfast of more goat cheese—this time with the delicious addition of honey—we drove off through the countryside, which was bursting with the first signs of spring. It felt exciting to be heading back to the challenges and joys of our Parisian lives, now entwined, hopefully forever.

Epilogue

"A dessert without cheese is like a beautiful woman with only one eye."

—BRILLAT-SAVARIN

THREE MONTHS AND THREE DAYS after my glorious first—proper—date with Serge, I was still in Paris to see the city transform back into its beautiful, sunny best. I'd now been living here long enough to see the influx of spring tourists and the slow decline of Parisians who, with the arrival of the sun, all began to escape to the coastlines for long weekends and public holidays. Occasionally, I'd stop to help a group of lost-looking foreigners and point out where the Louvre was or how to get to the Champs-Élysées. I finally felt at home.

Since that wonderful day driving around the Loire, things between Serge and me had been smoother than a slice of Brillat-Savarin. I finally told him the details of my breakup with Paul, about how I started dating him when we'd been visiting Paris and how I'd been wooed by his "knowledge" of French cheese. Funnily enough, I'd filled the void that Paul had left in my life with the exact two things that had brought us together, ultimately to have them both lead me to Serge.

Billie had been right when she'd told me I'd been dating the wrong type of guy. I had no idea I could be so happy with another person.

To celebrate my one-year anniversary of arriving in Paris, I organized a Sunday lunch at Serge's apartment—*our* apartment, although I still wasn't used to calling it that. I'd invited my odd collection of Paris-based friends and colleagues and had been cooking up a storm—or at least Serge had—all week in preparation.

The first guests to arrive were Clotilde and Papa Jean. Since we'd moved out of our little flat, I didn't see Clotilde or her father as much as I would have liked, and when I met them at the door their embraces were wonderfully warm and familiar. Papa Jean handed over a magnum of champagne as an anniversary gift, and as soon as Clotilde wasn't listening, he thanked me again for helping his beloved daughter through her "rough patch with the feet."

I laughed and looked over at Clotilde, who was as radiant as ever. She was the face of the new Balenciaga campaign, adorning magazines and billboards all over Paris. Camille's tenure had been short-lived after she was caught sleeping with an art director on set. From then on, Clotilde's modeling career had really taken off and she was constantly traveling—so much so that she was rarely in our apartment. Eventually, she and her father decided to sell it. Now when she was in Paris, she stayed in lavish hotels or with Papa Jean. Thankfully, he'd relaxed his stance on her modeling. As long as she remained clothed, properly shod, and classy, he gave her his blessing.

Clotilde offered to assist Serge in the kitchen and I rushed to assure her that everything was under control. From experience, I knew that she could do as much damage in five minutes as I could do in an hour. I asked her to pop open the bottle of champagne instead, a task she excelled at. As we clinked glasses, I had a pang of longing for our old apartment and the good times we'd shared getting to know each other.

When the time had come to move out of Clotilde's, Serge had suggested I move in with him. I'd thought it was too soon and had told him I preferred to just look for another share house, but he'd insisted.

I'd remained apprehensive, telling him that when I'd lived with Paul, I'd gotten lost in our relationship, something I wasn't in a hurry to repeat. But as my search for a new home became as painful as the first time around, Serge had begged in his irresistible French accent to give it a try, and I'd finally caved and said yes. Deep down, I knew I was a different person now and I could hardly lump Serge in the same boat as Paul. He'd even told me that if he saw me changing, he'd kick me out on the street and force me back to Australia. And while his threat seemed a little dramatic, I trusted him.

Next to knock was my favorite Parisian barista, Chris. He arrived armed with a takeaway coffee for me, which was cold from his commute, but I loved the gesture. He joked and said that Flat White wasn't the same without his favorite dish pig although I was sure he was exaggerating. I missed working there on weekends since I'd resigned, but thankfully, I could still always count on him for a good flat white. He saw Clotilde inside and smoothed down his hair. In the end, I don't think he'd ever built up the courage to ask her out on a date but judging by the look in his eyes, all hope was not lost.

Before I had time to shut the door, Tim rushed up the stairs announcing, "Ella, we closed the funding round."

I looked at him, lost.

"We've got more money coming in!" he said.

"Seriously?"

Tim had been working tirelessly to attract investors to raise Food To Go Go's biggest round of funding yet. His baby girl had arrived safely a few days before Christmas and he'd turned into a very serious and driven boss, at least when he wasn't falling asleep at his desk.

"No more slumming it for us, girl. I think we'll even be able to get our own office."

I smiled thinking about how cramped we'd been getting in the tiny coworking space we were renting. The company had been growing rapidly over the past few months, so much so that a month earlier, Tim had offered me a full-time gig that included a pay rise and a working visa, one that allowed me to legally stay in Paris. He made his way around the room saying hello to everyone before stopping to share the good news with Serge.

I saw Serge nodding despite looking completely lost, probably baffled by Tim's Scottish accent but too polite to ask him to slow down.

⁓

When we were all collected at the table—my boyfriend, my boss, my barista, my best French friend, and her dad—I made a terrible speech thanking everyone for their support over the past year. It was sappy and embarrassing but I felt like I needed to mark the occasion somehow, and I couldn't help getting emotional thinking about the life these people had helped me create here.

Although it'd been an easy decision for me to stay in Paris, Mum hadn't taken the news so well. Thankfully, Ray and I had been emailing beforehand and he'd helped me arrange a surprise trip for them to return at the end of summer. She was touched to find out that we'd been scheming something together and I think it helped soften the blow of me not moving back to Melbourne. I couldn't wait for them to get to know Serge better.

As for the cheese challenge, I finally resigned myself to the fact that I probably wouldn't succeed in tasting 365 types of cheese in 365 days. I'd certainly tried and had come close to hitting the goal—320 tasted—but I knew I'd never be able to get through another forty-five varieties in the time that remained, at least not healthily.

Of course, I still relished trying new cheeses at every opportunity and discovering their unique origins—which Serge continued to describe to me in wonderful detail—but trying all 365 varieties within the year had lost its urgency. I wanted to savor those that remained.

When I ate cheese with Serge now, my enjoyment was on a different level. When I'd first arrived in Paris, eating cheese gave me purpose. It provided me with some structure to my days and I had clung to the challenge like it was my *raison d'être*. It was also my entrée into French culture and—in hindsight—a way to get closer to my cheesemonger. Now my consumption was for sheer pleasure. I did however quietly continue with the Instagram account, both to keep my still-increasing number of followers happy and to share the joys of French cheese with the world.

A few weeks earlier, when Serge had been probing me about the bet, he admitted he'd thought I'd only get around to tasting maybe one hundred types; he was impressed at how wrong I'd proven him. Thankfully, he found my obsession with cheese—and my seemingly endless appetite for it—endearing and he encouraged me to make a final effort to reach my goal. I considered pushing through but ultimately decided that 365 types of cheese was far too many to try in one year. I finally admitted to him—and to myself—that the world of French cheese was untamable, even with my greedy nature. This seemed to quieten him and he begrudgingly agreed. I think his real motivation behind seeing me succeed was because he still wanted to take me to dinner at La Tour d'Argent, which was sweet—but now that we were dating, it didn't seem necessary.

Serge and Clotilde cleared the lunch plates and disappeared into the kitchen. Just as I was considering going to check on them, I spotted Serge's large wooden cheese trolley making an entrance into the dining area. The smell hit us before we were able to take in the full effect. I was momentarily stunned, seeing what looked like half the contents of Serge's *fromagerie* on display.

"What have you guys done?" I asked.

"To wish you a happy Paris anniversary, we got you forty-five new types of cheese to try," said Serge, standing next to a beaming Clotilde.

"But how did you know? How did you know which ones I haven't already tried?" I asked, stunned.

"Well, I've kept a rough list of the cheeses you've tasted from my store," Serge said. "Because honestly, I was worried you might exaggerate your efforts slightly. And then Clotilde hunted through your Instagram account to help me piece together what was missing. Turns out you have quite the diary of your cheese adventure on that social media thing."

"You guys! I can't believe you've done this," I said, more tears welling in my eyes.

"Now you've just got to sample everything here and you'll know more about French cheese than the majority of French people," Serge said. "And I'll get to take you to dinner, of course."

We got to work on the trolley while Serge told us the individual names for each one and gave us tasting notes along the way. Chris and Tim looked like they'd just waltzed into the best lunch of their lives and Clotilde and Papa Jean embellished Serge's descriptions with anecdotes. Then we stumbled across a cheese that nobody but Serge had tasted; everyone's first bite was met with a sort of sacred silence.

My adoration for Serge in that moment was at bursting point. Without him and Clotilde, I certainly wouldn't have had such a great first year in Paris and I probably wouldn't still be here to celebrate finally feeling at home. I'd needed to dump my Australian boyfriend, move to the other side of the world, and struggle to find my place in France for it to happen, but it had all been worth it.

Of all the cheese I've tasted, Comté still remains my favorite, and I quietly thank it for luring me to Paris, pushing me to explore different types of cheese, and, ultimately, discover a new type of love.

Acknowledgments

WHEN THIS BOOK WAS STILL a draft, my sister asked why Ella was always drinking champagne. It's probably because a lot of my writing was fueled by glasses of champagne (or sparkling wine when the budget was grim). Sometimes drinking when working is disastrous, sometimes it's magical; for a book based in Paris, it felt necessary.

France (and its whole array of food and wine) has been an ongoing source of joy and inspiration. From the first time I lived here when I was sixteen, I fell in love, and now much more than a decade later, I'm still finding things that surprise and delight me.

But perhaps more important than the place that inspired this book are the people who helped me finish it.

Thanks first to my agent Gregory Messina for his excitement and determination to bring this story into the world, and to my UK editor, Emily Yau (and the teams at Quercus and Amberjack), for being the first to see its potential and making it a reality.

A huge wave of gratitude goes to my family. To my ever-encouraging mum and two sisters, Lorna and Jules, for their enthusiasm and insightful feedback; and to my dad, both for reading outside his usual genre, and for making up fabulous stories when I was young. The Hollow Log was probably a precursor to arriving here.

Thank you to my favorite tea companion, Shaz, for making writing a book seem easy—oh, they were the days; to Robin Wasserman (and the instructors at the Paris Writing Workshop) for motivating me to keep going and for giving me the tools to do so; and to all my friends who have endured the soul-searching that accompanied my writing.

Finally, thanks go to my adorable daughter, Clementine, for giving me a nine-month deadline to start wrapping things up. And to my husband, Jamie, it's hard to express how much I appreciate your continuous support. Thanks for reading the very first (and very terrible) draft and then the better versions that followed. You're my Serge.

About the Author

VICTORIA BROWNLEE is an Australian-born food writer. She's spent the best part of the last decade eating her way around the world, including a two-year stint in China where she was the Food & Drink Editor at *Time Out Shanghai*. In 2016, she traded dumplings for cheese, and is now settled in Paris with her husband and daughter.